THE
PERFECT
MURDER
ASSIGNMENT

THE PERFECT MURDER ASSIGNMENT

BRIAN FINUCANE

The Perfect Murder Assignment
by Brian Finucane

Published 2022 by Peacoat Press.

Typeset in Goudy Old Style, Adobe Caslon Pro and
Ratio Modern by Eleanor Abraham.

ISBNs
Print: 978-1-8382244-3-1
Ebook: 978-1-8382244-4-8

Contents

"Crime is common. Logic is rare. Therefore it is upon the logic rather than upon the crime that you should dwell."

—Sir Arthur Conan Doyle, 'The Adventure of the Copper Beeches', a Sherlock Holmes Short Story

Prologue

If someone had told me a few weeks ago that I'd almost be murdered while doing a writing course in the countryside, I would have laughed. And yet that's exactly what happened. On the day I skipped class, I journeyed into the woods, driven by my mystery-obsessed curiosity. It wasn't long before I was running for my life from a deranged stalker, intent on killing me. Not my stalker, I might add. The stalker of internationally renowned mystery writer Edith Ramsey, who taught the course.

I shudder to think what might have happened to me that day. What if that maniac had caught me? Certainly, I wouldn't be sitting in the back garden of this grand country house, having afternoon tea with my classmates.

As I picked up a knife to butter my scone, my newest friend, Hazel, moved her chair next to mine.

"Cosy get-together this, eh, Bel?" she said, then stuffed a scone into her mouth.

"Indeed," I replied, observing the crumbs falling from her lips. "How is your scone?"

"Absolutely scrummy," she replied, with her mouth full. "You want some tea?"

"Please."

She picked up the silver teapot from the table and poured me a hot cuppa.

"Did I just hear someone use the word 'scrummy'?"

On the other side of the table, Robert reclined in his chair, aiming a scowl at Hazel. He had been the most vocal participant in this morning's class, insisting that the villain in detective stories is more admirable than the hero, given the ingenuity of his murderous schemes. It was obvious he didn't like Hazel, or myself for that matter, having earlier referred to us as "a pathetic pair of Holmes and Watson wannabes".

"Yes, I was talking about the scones," Hazel confirmed.

"Is that a word a professional writer should use?"

Hazel shrugged. "What's wrong with 'scrummy'?"

Robert folded his arms and laughed haughtily. "What's wrong with 'scrummy'?"

"We're not professional writers," I said. "We're amateurs."

"Amateurs?"

"Yes. That's why we're on this writing course."

Maintaining his folded arms, he straightened up in his chair. "Yes, and that's why we should make every effort to enrich our vocabulary. Take greater care in how we choose our words and avoid using childish adjectives like 'scrummy'."

"Well, we're not writing now, we're just talking," I pointed out. As I attempted to put the knife on the table, it slipped out of my hand, falling to the ground. Hazel reached down and picked it up.

"Would make a nice murder weapon," she said, examining the ornate handle before placing it back on the table.

"That knife?" Robert said with a touch of belligerence. "That could barely cut through cold butter, let alone flesh and bone. You'd need one of the kitchen knives to do some real damage."

While stirring my tea, I carefully considered his words. "A kitchen knife would not be a wise choice for a murder weapon."

"Why's that?" Robert asked.

"If, indeed, you wanted to murder someone with a knife, a kitchen knife would undoubtedly accomplish the deed. However, kitchen knives mostly come in sets, so if you dispose of the murder weapon, it will be obvious that a knife is missing. Or if you put it back into the set it will contain incriminating DNA. Either way, you risk being caught."

"Brilliantly observed, Bel!"

Robert rolled his eyes. "Bloody amateurs!"

I took a bite of my scone and relished the taste.

"How is it?" Hazel asked.

"Scrummy!" I replied.

"Guys, listen to this." Jamelia and Aaron had been huddled over Jamelia's tablet since we sat down. "The police let that psycho go last night," Jamelia said.

"Who?" Hazel asked.

"Jack," she said, leaning over the table. "He's back on the street."

A cold chill ran down my spine. Jack Burley, the man who chased me through the woods, had been released. I was shocked, to say the least. And scared. Not only for myself, but also for Edith, who had been the victim of that maniac's harassment for years.

As I pondered the police's decision, Robert started whistling. I glared at him as he lounged in his chair. His brash attitude throughout the week had earned my ire. He stared back at me as he continued whistling, clearly enjoying my irritation. Taking a sip of tea, I looked away from him to think. Across the garden lawn, Shirley, Edith's personal assistant, shuffled towards our table. As she approached, her shoe got caught in some uneven grass, almost causing her to lose her footing and fall over. Robert ceased whistling, saying to himself: "She's such a klutz."

"Edith has just handed me an assignment for tomorrow's final workshop," Shirley announced, holding up five small envelopes in her hand.

"An assignment?" Hazel said. "We haven't been given an assignment before. How exciting!"

Shirley adjusted her glasses. "Well, this is a special assignment." She fumbled the envelopes, dropping them. Robert sneered, not bothering to hide his disdain. She gathered up the envelopes and handed one to each of us. Curious, I opened mine quickly. Inside was a card containing the following words:

Write in one sentence how you would commit the perfect murder.

"You've all been given the same assignment," Shirley declared. "But you must all come up with your own individual answer."

There was blank space beneath the statement, where we would have to write our name and our answer. We looked at each other, amazed by the assignment. Shirley was smiling broadly.

"Well, enjoy the rest of your day," she said chirpily. "See you bright and early tomorrow." She turned and shuffled back to the house.

"Bright and early tomorrow" were the words I will always remember. For it was bright and early the next day that the body of Edith Ramsey was found.

1

Lesson Number One

I've always loved train journeys. The train's a great place to read a book, sip on a cinnamon coffee, make small talk with friendly strangers, and gaze at the countryside. It also makes the perfect setting for a murder mystery. *Murder on the Orient Express* was one of the first mystery novels I read as a teenager. It started my whole obsession with being a mystery writer.

During *this* train journey, however, I was too excited to read. Sitting at a window seat on the Thameslink from London to Cambridge, all I could think about was the seven-day writing course I was about to embark on. I was one of five chosen for a coveted place on the Cosy Mystery Masterclass, taught by mystery writer Edith Ramsey at a remote country house. I had brought her latest novel, *The Final Draft*, along for the journey. I'd read it four times already. The story's twisted plot is about five successful writers who are invited to a remote castle in the Yorkshire countryside by a mysterious publisher. They are each to write a chapter for a new mystery novel. After the first draft of each chapter has been completed, the writers are killed off one by one by the mysterious publisher who turns out to be a failed writer, driven by jealousy and the need for recognition. He completes the final draft by himself and publishes it as his own novel, becoming the successful author he always dreamed of.

The similarities between her latest novel and this writing course were more than obvious, and the irony did appeal to the darker side of my imagination. But there was one obvious difference: the book was about five *successful* writers. This course was for five unknown authors, who have yet to publish a novel and who would kill to be the next Edith Ramsey (not literally of course).

To earn a place on the course, we had to submit a five-hundred-word essay with the title "Why I Want to Join the Cosy Mystery Masterclass". Apart from my admiration for great mystery writers like Agatha Christie, Dorothy L Sayers and PD James, my reasons stemmed from my upbringing in a small village in Sussex. My mum ran a local haberdashery for many years, but reluctantly had to sell it due to her chronic fatigue syndrome. Her condition got worse as I got older, to the point where she rarely left the house and I had to stay in most evenings to take care of her. Dad spent most of his evenings in the local pub, not wanting to deal with what Mum was going through.

One night, when Mum was very bad, I went down to the pub to try to bring him home. I was only fifteen at the time. When I got there, I couldn't find him. I searched everywhere. Outside, I spotted him in the backseat of a car, all over another woman. Turned out he'd been having an affair for years, behind Mum's back. I agonised over telling mum, but I knew I had to. She broke down in tears. We later learned that the whole village had known what Dad had been up to. Their silence helped him live a lie that broke my mum's heart. We couldn't bear to stay. She took me and my younger brother to live with my aunt in Brighton.

And that's why I wanted to become a mystery writer. Not to indulge in murderous fantasies, or to show off the intellectual superiority of an amateur sleuth amidst the bumbling ineptitude of local police constables, but to confront the one thing that still goads me to this day about village life: *small-mindedness.*

I ended my application with this: "Although it is only in the realm of mystery fiction the murder rate in villages seems absurdly above the national average, yet it is equally in this fictional realm that truth and justice is ever-present, ever striving to overcome the narrowmindedness of traditional folk, bringing the light of reason to those dark nooks and crannies of village life, where gossip and hearsay habitually lurk."

Four weeks after I submitted my application, I received the invitation to the masterclass. I was overjoyed. Mum was too, although she worried about me whenever I wasn't with her. She insisted I ring her every day while on the course. At the very least, I assured her, I would send her a text.

At around midday, I arrived at Cambridge Station where I transferred to an old train that took me to the sleepy village of Beaglesford. It was a ten-minute walk from the station to the village high street, where I stopped to look at a map of the local area. Turnpike Road wasn't on the map. My phone signal wasn't great, so I couldn't look it up online. I needed help. Wheeling my suitcase behind me, I walked down the high street, taking in the surroundings. The village was typically quaint, leafy and – dare I say – *cosy*; lined with small, independent shops, houses with thatched roofs, and a fifteenth-century parish church whose stone

The Perfect Murder Assignment

turret towered above the surrounding buildings. I arrived at a charming little bookshop. A brass doorbell rang as I entered. The two elderly women sitting behind the counter seemed surprised by my entrance, as if they weren't used to customers at this time of day.

"How may we help you, dear?" said one of them, putting her box of gift cards to the side.

"I'm looking for Ainsley Manor," I said.

They exchanged glances. "It's at the end of Turnpike Road," said the other woman, who was reading a novel with a cover image of an anthropomorphic cat attired in a deerstalker and trench coat.

"Can you tell me how to get to Turnpike Road? It doesn't seem to be on the map."

"The best way to get there is to follow the road around the church, cross the bridge, then take the first left. From there, 'tis about a ten-minute walk straight ahead."

Nodding my head, I smiled, then turned to leave the shop.

"What brings you to Beaglesford?" said one of the ladies.

"I'm here for a writing class with Edith Ramsey."

They looked at each other again and smiled excitedly.

"Oh, we just love Edith Ramsey, we have all her books for sale here," she said, as she pointed to the shelf nearest the door. Looking in the direction of her crooked finger, I could see all of Edith's novels in the crime fiction section, right next to a section dedicated exclusively to animal cosy mysteries.

"We'd do anything to meet her. She's a hero of ours. What's your name, dear?"

"I'm Belinda."

14

"Belinda," she repeated affably, "I'm Joanne. This is Hilda."

"How do you do?" I said. "Well, I must be off. Thank you for your help."

I opened the door to leave.

"Be sure to tell Edith about our shop," Hilda said after me.

"Yes," said Joanne, "and we have a book club as well. We meet here every Thursday morning. We would love if Edith could come along, you know, make a special guest appearance."

"Yes, I'll be sure to tell her."

"Great. We hope you have a lovely stay in our village."

"Thank you," I replied. "I'm sure I will."

*

Walking by the old parish church, I passed a graveyard where a gardener hacked weeds at the bottom of a stone wall. He halted and leaned on his garden hoe, glaring at me through his deep-set eyes. I smiled at him but his face remained wholly unchanged, which made me feel quite unsettled. I crossed the road and then a stone humpback bridge over a tranquil river that flowed through the centre of the village. Past the bridge, I took the first turn left and walked carefully along the grassy edges of a narrow, uneven road.

I had walked for five minutes when I heard a car fast approaching. I flattened myself against a hedgerow to let it pass, scratching my legs on the briars. The car passed me at a phenomenal speed, only missing me by a couple of inches. I was left shaken and outraged. Was there no speed limit round these parts?

Defiantly, I marched onwards. After ten minutes, I could see the manor house: a grand, elegant Edwardian mansion, whose splendid exterior was partly covered in lush green ivy. Arriving at the large iron gates, I pressed the intercom button and waited.

"Ainsley Manor House, how may I help?" said a female voice.

"I'm here for the masterclass... the one with Edith Ramsey," I replied, feeling slightly nervous.

"Name please?"

"Belinda Boothby."

The mechanical gates creaked open slowly. Holding firm to my suitcase, I briskly walked up the winding driveway. A young woman came out into the courtyard to greet me. She was very pretty, brunette and blue-eyed, probably mid-twenties and wore an old-fashioned black-and-white maidservant outfit.

Very retro!

"Hello, Ms Boothby," she said, with a warm, welcoming smile. "How was your journey?"

"Not too bad, thank you," I said.

"May I take your case?" she asked.

"Oh, yes please," I answered. "If you want."

She took my suitcase and led me inside the front door. The grandeur of the elegant hallway made me feel like a cast member of Downton Abbey. Above me, hung a crystal chandelier, while beneath my feet a soft luxurious carpet spanned the spacious hallway, continuing up the mahogany staircase.

"I'm Rita by the way," she said, as she laboured up the staircase with my suitcase. I felt I should have carried it myself – what was the etiquette in these situations?

"What a lovely house!" I said as I followed her up the stairs. "Does it have any dark secrets?"

She looked back at me and smiled. "Not that I've heard of. Maybe after this week!"

We reached the second floor. Rita carried my bag to a door, then laid it down. Near the door was a glass statue of a peacock on top of a wooden column. Rita took out a set of keys and opened the door, inviting me inside the room with a wave of her hand. It was probably one of the quaintest bedrooms I'd ever seen: exquisitely neat and tidy, with not one single crease visible on the ochre bedsheets. The floor was made from varnished oak wood, with a matching wardrobe and chest of drawers. Most importantly, it had its own bathroom. I sat on the edge of the soft bed.

"Have the others arrived?" I asked Rita, who stood at the door.

"No, you're the first,"

"What about Edith?"

She paused to think for a few moments. "Edith will be available later this evening for the meet and greet. Can I get you anything for now?"

"No, no. I'm fine. Where will the meet and greet take place?"

"In the drawing room at seven," Rita said. "If you need anything before then, just let me know." She smiled then closed the door, leaving me to take in my surroundings.

Feeling excited, I leapt to my feet and walked to the window where I could see the stately back garden, populated with trim flower beds and cone-shaped trees. In the middle of the garden was a labyrinth, measuring about ten metres in diameter.

Beyond the garden, spanned the picturesque Cambridgeshire countryside with its infinite blanket of green, brown and golden fields that rolled into the horizon.

Under the window, a desk with a flexible lamp, three spiral notebooks and a row of ballpoint pens. I'd chosen not to bring my laptop for this writing course, since I always found it to be too distracting, with its addictive games and internet access. A good old-fashioned notebook and pen was ideal for fleshing out new story ideas.

I sent my mum a text to tell her I had arrived safely, and laid down on the bed, tired from the journey. I thought about Mum, who was probably also lying in her bed at this time.

*

It was almost six o' clock when I awoke. Mum hadn't replied to my text. I decided it was time to explore the house. I walked downstairs and paced around the hallway, fantasising about being a member of the upper class. The house had many rooms, to be sure. About fifteen in total, by my estimate. Seven of which were located downstairs. The doors of each were all firmly shut. I remembered that Rita said the meet and greet was at seven in the drawing room. But which room was the drawing room? I decided to don my detective hat and open a door at random.

The first door I tried was closest to the foot of the stairs. Inside was a small antiquarian library, filled with the musty but familiar smell of old books. Perched on a writing table in the corner was an antique armillary sphere. I walked over to it and pushed one of the spheres, which rotated with a squeaking sound. Just then, there was a loud crash, followed by a shrill voice, exclaiming: "Oh fiddlesticks!"

I rushed along the few rows of bookshelves until I came to the final aisle, where a woman was bent over a toppled pile of old books.

"Are you alright?" I asked.

The woman straightened up, startled. She squinted her eyes at me through a large pair of red-framed glasses.

"Oh yes," she said in a timid voice. "I'm quite alright. Just had a slight accident."

She was middle-aged with a slightly stooped posture. Her hair was greying blonde, with a frizzy dry texture. Her large red specs, which resembled novelty glasses, made her overall appearance unintentionally comical. She looked down at the pile of books and winced.

"May I help?"

"No, no, I'm fine," she said. "I was just trying to rearrange some books. What's your name?"

"Belinda."

"Belinda..." Her eyes rolled upwards as if trying to remember something. "Belinda Boothby?"

"Yes, that's correct. And you are?"

"Shirley Atkins. I'm Edith's assistant."

"Oh, well, very nice to meet you. So, has she arrived?"

"Who do you mean?" she asked.

"Edith."

"Well, yes, well, I mean, no, not exactly. She's... on her way." She bent down to pick up a few fallen books and stacked them next to a Newton's Cradle on a vintage pedestal desk.

"Oh, I see. So, you didn't travel together?"

"Well, yes, we did," she said, as she placed the rest of the fallen books on the desk, "but she decided to stop in the village. To do a bit of shopping I think."

"I see," I said. "Well, it was nice meeting you."

She adjusted her glasses with her finger and smiled awkwardly. "Nice meeting you too. See you later for the meet and greet."

*

Outside the library, I surveyed the other closed doors and opened another at random. Inside, was the dining room, which had a large oval table surrounded by a matching set of high-back chairs. The wooden floor creaked under my feet as I wandered around the table. I stopped to examine a large heraldic plaque on the wall behind the top end of the table. The plaque bore the name Ainsley and depicted two lions fighting with each other beneath a knight's helmet. At the other end, a stag's head with an enormous pair of antlers extending outwards was mounted on the wall. Looking at the stag's lifeless eyes, I felt uneasy.

Time to look behind another door.

Back in the hallway, I opened another door and found the living room. The splendid interior was decorated with a suite of mahogany furniture, a fireplace, and framed oil paintings depicting scenes of fox hunting. Above the mantelpiece, hung an imposingly large-framed painting of a middle-aged gentleman, clad in nineteenth-century hunting attire, holding a double-barrelled shotgun in his hands. To his side, stood a bloodhound, poised for the hunt his master was to embark upon. The inscription at the base of the painting indicated the identity of the gentleman – Lord William Ainsley – presumably, the original owner of this stately house.

Turning my attention to the table in the middle of the room, I spotted a selection of board games: Guess Who?, Draughts, Dominoes, Snakes and Ladders, Monopoly. At the top of the pile of games was the legendary Cluedo. I smiled to myself as I remembered playing this as a little girl. As I was about to pick up the box, a high-pitched voice sprang from the corner of the room: "Hi there!"

Startled, I looked in the direction of the voice and saw a petite girl in her twenties, sitting alone by the window, polishing a pair of round glasses.

"I'm Hazel," she said in a friendly manner, putting on her specs.

"Hello," I said, clearing my throat. "I'm Belinda."

She walked towards me and extended her small hand. "Nice to meet you, Belinda."

"Nice to meet you," I said, shaking her hand.

"Have you met any of the others yet?"

"No, you're the first. Except for Shirley. Met her in the library."

Hazel nodded. "Yeah, I met her too. She said Edith's train was delayed. She had to get a later one."

I frowned. "Really? She told me they travelled together and Edith's in the village doing some shopping."

"Huh," Hazel said. "That sounds..."

"Odd," I said.

Hazel smiled. "Already, we have a mystery."

"So, do you think this house has any dark secrets?" Hazel said playfully.

My eyes wandered to the painting of Lord Ainsley. "I was wondering that myself. I'm sure we'll find out."

Hazel followed my gaze toward Lord Ainsley. "Do you think he was married?"

I pursed my lips, thinking about her question. "I'm sure he was. This house must have come down through many generations, since it bears his name."

Hazel looked around the room. "That's exactly what I was thinking. But there are no paintings of his wife anywhere."

"Women probably didn't appear in paintings as often as men did back in those days."

Hazel looked at me, with a wry smile. "Or maybe... there's *another* reason."

"Another reason?" I asked.

She leaned in toward me, as if to tell me a secret. "Maybe he got rid of her and buried her body somewhere in the grounds?" She leaned back and smiled. Her mind was clearly filled with ideas from reading murder mysteries. Perhaps too many murder mysteries.

"You really think so?" I replied, sounding unconvinced.

She continued smiling and wandered over to the table with the board games.

"You a Cluedo fan?" she asked.

"Oh yes," I said. "Certainly, brings back memories."

"Me too," Hazel said. "Played this so many times when I was a kid."

Sitting down on the leather sofa, Hazel opened the box and emptied the contents onto the table. I took a seat beside her and sifted through the miniature murder weapons.

"Huh, that's strange."

"What's that?"

Picking up the tiny candlestick, I began to ponder. "If I remember correctly, there should be six murder weapons. There are only five here. I wonder which one is missing?" The candlestick, the revolver, the rope, the pipe and the spanner were all present.

"Wait," said Hazel, picking up the instruction leaflet. "I'll look it up."

After a few moments, it hit me: "The dagger."

"Yes, you're right."

"I wonder what happened to it?" I asked, while searching inside the box.

"Maybe the last player got away with his crime," she chuckled.

I chuckled along with her. At that moment, I got the impression we had a lot in common. As well as honing our skills at writing, this course was a chance to make new friends. I hadn't really made any friends since I left uni, which was four years ago. Most of the girls I still knew didn't have time to read mystery books, being too busy with work and girls' nights out. But Hazel didn't seem like the socialising type. She was clearly bookish and introverted. You could say she was nerdy, but I wouldn't describe her so, since I always hated when people in school called me nerdy.

We left the living room together and ventured though another door, which turned out to be the kitchen. It was very spacious and rustic, with exposed beams and rugged stone walls, culminating in a cosy farmhouse interior décor. Etched on a wooden plaque on the wall were the words:

Beware of hurting the cook's feelings.

He has access to all the knives.

On the kitchen table was a chopping board, with chopped vegetables and a large carving knife. The cook, it seems, had been chopping here only recently.

"Wow, check this out," Hazel said, gazing out the window into the back garden. I could see the garden labyrinth, beckoning us to explore its design. We looked at each other and smiled. Exiting through the kitchen's back door, we strolled onto the magnificent lawn towards the labyrinth. Its hedge walls were about knee-high and trimmed to perfection, and its smooth stone pathway coiled towards the centre like an ouroboros.

"I love mazes," Hazel said, approaching the centre.

Trailing behind her small steps, I responded: "It's not a maze. It's a labyrinth."

"What's the difference?" she asked.

"Mazes have many ways to the centre and many dead ends. A labyrinth has one single path, which leads to the centre and back."

"I see," she said, as she reached the centre. "Made it! Nice view from here, isn't it?"

I stood next to her in the centre and gazed around at the surrounding countryside. In the distance, was an old windmill, perched in the middle of a golden field, with its blades rotating slowly in the wind. Memories of Mum reading Don Quixote to me as a child came to mind, which inspired a love of reading from an early age.

"Here's where the adventure begins," she said excitedly, as she raised her arms in the air. She seemed genuinely inspired by the surrounding natural beauty. After a few moments of contemplative silence, she turned to me. "Where to now?"

There was a wooden bench hidden within a group of cypress trees at the other side of the lawn. "Let's go over there," I said, pointing. Hazel looked towards the group of trees and nodded.

In front of the bench was a small herb garden, which emitted an enticing aroma.

"Mm, that's lovely," Hazel said, sniffing in the air. "I smell lavender, basil, and rosemary."

"I detect sage and fennel," I added, "and a hint of thyme." Hazel and I sat down and soaked up the relaxing atmosphere.

"This is a cosy little place," Hazel said, gazing upward at the tall, slender cypress trees behind her. "Hidden from the prying eyes of the house."

"Yes, it's like a secret garden," I said, as I stretched out my feet on the grass.

"I wonder what Edith will be like," Hazel mused.

"I'm sure she'll be very witty. Intelligent. Charismatic. And will have much to teach us."

She looked at me. "Is it your dream to be an author?"

"Yes, indeed," I said. "It's what I want to do more than anything else. What about you?"

Her hands fidgeted. "I'd like to be a real detective."

"What's stopping you?"

She looked down at her feet, as she continued fidgeting her hands. "I'm not cut out for that kind of work, I think. I'm a bit too shy. I love reading and don't have many friends. I find it hard to talk to strangers." She raised her head to look at me. "But you're easy to talk to."

"Thanks," I said, smiling at her. "I feel the same way about you."

We both sat comfortably in silence for a few moments. My nose began to feel slightly runny from the strong-smelling herbs.

"What do you do for work?" I asked in a slightly nasal voice.

"I work in a library. Digital archiving mainly. What about you?"

"I was a PA but lost my job recently. Been looking for a new career path."

"Oh, I'm sorry to hear you lost your job."

"It's fine," I said, taking out a handkerchief. "I'll live. Hated my job anyway."

"What kind of work did you do?" she asked.

I dabbed my nose with the handkerchief. "I worked for a PR company in London, but couldn't put up with my manager's abusive attitude, so I quit."

"What did he do?" she asked.

"It was a she. Wendy Simmonds. She treated me like her servant. Had to do her laundry, book her dinners, buy her friends coffee, arrange to have her kids picked up from school. Things that had nothing to do with my job description. And when I didn't do things to her impossibly high standard, she'd rant and swear at me in front of everyone in the office. On my last day, I told her what I thought of her in no uncertain terms, then stormed out of the office with my head held high."

"Good for you!"

Smiling, I added, "Broke her favourite coffee mug on my way out too."

Hazel laughed out loud. At the end of the garden, a hare appeared and started nibbling at some of the herb plants. As I observed the hare, Hazel's laughter transformed into heavy coughing.

"Are you OK?" I asked

She nodded her head to indicate she was, but her coughing became worse. She started wheezing.

"Hazel, what's wrong?"

"It's," she struggled, clutching her chest. "My asthma. I... need... my... inhaler."

"Where is it?"

"In my room."

"Oh dear," I rose from the bench. "I'll get it for you. Which room are you staying in?"

"Third... door... on the left... of the... stairs," she barely got the words out.

"OK, wait there, I'll be back in a jiffy."

I sprinted back to the house. Dashing through the kitchen, I made it into the hallway, where I stopped suddenly, slightly out of breath. Rita was standing there with a young man with two suitcases at his feet. He was dashingly handsome, dressed in a Ralph Lauren polo shirt and creaseless chino pants. He looked like one of those posh lads that went to Eton. Both stared at me curiously as I caught my breath.

"What's wrong?" asked Rita.

"It's Hazel," I uttered. "She's having an asthma attack. I need to get her inhaler from her bedroom. It's quite urgent."

"Alright, I'll come with you." She turned to the young man. "Sorry, I have to run. Here's your key. Your room is up the stairs, third door on the left."

"No worries," the young man replied, as he picked up his suitcases.

Rita and I dashed upstairs. I tried to open the door to Hazel's room but it was locked. Rita briskly took out a set of keys and opened the door. Rushing inside, I immediately spotted the asthma inhaler on the bedside table. I grabbed it and ran back to Hazel. To my horror, Hazel was slumped on the bench, struggling to breathe. I held the inhaler to her mouth and she took two deep puffs. Within moments, her breathing improved enough for her to sit up.

Rita arrived on the scene seconds later, a panicked look on her face.

"Are you alright?"

Hazel nodded, as she took two more puffs.

"You need a doctor?"

"No," she said, as she sat up. "This happens a lot." She stood up and wobbled slightly. Rita and I took one of her arms each and helped Hazel back inside the house. We entered the hallway, where the man was coming back down the stairs. "Is she alright?"

"She's fine," I informed him. "Had an asthma attack. I'm Belinda, by the way. This is Hazel."

"I'm Robert." He smiled, which made me blush momentarily.

Gosh, what nice teeth he has. He's quite a fox!

"So, you're on the writing course," he said.

"Yes, we are," I said, smiling in return.

He glanced around the hallway. "Any sign of Edith Ramsey?"

"She'll be here soon," Rita said, though she didn't sound sure. "She's running a few errands."

"I see. Looks, like I've got a bit of time to look around." He turned to Rita. "Fancy giving me the grand tour?"

Rita smiled. "My pleasure."

She led Robert towards the library while Hazel and I walked to the living room where we relaxed until the meet and greet.

*

Seven bells came and we followed the sound of chat to the drawing room. Robert and two more young people were there when we entered. I greeted them as I took a seat beside Robert, while Hazel took a seat opposite me. There was a beautiful silver tea set on the table in the middle of the room, accompanied by a selection of sumptuous cake slices: lemon drizzle, chocolate fudge and Victoria sponge. Hazel picked up the elegant silver teapot and poured me a cup of tea. Choosing a slice of lemon drizzle, I sat back in my chair and relished the sweet taste. As I ate the slice, I gazed at a fox's head mounted in the centre of the wall in front of where I sat. Its mouth was frozen in a snarling sneer, while its eyes, like two pale amber marbles, glared at me, making me feel quite disconcerted. I turned in my chair ever so slightly to avoid its predatory stare.

"Right, should we go around the room and introduce ourselves while we wait for our host?" Robert suggested.

"Sounds like a good idea," Hazel replied.

"Alright then. I'll go first. My name is Robert. I'm twenty-five and training to be a CA. In my spare time I enjoy reading, writing, gaming and lacrosse. I've published two short stories in *Young Mystery Writer's Digest* and I own a goldfish named Sam. Anything you want to ask me, feel free to ask."

"What's a CA?" Hazel asked.

"Chartered accountant," Robert answered.

"Well, I'll go next. I'm Hazel, I'm a library assistant. I love reading books, especially detective stories. Arthur Conan Doyle is my all-time favourite writer, but I'll say Edith Ramsey while I'm staying here." She smiled. "As I demonstrated today, I have chronic asthma. I would love to be a detective, to solve mysteries in real life, but my condition makes that too difficult. I'm content to read about them instead." She smiled when she finished, then ate a piece of sponge cake.

"Who's next then? How about you?" Robert said to a girl sitting beside Hazel.

The girl shifted in her seat, looking slightly nervous. She was pretty, slim-athletic, with a dimpled, radiant smile that could light up a small village.

"Hi. My name's Jamelia. I'm currently studying at the Royal Academy of Dramatic Art, hoping to become a professional actor. I'd love to star in a detective TV series one day, like *Line of Duty* or *Death in Paradise*. And, of course, be a mystery writer. Would be really cool if a book series I'd written were made into a TV series. Then I could cast myself in the lead role," she smiled broadly to everyone.

Everyone smiled in return.

"So, anyway, nice to meet you all," Jamelia concluded.

"Nice to meet you, I'm sure," Robert said. "Who's next?"

All eyes turned to the young man sitting next to Jamelia. He was neatly dressed in a navy blazer, white shirt – top button open – and camel-coloured slacks. His hair was perfectly combed to one side, with a cool, wet-look finish and he had a designer-trimmed beard.

"Hello," he started, sitting upright in his chair. "My name's Aaron. I'm twenty-four. Studying for a Masters in Politics and International Relations at Oxford. I love mystery novels. My favourite writers are Ruth Rendell and Patricia Cornwell and, of course, Edith. I've read all her books. I hope to learn new skills on this masterclass, like improving story structure and character development. Things like that. So, yeah, I'm really looking forward to getting to know you all and hope this is something we'll all remember."

"Thanks, Aaron. Well, I guess that leaves only you then," Robert said, turning everyone's attention on me.

I took a quick sip of tea. "Yes, indeed, and then there was one." As soon as I said those words, I cringed, but I carried on. "My name is Belinda. I'm twenty-six. Recently unemployed and looking for a new direction in life. My hobbies include reading, theatre, hiking and badminton. I love to write in my spare time and..."

As I was speaking, a woman entered the room. A very strange-looking woman. She had long, bushy brown hair and wore a large pair of tinted glasses, much too big for her face, and a lit cigarette was balanced precariously between her lips. She was dressed very shabbily, looked to be in her late fifties, and the smell of her cigarette immediately stank up the room.

I refocused on myself. "Um, I'm currently writing a murder mystery set in Elizabethan England, during Shakespeare's time. Well, I just started it, not sure when it'll be finished. But, um, yeah, that's me. Hope to see all your names in bookshops one day," I said, smiling awkwardly at everyone.

"Thanks, Belinda," said Robert, who had focused his gaze on the strange-looking woman. In fact, everyone had their eyes on the strange-looking woman, who was pouring herself a cup of tea while puffing on her cigarette. She sat in one of the few remaining chairs and exhaled a thick plume of smoke, then took a long, emphatic slurp of her tea. Who was this woman?

"Hello there," Robert took the initiative in addressing her. "And who might you be?"

She sat in silence for a few moments, stirring her cup of tea noisily with a spoon.

"My name... is Margot," she said in a husky Scottish accent. She slurped her tea loudly, then placed the cup and saucer carelessly on the table. She took a long drag on her cigarette and exhaled an almost perfect smoke ring that wafted through the air, before dissipating above Robert's head. Hazel began coughing.

"Excuse me," I said to the woman, "I don't mean to be rude, but do you mind smoking elsewhere? Hazel has asthma and the smoke is clearly affecting her."

"Yeah, yeah," the woman said indifferently, "whatever you say, lassie." She dropped her half-smoked cigarette into her tea then stared at the group in silence. An awkward silence passed before Aaron made an observation.

"I thought there were meant to be only five people on this course."

He was right. The masterclass was meant for five people. Presently, there were six sitting in the drawing room.

"Yes," said Robert. "That's what I was led to believe. That's weird. There's one too many."

"I'm not on this course, lad," Margot said. "That explains the discrepancy."

"Oh," said Robert. "So why are you here exactly?"

She sighed deeply. "I'm here because Edith Ramsey owes me money."

"What do you mean?" asked Aaron.

"What do I mean?" she retorted. "I mean, I was her agent. Then when she got famous, she ditched me for a fancy London agent. That bloody bitch still owes me money! I tracked her down to this village to confront her. Things, however, didn't go down well..." She put her hand close to her face, examining her fingernails. That's when something dawned on me...

She's got blood on her fingers!

Dried blood to be exact. Suddenly, I felt very uneasy. Shirley appeared in the doorway.

"You!" she exclaimed. "What are you doing here?"

"I've come to get what's mine," Margot said coldly.

"What? But... how? How did you get in here?"

"I ran into Edith earlier in a bookshop," Margot calmly explained. "She was, as you can imagine, not very happy to see me. She left the shop, so I followed her out to her car where we had an argument. She threatened to call the police, so I..." she produced a bloodstained dagger from her purse, "settled the dispute."

Everyone in the room stared at the woman in disbelief.

"What do you mean?" Shirley stridently asked. "Where is Edith now?"

Margot held the dagger up to her face, examining the blood on the blade. "Probably where I left her. By the side of the road. Took her keys and purse and drove here. Now... you need to get my money, lassie. Or you'll end up the same way."

Shirley grimaced. "You're lying! You... you... you can't be telling the truth. I don't believe it... you..."

A panicked Shirley took out her mobile and frantically dialled a number. A phone started ringing in Margot's pocket. Margot held up the phone, with a look of triumph on her face.

"Oh my God," Shirley shrieked. "Edith's phone! What have you done with her?"

Margot rose from the chair and approached Shirley, aiming the dagger directly at her. Observing the scene, it felt like I was in a dream.

Could I have been dreaming?

"I'm not leaving here empty handed!" Margot bellowed, as Shirley cowered from the knife. "I want my money and you're going to get it for me!"

"No, no, no," Shirley squealed, as she backed into a corner. "I don't have... I don't have your money."

"Don't have my money?" Margot asked, as she walked right up to Shirley. "Then die, you miserable little bitch!"

Margot plunged the dagger into Shirley, who immediately slumped to the floor. We gasped in horror, leaping from our chairs. Margot turned to us, her face hell-bent on bloody murder. Petrified, we backed away from her and huddled together at the other side of the room.

"Have you seen enough?" she asked menacingly. "I know I have." She took off her glasses and ripped off her brown bushy hair. Margot was in fact... *Edith Ramsey! The* Edith Ramsey. We gazed at her in bewilderment. She looked at us and grinned.

"Surprise," she said in her natural English accent. "You may assuage your worst fears. Edith Ramsey is very much alive. As is her personal assistant, Miss Shirley Atkins."

Shirley stood up from the floor and brushed herself off. She smiled awkwardly at the group.

"Lesson number one," Edith declared, with her index finger raised. "Learn how to suspend your audience's disbelief. You'll never be a mystery writer if you can't accomplish that most fundamental deed. Make the audience believe in your plot!" She demonstrated how the dagger had a retractable plastic blade by pushing it in and out with her finger. "Anyway, I want to welcome you all to the masterclass. I'm sure we'll get better acquainted over the next few days. My team have prepared a wonderful meal for you. I have things to prepare, so must bid you goodnight. I hope to see you bright and early tomorrow." Edith took an ostentatious bow, then marched out of the drawing room.

"Dinner will be served in ten minutes in the dining room," Shirley said, smiling. "See you tomorrow." She shuffled out of the drawing room after Edith.

We were left standing in silence. Each of us, equally astounded. It was certainly a dramatic introduction. Unexpected and twisted. I loved it.

Hazel finally broke the silence: "Well, she was everything I expected," she said with a giggle.

Robert shrugged. "Didn't believe it for a second," he said unconvincingly. "The knife looked fake from the moment she pulled it out."

We had finally met the great Edith Ramsey. What an introduction! One that each of us would remember for a long time.

Dinner was very welcome after my eventful day. At ten o'clock, I left them all to it and went to my room. I was relieved to see that Mum had replied to my text, to say that she was fine. Before turning out the lights, I texted her back telling her about Edith's shocking act and how I was both excited and nervous at how this masterclass was going to turn out.

2

Quiet Little Backwater

Good heavens!

The sound of a bell ringing ripped me from my slumber. It was soon followed by the maidservant's voice: "Breakfast is served!"

It was morning – 8 am to be exact. I'd slept like a log. At least, I think I did. My belly rumbled as the mouth-watering aroma of fried sausages and bacon wafted into my bedroom. That smell meant one thing: traditional English breakfast! Time to get dressed.

Entering the kitchen, I received a warm greeting from Aaron, Jamelia and Hazel who were being served breakfast by Rita. Standing with his back to us at the stove was a stocky young man whose hair was styled in a man bun. I took a seat opposite Jamelia, who was eating scrambled eggs on toast.

"What do you fancy, Belinda?" Rita asked. "Eggs on toast, cereal, fruits and nuts or full English fry-up?"

"Full English fry-up please!"

Hazel, whose plate was filled with bacon, sausages, fried tomatoes and perfectly poached eggs, smiled at me, conscious of how spoilt we were for breakfast.

The chef walked over to me and placed a full plate in front of me. "I'm Simon. Nice to meet you." He had a plump, friendly face with a very shiny forehead.

Smiling back, I said: "I'm Belinda. Pleased to meet you. You're the eighth houseguest then?"

He shook his head. "I'm not staying here. I only come in to do the cooking. I live about a half-hour drive from here."

I ate a juicy piece of sausage. "Mm, this is really good!"

"Thanks," he said, cheerfully. "Plenty more where that came from."

Robert entered the kitchen, looking decidedly jaded. He yawned, while saying: "Morning everyone." He took a seat at the top of the table and yawned again.

"What would you like?" Rita asked him.

"Just cereal for me. Bowl of muesli if you have it."

"Coming right up," Rita said.

"Sleep well?" I asked.

"No," he said, as he yawned again. "Kept hearing these strange noises outside my window. Like an owl or something. Anyone else hear it?"

Rita served Robert his muesli. "I think I heard it too," she told him. "Sounded like a tawny owl."

"A tawny owl?" he said.

"Yes. I believe it's a mating call," Rita informed Robert, with a smile. It didn't take a great detective to see that her smile had a flirtatious element. Robert nodded, mulling over Rita's words.

"Tawny owl," he said. "Yeah, that could explain it."

*

When breakfast was finished, Rita instructed us to proceed to the library with our writing materials. When we entered the library, there were six chairs positioned in a circle. Each chair had a wooden writing tablet. We each took a seat and waited excitedly for Edith to arrive. I opened my notebook and wrote my name and address on the inside. Aaron and Robert had brought notebooks too, while Hazel had opted to bring her laptop and Jamelia her tablet computer.

Shirley entered the room and placed a glass next to Edith's writing tablet, then left again without saying anything. A few moments later, Edith entered the room. She wore a full-length turquoise dress, with a lavender silk scarf draped casually over her shoulders, and a magenta beaded necklace. Her greying hair was permed to perfection, while her piercing blue eyes, accentuated by eyeshadow, seemed like they could penetrate the deepest recesses of your soul. Refined, elegant, and eccentric, she was so different from how she looked the night before. Sitting down on the only vacant chair, she drank back the iced drink that Shirley had left and gasped in satisfaction.

"We meet again," she said with a teasing smirk. We couldn't help but smile back, intrigued by her peculiar presence.

"What class is this again?" she asked, at which we all laughed.

"The Cosy Mystery Masterclass," Hazel said.

"Ah, yes, cosy mystery. Tell me something... oh, wait a second. Shirley?" she shouted towards the door, which was slightly ajar. "Shirley! Shirley!" Her voice was quite strident. "Oh God, where is that bloody woman!"

At that moment, Shirley entered the room. "Yes, Edith?"

"Be a dear and fix me another drink."

"Another drink?" Shirley said.

"Yes, another drink," Edith snappily replied.

Shirley humbly picked up the glass and shuffled out of the room.

"And don't dillydally!" Edith shouted after her, then turned to us and rolled her eyes. We laughed again, enjoying her exaggerated cantankerous attitude.

"Where was I?" she continued. "Oh yes, I wanted to ask you something." She paused for a few moments, looking up at the ceiling. "Why murder? Why do we want to read and write about murder? Any idea? I mean, are we all sick-minded, bloodthirsty, borderline psychopaths?"

We laughed again. This time, a little more subdued.

"I'm serious!" she said. "Why are we so interested in murder mysteries?"

There were a few moments of silence.

"Because we want to solve a mystery," Hazel said. "We want to know who the killer is and see him brought to justice."

"Okay," said Edith. "Mysteries are indeed interesting. And we want to see the triumph of justice. But aren't there mysteries without murder? And aren't there other ways to see justice triumph than through the resolution of a whodunnit?"

"Murder makes us question our core communal values, you know, it forces to ask where things have gone wrong in society," asserted Aaron.

"Okay," said Edith. "Anything else?"

"Murder, being the worst of crimes," I put forward, "usually requires the best of minds to solve it. Murder mysteries gives us heroes to believe in."

"Okay, okay, all very interesting answers. All very thoughtful and insightful and intelligent but all just completely... *wrong*."

The class looked at Edith, perplexed. Shirley entered the room with another drink for Edith. She placed the glass on her writing tablet, then left the room again. "Thank you, Shirley," she said after her. She picked up the glass and took a long sip.

"The answer lies in the *setting*. Look around you. We're in a sleepy little village in the middle of nowhere where there isn't much to do. Such are the typical settings of murder mysteries. Small, intimate, cosy little corners of society. So why are we obsessed with murder? The answer is: because life is so bloody boring in these places! There's nothing quite like a murder to liven things up!"

We paid attention. Edith drank the rest of her glass.

"A boring setting makes murder exciting! In a built-up setting such as a city, there are so many distractions. So many things going on. Subplots, backstories, multiple-character points of view and story arcs, yah-dee-yah-dee-yah. It's easy to lose focus. Villages are perfect for murders. Life is so still, so quiet, so slow-paced and peaceful. Suddenly there's a murder and everyone has their knickers in a twist!"

Another round of laughter.

"Right, so, who here has written a murder mystery? Or is currently writing one? What about you?" Edith pointed her finger directly at me.

"Um, well, I am currently writing one."

"Okay great. What's the title?"

"It doesn't have a title."

"I see. Well, tell us the plot?"

"Um, it's set in Elizabethan England. During Shakespeare's time."

"Oh dear," Edith interrupted. "A historical murder mystery! I would say stay away from this genre at all costs, but it seems it's too late for this young lady. Carry on, dear, tell us about your Shakespearean murder mystery."

"Well," I continued, a little taken aback by her comment, "it's set around the time when 'Hamlet' played in theatres, and a woman is found murdered in an alley, but no one really cares because she was a prostitute. Her brother is determined to find the killer, so, um, he stages a play showing how a famous thespian is the killer, similar to how Hamlet stages the 'play within the play' of the murder of his father in Shakespeare's play. And that's the basic outline. It's still in its early stages, but I hope to finish it this year."

"I see," said Edith. "You must have done a lot of research?"

"Um, yes, I did. I find I have lots of spare time these days, since I lost my job."

"Well," Edith smiled, "good for you. I must say I have deliberately avoided writing a mystery novel set in a historical period, for fear of getting the details of the milieu wrong. It's a very difficult thing writing in a different time period. The level of detail, the mannerisms, the fashion, the way people spoke. You will have to research your historical period down to the finest detail. Not an easy task! So I admire your efforts. It sounds like an intriguing plot and I sincerely hope you do complete it this year. Heaven knows how many people tell me that they are writing a book and years later they are still writing it!"

"Sounds great!" said Hazel. "I'd buy it!"

"And what about you? What are you working on at the moment?"

"I'm not working on anything at the moment," Hazel answered, a little caught in the spotlight. "I'm waiting for inspiration. That's why I wanted to do this masterclass."

"Okay, well, the Muse comes when we least expect it. How about you, young man?"

Robert straightened up in his chair. "Well, I have been writing something. At least, I've been writing a detailed outline of a book that I plan to write next year. After I finish my training. The story is about a detective who, in the pursuit of catching a serial killer, comes to admire his adversary. Over time, his admiration leads him to become the killer's accomplice: if he finds clues left behind at a scene, he deliberately conceals them. As the story progresses, the two develop a working relationship, culminating in a series of perfect murders."

"Oh, very interesting," said Edith. "I'm intrigued about your admiration for the murderer. Have you any sociopathic tendencies that we should know about?"

"Yeah, well," Robert said smiling, while scratching his head, "I'm an accountant, so sociopathic tendencies are an advantage."

Edith chuckled.

"I've always recognised the interdependency of the villain and the hero in detective novels," he continued. "But I have more empathy for the villain, since he comes up with all the good schemes. You see, for me, how to get away with murder is more interesting than solving it."

"What an unconventional attitude for an accountant to have," Edith said. "Remind me to ask for your card before you leave and you can take a look at my tax returns."

The class laughed together again. Robert's story did sound intriguing. It was clear that he had a dark mind. But I wondered whether his dark mind was genuine or something he feigned to make himself interesting to others.

*

During the break, I took a cup of tea into the garden. There was a small hole beneath a hedge that I presumed was created by a rabbit. As I examined the hole more closely, something brushed up against the back of my legs causing me to jump with fright.

I spun around and saw the droopy eyes of a bloodhound, panting frantically while excitedly wagging its tail. Behind him stood a man in his fifties, wearing a tartan flat cap, hunting jacket and wellingtons, and posed with his hands behind his back.

"Afternoon, young lady," he said. "Lovely weather today."

"Yes, indeed," I replied. "What an adorable dog. Yours, I presume?"

Closing his eyes, he nodded. "Name's Henry."

"I'm Belinda," I said, smiling. "What's your dog's name?"

His eyes opened wide. "Name's Henry," he repeated.

"Oh," I said. "So, both your names are Henry?"

He frowned. "No, my dear. This is Henry," he said, pointing at the hound. "My name is Gregory. I'm the groundskeeper. I live in the coach house with this lovable rascal." Towards the west side of the garden, hidden beneath a giant sycamore tree, I could see a small, cottage-sized house with a pointed roof.

Henry scampered away from his master and returned to the rabbit hole, wedging his entire head inside the small hole. As lovable as he seemed, I prayed he wouldn't catch a rabbit. *I bet those rabbits don't consider ol' Henry lovable!*

"How long have you lived here, may I ask?"

"For the past twenty years," he said. "Before me, there was another groundskeeper who worked here for almost fifty years. He knew Robert Ainsley Jr., the great grandson of Lord Ainsley."

"Oh, I see," I said. "So, it's still owned by the Ainsley family?"

"Not any more. Robert Ainsley Jr. was a rake in his day. Squandered his money for many years and couldn't pay off his gambling debts, so the house was auctioned off to the National Trust in 1958."

Gregory looked at his watch, then took out a whistle and blew into it. Immediately, Henry withdrew from the hole and scrambled back to his master's side. He gazed up at his master, while his drooling tongue dangled out of his mouth.

"Time to get you some grub, eh, ol' boy?" he said, stroking Henry's head. He turned to me and nodded. "Good day to you, Belinda. Need anything, just knock on my door."

*

Before class recommenced, I popped up to my room to see if Mum had texted me. At the top of the stairs, I could hear Edith in her room yelling at Shirley. What was she so angry about? Not wanting to draw attention to myself, I quietly entered my room and checked my phone. Mum hadn't texted. I crept back down the stairs and into the library. After about ten minutes, Edith re-joined the group – with another drink in her hand.

"So, who can define the word *cosy*?" she asked stridently.

"As in cosy mystery?" asked Hazel.

"Yes," replied Edith.

"Something insular?" Aaron said.

"What do you mean by insular?" Edith asked.

"A closed world," Aaron said. "Where things happen in a closed environment, far from everyday life."

"Like in a village," said Jamelia.

"Or a mountain resort," I said.

"And where there's usually no sex and violence," said Aaron.

"Sadly," quipped Robert, which made the group laugh.

"Okay, good. So, as we mentioned earlier, we are talking about an isolated location, such as a village. Anyone here grow up in a village?"

Robert and myself raised our hands.

"Ever witnessed any murders?" Edith asked.

I shook my head.

"Yes," said Robert hesitantly. "Well, sort of. I knew a girl who went missing. She went into the woods one day and never returned."

"Oh, how awful," said Edith. "And she was never found?"

"No," said Robert solemnly. "No one ever discovered what really happened."

"That's tragic," Edith said. "Then you'll know from first-hand experience how crime can impact a small community?"

Robert pursed his lips and nodded. "Yes, I know only too well."

There was a brief pause, before Edith continued. "We've mentioned villages. What are other examples of cosy mystery settings?"

"Hotel," said Hazel.

"Island," said Jamelia.

"University," said Aaron.

"Train," I said.

"Let's not forget," Edith raised her hands, "the country house."

We looked at each other momentarily, then Shirley entered the library.

"Shirley, have you heard of knocking?" Edith snapped.

"Sorry, Edith," Shirley said with a quiver in her voice, "just wondered if you wanted another drink?"

"I will tell you when I need another," Edith barked at her.

"Sorry," she said. "I'll be outside if you need me."

She left the library and closed the door. Edith finished her drink.

"Oh, Shirley," Edith shouted.

The door opened slightly with Shirley peeping in.

"Could you get me another drink?"

The class were bemused as Shirley entered the room like a timid mouse and took the empty glass from Edith. I was beginning to feel quite sorry for Shirley. We spent the rest of the afternoon discussing the importance of settings in mystery novels. During that time, Edith downed another three glasses.

*

"What do you think is in her glass?" Hazel asked, as the five of us walked to the local pub in the evening. The dusk had begun to settle across the sky, as we walked cautiously in single file along the edge of Turnpike Road. I kept my ears open to speeding drivers.

"Soda water, I'd say," said Jamelia.

"I personally think it's an alcoholic beverage," I said.

"I agree," Hazel replied. "Must be hard teaching a class while drinking."

"I don't think it's alcohol," proffered Jamelia. "She was drinking them from early morning. That would mean..."

"She's an alcoholic," Aaron said.

"Well, that's what a lot of famous authors end up as," I stated.

"I still don't think it was alcohol," said Jamelia.

"They were G&Ts," declared Robert. "I smelled the empty glass in the kitchen."

I turned to look at him.

"Wow, that's good detective work."

"Yeah, real nosey, Robert," jeered Jamelia.

"Well, I was helping Rita with the washing up and I had the opportunity," Robert explained.

"You and Rita might well become a detective team," I commented.

Robert shrugged his shoulders. "Who knows what will happen this week."

*

Five pints of local ale stood before us at a table in a quiet corner of the Greyhound Arms. The pleasant smell of burning logs wafted from a fire close to where we sat. The place wasn't packed but you could tell that practically every person in here lived locally.

"Cosy little corner, isn't it?" Jamelia observed.

I took a sip of my pint and shuddered slightly from the bitterness. Hazel, to my surprise, was almost halfway through her glass and seemed to be enjoying it.

"Hazel," I said, "you're outpacing the rest of us."

"Yeah, slow down, girl," Jamelia said.

Hazel giggled, holding up the pint in her hand. "It's a shandy."

Robert hadn't touched his drink. He sat with his head resting on his hand, looking very despondent.

"Rob, you're very quiet," said Jamelia. "Everything alright?"

Robert sighed deeply. "Yeah, I'm fine. Just thinking about something."

"Anything you want to share?" Jamelia asked.

He picked up his pint and drank a large mouthful. "You know the missing girl I mentioned to Edith earlier?"

"The girl who went into the woods and disappeared," said Jamelia.

"Yeah," said Robert, nodding his head. "Well, I actually know what happened to her. I've never told anyone."

"What happened to her?" I asked.

Robert eyeballed me directly, before refocusing on his pint. "Me and this girl... we'd been on a few dates. I started to have feelings for her. One night, we were walking home together and took a shortcut through the woods. I decided to reveal my true feelings. I told her I loved her but turns out she didn't love me. In fact, she told me she had been seeing my best mate behind my back. We had an argument. Things got out of hand. To cut a long story short, I, um, hit her."

"You hit her?" I said, aghast.

"Yes," he confirmed. "With a rock. Then I covered her up with leaves. I went home and returned later with a shovel and dug a shallow grave. That's where she lies to this day."

We looked at him in stunned silence.

"Anyone fancy another pint?" he asked casually. "My shout."

There was a full minute of silence before Aaron spoke up: "You're full of crap, mate!"

Robert burst out laughing. "You got me! I'm just taking the piss, ladies," he said, smiling at us. "You know I'd never hurt anyone."

"Yeah, nice gag, Rob," Jamelia said, unimpressed.

Hazel and I looked at each other. We were both shocked by Robert's bizarre sense of humour.

*

By 9 pm, Robert and Aaron were playing pool, not far from our table. Robert seemed to be in the lead, having fewer balls on the table than his opponent. I observed him carefully chalking his cue. Behind him, each holding a pint of lager, stood two girls who clearly fancied him. Robert leaned over the table and sized up his next shot. He potted the ball effortlessly then looked back at the girls and gave them a cocky wink. They turned to each other and giggled.

This guy is so full of himself.

"Isn't that Shirley over there?" Jamelia asked, squinting over to the bar.

I scanned the small crowd at the bar but couldn't see any sign of Shirley.

"Can't see her," I said. "Where?"

"She was there a second ago," Jamelia said, "She's probably gone to the loo."

"Can't imagine her as the type that socialises in pubs," I said.

Jamelia shrugged. "Yeah, true, she's a bit of a shrinking violet. They're quite the odd couple, Shirley and Edith."

"Yeah," agreed Hazel. "Edith seems to pick on her a lot."

"I'm sure it's just for show," said Jamelia.

"I'm not sure," I said. "I think there's real hostility there."

Jamelia placed her hands together and smiled. "This masterclass could get ugly. Who do you think would win in a fight? Shirley or Edith?"

Hazel and I looked at each other and remained silent.

"Come on," goaded Jamelia. "They're both roughly the same size, age and weight. Who'd you put your money on?"

Hazel shrugged. "I suppose I'd have to say Edith. Only because I don't think Shirley has the courage to stand up to her."

Jamelia shook her head. "Nah, you see I think Shirley would win. On the surface she's like this doormat for Edith's passive-aggressive behaviour but, deep down, she's a wildcat waiting to pounce on her enemy and scratch their eyes out."

Hazel took a long drink of her shandy. "I don't know," she said. "Shirley wears quite large frames. If she took them off to fight, she would probably be very poor-sighted. Therefore, Edith would win based on her ocular advantage."

"Shirley could just wear contacts?"

"True, I suppose," Hazel admitted. "But I think Edith's arms are slightly larger than Shirley's."

"Only because Shirley wears loose cardigans, which makes her arms look smaller." Jamelia raised her arms to illustrate.

As Jamelia and Hazel debated who would win the fictional fight, I spotted Gregory sitting in a corner, with Henry by his feet. He was feeding his bloodhound with what I guessed were pork scratchings or something like that. Whatever they were, Henry seemed to be enjoying them, judging by the speed at which he wagged his tail while he ate.

"Isn't that cute?" I said, interrupting their debate.

"What's that?" Jamelia asked.

"Over there. Man's best friend."

Jamelia and Hazel looked over at Gregory feeding his dog and smiled. As we observed them, a tall, powerfully built man came to stand right in front of our table, obstructing our view.

"Well, ladies? Having fun, are we?" He was maybe in his mid-forties and looked very unappealing. His greasy, dirty blond hair was thinning and badly combed to one side, and he wore a shabby black donkey jacket. He took a drink of his pint then smiled, revealing a prominent gap between his upper front teeth. Without being invited, he sat down at our table.

"I'm Jack," he said, as he settled in beside a very awkward-looking Hazel. "So, what brings you all to this quiet little backwater?"

"We're here for a writing course," Hazel said, straightening up in her seat.

"Writing course," he said. "That's fancy. Is that with Edith Ramsey?"

"Yes. She's our tutor for the week."

"Wow, that's amazing," he said. He gulped back most of his pint, leaving mainly backwashed lager at the end of his glass. He belched loudly. "What's she like then?"

"She's very nice," Hazel said, appearing more uncomfortable in the wake of the stranger's vociferous belch. "She has lots of wisdom to share."

"I bet she does," he said, swirling the remaining lager in his glass.

"Have you read her books," I asked.

He glanced at me and narrowed his eyes. "Of course, I have. I've read her new one about five times already."

"You mean *The Final Draft?*" I asked.

"That's the one," he said. "But it was nowhere near as good as her bestseller *Shedunnit*. Bloody loved that book."

"Yes," I agreed. "It's one of my favourites."

Although he sat across the table from me, I could smell the lager on his breath. It was very strong. Coupled with his bleary eyes, it was obvious he had drunk several pints by this stage.

"I just love the way she described how that rich woman was killed in the middle of the book," he continued in a slurred manner. "A knife in the back, while she was out pruning her rosebush." He knocked back the rest of the backwashed lager then slammed his glass on the table, causing Hazel to jolt with fright. "That's how you get it done," he drunkenly declared. "There's no comeback from a knife in the back, eh?"

Robert and Aaron stopped their game of pool as they observed the boisterous stranger at our table.

The man laughed haughtily, seemingly unembarrassed by the gap in his front teeth. "Ah, I love a good murder mystery, don't you, ladies?"

We remained silent. Just then, Henry walked up to our table and began sniffing at the man's jacket. The man quickly became agitated.

"Get out of here," he snapped at the dog. "Go on! Get! Bloody mongrel! Why do they allow these animals indoors in this country?" The dog continued sniffing at his jacket. "I said get out of here, ya bloody mutt!" he shouted harshly.

Gregory came to our table and placed his hands on Henry's collar, gently pulling him back.

"Alright fella, no harm done."

"No harm done?" the man retorted. "Your stinkin' mutt has put his filthy nose all over me coat."

Gregory's face became stern, frowning at the man. "Take it easy. No need for that kind of talk."

"I tell you what," bellowed the man. "That mutt comes near me again, I'll put him down right in front of everyone here."

Gregory was taken aback.

"Now listen here, Henry's a good boy. I've been bringing him here for years and there's never been any trouble. You need to calm down. Alright?"

The man rose from the table, clutching his empty pint glass. He smashed the pint glass on the floor. Henry leapt back and barked. The man, whose face now contorted with rage, pointed his finger right into Gregory's chest.

"You better go back to your corner, old man, and take your mongrel with you, or this'll be the last outing you'll have together!"

The pub fell silent. Gregory slowly backed away, gently pulling Henry with him. The pub owner, a scrawny man in his fifties with tattooed arms, marched over to the man and told him to leave the premises immediately. With a searingly contemptuous gaze, the man looked around the pub then stormed out. Robert and Aaron walked over to our table with their pool cues.

"Are you alright?" Aaron asked us.

"Yeah," I said.

"Who the hell was that?" Robert asked.

"No idea," said Jamelia. "Just some random stranger."

*

Hazel and I left the pub around ten, while Jamelia, Robert and Aaron stayed behind playing pool. A deathly silence pervaded the entire village as we walked towards Turnpike Road.

"Jeez, it's really creepy at this time. No one around at all," said Hazel.

"It is," I replied. "Though I grew up in a village like this, I should be used to it."

"You miss village life?"

"Oh no," I said. "My mum, my brother and I moved to Brighton when I was fifteen, to get away from all the small-town gossip. I was glad to leave it all behind."

Hazel nodded. "I wish I moved when I was fifteen. I hated my school."

She stared at the ground as she walked, looking quite glum. I had been bullied at school on occasion myself, and knew the horrible feeling of being stuck in a place where you were made to feel you didn't belong. Perhaps we had that in common too.

"How bad was it?" I asked tentatively.

"Very bad. Got picked on a lot. Almost every day. Hated the nickname they gave me."

"What was it?"

She looked at me, unsure whether to reveal the horrible nickname she had to endure all those years ago. She lowered her head again and said in a subdued voice: "Penfold."

Penfold?

"You mean... Danger Mouse's sidekick?"

She nodded her head despondently.

For a moment, a giggle almost escaped my lips. The nickname certainly had a humorous quality. And it was easy to see how Hazel had been given it. She was timid, wore spectacles, and was overall quite small. But judging by her sullen face, the name had scarred her. My initial flippant reaction quickly turned to pity.

"I'm sorry to hear that. Nicknames can be so cruel."

"What was your nickname?"

Good question. There was a rather stupid one I had to put up with when I was in school. But I don't think it caused me any long-term damage.

"They used to call me... Bel jar."

Hazel looked at me, squinting her eyes. "Bell jar?"

I nodded. "After Sylvia Plath's novel. I was sort of an oddball in school. I liked to read on my own and wear a French beret, thinking it made me look intellectual. I told everyone I was going to be a famous writer one day. So, they added 'jar' to the shortened version of my name."

"So, people call you Bel rather than Belinda?"

"Yep, I prefer Bel, I think. But without the jar bit."

Hazel smiled. "I think I prefer Bel as well."

*

We walked along the narrow road in almost total darkness. In the background, we could hear an owl hooting.

"Do you hear that?" asked Hazel, as she walked behind me.

"Yes," I said.

"Makes me scared," she said.

"Don't worry," I said. "We're not far from the house."

The hooting became louder, as if it was following us. I turned around and could see the dark outline of someone walking not far behind us. Hazel turned around as well.

"Is someone there?" Hazel asked.

As the figure got closer, I realised who it was: that drunken stranger from the pub! He stopped in his tracks and put both his hands to his mouth, creating the sound of an owl's hooting. A cold chill ran down my spine.

"Come on, Hazel," I said in a lowered voice, "let's speed up the pace."

Hazel was right on my heels, walking as briskly as I was.

"Isn't that the guy from the pub?" she asked with a quiver in her voice.

I didn't answer her. The owl's hooting became even louder, as if it was coming right up behind us. I decided there was only one sensible thing to do at this stage.

"Hazel, run!"

We sprinted into the darkness ahead of us. As we ran, I could hear the hooting recede into the background. Within minutes, we reached the gates of the manor house, petrified and out of breath. I looked at the dark road behind to see if the man was pursuing us but couldn't see anyone. I pushed the buzzer frantically until Rita answered.

"Rita, it's us," I said, "let us in!"

The gates slowly opened. We sprinted up the driveway and ran through the open front door, where Rita stood.

"Why are you running? Did you have a race?"

Hazel and I exchanged glances, as we stood bent over in the hallway, trying to catch our breaths.

"Any chance of a cup of tea?" I asked.

Rita looked at her watch. "My duties ended an hour ago," she said, staring at us blankly. Then she smiled, adding, "But I guess I can make an exception."

*

In the middle of the night, I was awakened by the incessant sound of an owl's hooting outside my window. I peered out into the darkness but couldn't see anything. Or anyone. The image of the drunken stranger from the pub lingered in my mind. Had he followed us home? After a few moments, there was a thud outside my door. *What could that be?* My heart began to beat faster and faster as I opened my bedroom door and peered out into the dark hallway.

The glass peacock was lying on the floor, having fallen from its stand. At the top of the stairs stood a figure dressed in a white ankle-length nightie and matching nightcap. Who on earth owned clothes like that anymore?

"Hey," I whispered. "Hey."

Their head slowly turned to face me: *Edith!* She stared at me vacantly for a few moments then proceeded to walk slowly down the stairs.

That's creepy! She must be sleepwalking.

Keeping a slight distance, I followed her downstairs. Edith moved through the hallway and approached the kitchen door. She turned the knob and tried to enter the kitchen, but the door was locked. She stood outside the door for a few moments then turned around, making her way slowly back towards the stairs. Watching her move in her long, flowing nightie was like witnessing a scene from a ghost story.

I followed her to the foot of the stairs and observed her slow, plodding ascent. The staircase creaked ominously with each step. As I watched her, I heard what sounded like murmuring nearby. I listened more carefully. It sounded like people talking at a very low volume. Then I heard giggling. Turning around, I noticed the library door was slightly ajar.

I gently pushed the door open and peaked inside. It was Rita and Robert embracing each other.

Rita giggled as Robert repeatedly kissed her neck, moving down to her chest, like a steamy scene from a romance novel.

Embarrassed, I rushed back upstairs. When I got to the top, the landing was empty. Edith must have returned to her room. I picked the glass peacock off the floor and placed it back on the stand. What a strange night this was!

A ghostly romance novel in the making?

I won't be writing it, I thought, as I went back inside my room. I'll stick to clean, good ol' fashioned murder, thank you! Settling down in my cosy bed, I noticed the hooting from outside my window had stopped. *At last!* Time to get some much-needed rest.

3

The Case of the Missing Groundskeeper

Ahhhhhhhhhhhhhhhhhhhhhhhh!

Standing in front of the bathroom mirror, I had just begun brushing my teeth when I heard the terrible scream. *What on earth was that?*

I dashed out on to the landing to find Jamelia, Hazel and Aaron looking equally horrified.

"Did you hear that?" I shouted.

"Yes," Jamelia answered, "it came from downstairs."

The four of us, still in our pyjamas, rushed down the stairs and found Shirley standing outside the open library door, with her hands cradling her face, looking distressed.

"What's wrong?" I asked her.

She looked at me but didn't seem able to speak, such was the terror in her eyes. She pointed towards the library. Looking through the open door, I could see an arm stretched out on the floor. I entered the room, closely followed by Jamelia, Hazel and Aaron. We stood aghast at what we saw: Rita lying motionless on the floor. A thin trail of blood ran from her mouth.

"Oh my..." I started.

"... God!" Hazel finished.

"What's happened?" thundered Edith's voice from behind us. We turned and saw her staring at Rita's body, wide-eyed and open-mouthed. "Dear God!" she shouted. "There's been a murder!"

Her vociferous voice made us shudder even more with fright. Was Rita really dead? Who would have reason to kill her? As I looked at the shocked faces of the others, a question sprang to mind: *Where was Robert? Was this another game?*

"Someone call an ambulance!" exclaimed Aaron.

Jamelia knelt down beside Rita and listened for a pulse. "I don't think she's breathing. Does anyone know CPR?"

"No, no, no," said Edith. "Don't touch her. This is a crime scene. Everybody stay back. Stay well back!"

We backed away as Edith stood over Rita's body.

"Poor girl," she said, looking down upon Rita. "She was so young. So much to live for. Despite being a servant." She wiped a tear away from her eye, then looked at us intensely. "Look, what we have, class: a murder in our very midst. How does this make you feel?"

We stood in stunned silence for a moment.

"I *feel* we need to call the police," Aaron said, with which we all agreed.

"I'll call them," said Jamelia about to exit the room.

Edith raised her hand. "No. Stay where you are. Nobody move. Nobody go anywhere. I want to know your feelings."

Why on earth was she asking us about our feelings in this situation? Something did not sit right with me. Something was amiss. Rita was so still...

"Excuse me, Edith, I think we need to call the emergency services right away," I said bluntly. It didn't seem like a game to me.

Edith looked focused and turned to address us. "We have plenty of time to call the police. Rita's dead. She's not going anywhere. Now, class, again I ask how does this make you feel?"

We looked at each other in disbelief.

Hazel decided to speak up. "Maybe we should search for clues."

"Search for clues? Okay, good," said Edith. "What else?"

"Perhaps the murderer is still about?" said Aaron.

Edith pursed her lips, nodding. "Perhaps he is. Or indeed, she. What else?"

This was getting ridiculous. Here we were being asked about our feelings, while someone lay dead on the floor. Possibly murdered. What was Edith playing at?

"Examine the body?" Jamelia said.

"Okay," said Edith objectively. "We can examine the body. Notice how we refer to her now as the body."

"Well, she is dead," said Hazel.

"Yes, I know she's dead," said Edith in a slightly elevated voice, "but she's not only dead, she is now a riddle to be solved. An enigma to be unfolded. She is now *the* victim. And what is the victim, class? It is the centrepiece of every mystery novel. It sets the investigation into motion. It's as if the person the victim once was, is now unimportant, and primarily serves as a catalyst for the detective story to begin." She cleared her throat. "Okay, Rita, you may get up now."

Rita sat up on the floor and wiped the blood away from her mouth.

Robert entered the library. "Sorry I'm late everyone, I was..." he looked at us curiously. "Why are you still in your PJs?"

We looked at him mutedly.

"Good morning, Rob. How are you today?"

"Morning, Rita. Never felt better," he replied chirpily. His eyes narrowed. "Is that blood on your face?"

*

Half an hour later, we were sitting at our desks, having got showered and properly dressed, and had another of Simon's excellent breakfasts. Edith sat in the centre of the class, polishing her glasses. "Today, class, we will be discussing the victim. Shirley?"

Shirley, who sat in a chair in the background, perked her head. "Yes Edith?"

"Be a dear and fix me a drink."

"Yes, Edith," Shirley dutifully replied, then left the library.

Edith put on her glasses and looked directly at us. "Right. Who here would like to kill someone?"

The class remained silent. She looked at us, as if to criticise our silence. "Well? Nobody here wants to kill anyone?"

The silence continued. She pursed her lips. "You may need to get in touch with your darker impulses if you want to be a mystery writer. The reader wants to know who killed the victim. The 'whodunnit' element. As authors, we must create a plausible victim and find a reason for them to die. The motive for killing this person must be convincing. The key to succeed at this is to first associate the victim of your story with someone you really dislike. Someone you just can't stand. It's easy to come up with ways of killing someone we detest, we do it every day in our thoughts. Our secret revenge fantasies."

Shirley entered the library carrying a glass of what we now presumed to be gin and tonic. It certainly fizzed like a gin and tonic. She placed it on Edith's writing tablet.

"You can't believe how many times I've wanted to kill Shirley because she drives me up the wall so often. Thank you, Shirley."

Shirley smiled at Edith in return. Her smile was wholly hollow to say the least. She left the room in her usual quiet manner. Edith paced up and down the floor. This was beginning to feel more like a drama class than a writing class. What would be her next performance? It felt like we were all guinea pigs being tested to see how much we could tolerate murder-themed theatrics.

Robert began tapping his pen repeatedly on his writing tablet, which irritated me. His pen was not the pen that we had been given as house guests. This being Robert, his was a swanky Montblanc pen – probably worth more than the contents of my suitcase. Eventually he stopped tapping his pen, only to begin spinning it around his fingers. He was quite skilful at it. He was probably skilful at many things in life: education, sport, socialising, getting girls. Getting Rita. Things probably came easy to him. An academic golden boy, overconfidently going places, and, as such, able to afford to express an open admiration for villains and anti-heroes. He was above criticism and he knew it. I wondered what his writing was like. He mentioned he had published something before. I reckoned he secretly wanted to become the next Bret Easton Ellis.

Or the next Bret Easton Ellis anti-hero!

Yes indeed. Robert certainly had a Patrick Bateman quality about him.

"So, who would you like to kill?" thundered Edith. She stopped pacing and stood behind her seat, her hands behind her back, casting a frowning stare at each member of the class, as if to scrutinise our secret thoughts.

"You there," she said in a militant manner to Robert. "Who would you like to kill?"

Robert's pen remained perfectly still in his hand as he looked at Edith, confounded by her question.

"Who would I like to kill?" he repeated.

"Yes," said Edith. "Don't be shy. Tell the class. And it can't be your father. There's no room for Oedipal complexes in this class."

Robert smirked as he thought for a few moments. "Well," he pondered, "I suppose I would like to kill... Evan Davenport."

"Ah," said Edith. "And who is this Evan Davenport?"

"We played lacrosse together back in sixth form. I was better than him, but because of bullshit politics and nepotism he was made captain and I missed out. I really wanted to be captain at the time. I deserved it. And everyone knew it. But I was robbed. I hated him. I really wanted to put my lacrosse stick through the back of his head."

The class gasped at Robert's comment. Edith was silent for a few moments. Then, in typical Edith fashion, she began clapping.

"Bravo," she said as she clapped. "Bravo. We have a writer in our midst."

Robert smiled proudly at the class, who were not smiling back.

"Who's next?" Edith asked. "How about you, my dear?" pointing her finger at Hazel. Hazel jumped slightly in her chair.

"Um, not sure. I'd like to kill, um, I guess I'd like to kill my former classmate, Rebecca."

She blushed once the words came out. Honestly, I'd expected her to avoid answering the question, given her usual shyness. This was a big, dark, revelation. Now, I really wanted to know what it would take to make Hazel into a killer.

"And why do you want to kill Rebecca?" Edith asked.

She shrugged her shoulders, looking uncomfortable. "We didn't get on in school. She was mean to me. She was mean to a lot of girls. But she picked on me the most."

"I see," said Edith. "You want to kill the former bully. No shame in that. How about you, Belinda?"

I didn't know what to say. It was a stupid question. There wasn't really anyone I wanted to kill. I had never really hated anyone, although I have hated the things certain people have done. Dad's infidelity I hated. But I didn't hate Dad. My former boyfriend cheated on me with one of my best friends, but I got over it. I certainly didn't want to kill them.

"I'm not sure if I can answer that question," I said. "There's no one that immediately comes to mind."

"There has to be someone you'd like to kill," said Robert, leaning towards me.

I shook my head.

"Then why are you doing this course?" he pushed.

"To improve my writing skills," I replied, looking at Edith and Hazel, anyone, to help me out here. Robert leaned back in his chair, clearly looking like he'd won something.

"Now, now, let's not get confrontational," Edith came to the rescue. "Infighting isn't the best idea for a murder-mystery masterclass. Come on, Belinda, surely there is one person in your life who has earned your infinite loathing."

"No," I stated blankly. "There's no one."

The class was silent for a few moments.

"What about the guy from last night?" Hazel asked.

I looked at her, recalling our escapade from the previous evening.

"Which guy do you mean?" Edith asked, before taking a long sip of her drink.

"Um, it's nothing," I said, as I straightened up in my chair. "We just encountered a very strange man in the pub last night."

"Oh, you mean Jack the nutter," Jamelia said. "He *was* a strange character. Bloody smashed a glass in front of everyone."

Edith spurted her drink, then started coughing. It took a few moments for her to regain composure. "I'm sorry, did you say Jack?"

"Yes," confirmed Jamelia. "Dodgy looking bloke, with a gap in his front teeth. Totally hates dogs. Or at least, Greg's dog. He was drinking in the pub when we were there yesterday. He's a big fan of yours."

Edith looked around the class with an expression of burgeoning horror. Her face became pallid, as if the name Jack had brought on sudden nausea. Clearly, she recognised the man Jamelia had described. Did she know him personally? She looked down at her feet for a few moments then stood up, visibly distressed. She excused herself then left the library. The class sat in silence, not really sure what to make of Edith's sudden departure. I looked at Robert, who stared back at me, with a slight grin on his face. Edith's behaviour didn't seem to bother him at all. Was his nonchalance an act, or a symptom of latent sociopathy? I looked at his hand – he was spinning his pen again.

*

I spent the afternoon in the living room, ruminating upon this morning's class. Opening my notebook, I thought about Edith's question. Who would I like to kill? There was one name that kept popping up in my mind, which I didn't want to mention in front of the class: Wendy Simmonds. I wrote the name down on a page. I wrote it several times. Wendy. Wendy. Wendy. I really hated that woman. Not that I wanted to kill her, but I could see Edith's point. If I wanted to write a believable murder mystery, I needed to know my victim. How were they killed? What was the motive behind the killing? I drew a crude little caricature of Wendy on the page, exaggerating her high cheekbones and aquiline nose. Then I drew a dagger in her back, which made me smile. Wendy would be my victim. Suddenly I could think of so many ways of killing her. Indeed, she would be my inspiration for my next mystery novel.

I continued to doodle images of murdering my former boss, until I became distracted by a dog's barking. I went to the window and looked out. It was Henry the bloodhound. He seemed rather agitated, judging by his incessant barking and his fiercely wagging tail. Jamelia, Rita and Hazel were below with him, trying to calm him. I decided to go downstairs to investigate.

When I entered the patio, Jamelia was patting Henry on the head, telling him to calm down. But he kept barking.

"What's wrong with him?" I asked.

"Don't know for sure," said Rita. "But something's got him upset."

"Where's Gregory?"

"No idea," Rita answered. "He doesn't seem to be home. Rang the doorbell several times and tried his phone. He's not answering."

Just then, I noticed Gregory's tartan peaked flat cap on the ground.

"How did that get there?" I asked, pointing at the cap.

"The dog had it in his mouth when we first saw him," said Jamelia. "He dropped it there then started barking like crazy."

Rita folded her arms, while observing the barking hound. "I think he's trying to tell us something. Like Gregory's maybe lost or something."

"Or maybe had an accident somewhere," proffered Jamelia.

"Or maybe," Hazel said, "he's in danger."

Hazel and I looked at each other, remembering our frantic flight from the strange man last night. Shirley silently appeared on the patio.

"What's with all the barking?" she asked. "Edith is trying to rest in bed."

Jamelia gave up patting the dog and turned to Shirley. "Gregory seems to be missing."

Shirley looked worried.

"Something bad may have happened to him," Hazel stated.

"Oh dear, that's awful!" Shirley exclaimed, as she fiddled with her large glasses. "Why do you think that?"

Hazel and I looked at each other again.

"He had a run-in with that man in the pub last night," I said, raising my voice above the dog's barking.

"Which man?"

"Jack!" Hazel and I said at the same time.

Shirley grimaced then looked down at the ground. "Oh no, this isn't happening. This cannot be happening. Not here, of all places."

I stepped closer to her. "Shirley, why don't you tell us what exactly is going on?"

She raised her head and looked at each one of us. "Why don't we go inside, and I can explain everything."

*

Robert and Aaron joined us in the drawing room as Shirley filled us in on the details about Jack. His full name was Jack Burley, a twice-divorced, London-based bricklayer with a history of alcohol abuse and domestic violence. He had been arrested and cautioned for stalking and harassing Edith in London. He would show up at book signings and cause a scene. He would follow her around the streets, in the subway, in restaurants and cafés. He would send her letters, emails, text messages, and leave notes outside her front door. He was obsessed with her. Despite Edith's legal team taking out a restraining order on him, the harassment didn't end. Whenever she went, Jack would show up at her destination. It was a mystery how he'd know Edith's whereabouts. Despite Shirley arranging all of Edith's travel in the strictest confidence, Jack would always show up. He was more than an obsessed fan, Shirley assured us. He was dangerous and disturbed.

"One of the local residents probably tipped him off about this place," guessed Aaron.

"I don't think so," said Shirley. "It's unlikely anyone here would even know about Jack. That's why we thought this little village would be safe. We revealed the location of the manor house only to the five winners in the invitation cards we sent out."

"Well then," I said, "perhaps another one of Edith's staff members let it slip to a journalist, or someone posing as a journalist?"

"Only myself and Edith knew about this location," Shirley stated.

"Then that leaves Rita," Hazel said.

Robert frowned at Hazel. "Rita has nothing to do with any of this. All this is news to her, like it is for us."

"It's just unfortunate he's shown up here," Shirley said as she took off her glasses. "I've tried so hard to make this a safe experience, where everyone would be..." she paused for a few moments, trying to compose herself. "Oh, I hope nothing has happened to that poor man."

"Should we call the police?" Hazel asked.

"He hasn't been missing long enough. You have to wait at least twenty-four hours," said Jamelia.

"Actually, that's a common misconception," I said. "You don't need to wait twenty-four hours. You can make a report to the police as soon as you think a person is missing."

Jamelia leaned back in her chair. "Really? Did not know that."

Shirley furrowed her brow. "I'll call the police. They need to be informed about Jack's presence in this village. I think it's best everyone stays indoors for now and doesn't go into the village for the time being."

The room remained silent. Shirley walked to the door and opened it. Before she left, she turned to us. "I'm really sorry about all this. I hope this doesn't spoil your experience." She left the room.

We continued to sit in silence for a few moments, until Robert started laughing. We stared at him, as he sat in a chair beneath the fox's head.

"What's so funny?" Jamelia asked him.

"Looks like things are getting exciting," he said, placing his hands behind his head. "I knew this masterclass would be worth it!"

*

I spent the evening in my bedroom trying to read a book from the library but found it difficult to concentrate with the dog's continuous barking outside. I decided to text my mum to ask how she was doing. Already, I was beginning to miss her. As soon as I sent the text, a note was slipped under my door. I walked across the floor and picked up the note, which had the words

> meet me by the rosebush
> in five minutes

written on it. There was no name on the note. I opened the door and peered out. No one was there. Closing the door again, I wondered who could have written it. I went to the window and gazed out. The rosebush was situated towards the rear of the garden but was visibly shrouded by a hedgerow. I looked at the note again in my hand. Should I ignore it? Would Holmes or Poirot ignore such a mystery? I was getting bored of being stuck in my room all evening.

And that dog's barking doesn't sound like it'll end anytime soon!

I decided to meet the mystery author.

*

I waited by the rosebush alone. Ten minutes had already passed. Was this person going to show? Admittedly, I was slightly nervous about who the person was. Could it be Robert playing a twisted prank? Or Jamelia having a wind-up? I heard a "pssssssssst" from behind the hedgerow. I cautiously crept around the side of the hedge only to find Hazel standing at the other side, grinning at me.

"Surprise!" she said.

"Hazel. Should have guessed. "What's with the secret meeting?" I asked.

"Follow me," she said excitedly.

We walked across the garden towards the coach house and Hazel led me to the dog kennel at the side which was built like a miniature house with a pitched roof. From inside, Henry continued to bark ferociously.

Hazel turned to me and spoke above the noise: "We may not be the police, but we do have a strong lead for this case."

"What case?" I asked.

She beamed. "The case of the missing groundskeeper." She unhooked the lock of the small front door, which caused Henry to bolt out into the open. He circled around myself and Hazel a few times, barking and wagging his tail.

I turned to Hazel, raising my hands. "What exactly are you doing?"

"He wants us to follow him," she said, shrugging her shoulders. "So, let's follow him."

Hazel proceeded to walk towards an old, rickety gate, shrouded in ivy, situated behind the coach house. At the gate, she turned and patted her knees with her hands, to entice Henry to follow her. "Come on, boy."

Henry scampered towards Hazel, with his tongue dangling from his mouth. Hazel crouched down and rubbed the dog's neck affectionately, which he seemed to appreciate. She then looked at me. "Aren't you coming?"

Curious to see where Hazel's initiative would lead, I decided to follow her.

We walked at a very brisk pace along Turnpike Road, trying not to lose track of Henry, who intermittently sprinted ahead of us only to return, when he realised we were almost out of his sight. Clearly, he was eager for us to follow his lead.

"It's a pity we don't have a leash," Hazel lamented.

"Gregory must have taken the leash off of him in the pub last night," I said.

"He and Henry were still in the pub by the time we left," Hazel said. "And Jack left the pub before us."

"Jack followed us home on this road last night, which means he could have encountered Gregory on the same road at a later time."

"That's very probable," agreed Hazel. "You think he did something to Gregory?"

I shrugged. "Who knows? Let's hope nothing serious has happened."

Henry stopped about a hundred metres ahead of us by the side of the road, which was bordered by dense woodland. He barked in our direction. As soon as we had caught up with him, he darted into the woodland. Hazel and I looked at each other.

"Hey," I shouted after Henry. "Come back! Hey! Come back, boy!"

I stared into the dark woodland in dismay. The dog had vanished. I turned to Hazel. "What do we do now?"

She raised her hands. "Fancy a stroll in the woods?"

*

We walked through the brooding woodland for about twenty minutes trying to find Henry but had no luck. It was getting darker and, worryingly, we could no longer tell which way we had come.

"I think we're lost," Hazel said, gazing around at the infinite cluster of towering trees. "We should try to head back."

"Good idea, but head back which way?"

Hazel scratched her nose then pointed her finger in a particular direction. "This way, I think."

Without having an alternative idea, I agreed, and we began to walk in the direction Hazel presumed was the way back.

It became obvious, however, after another twenty minutes of walking, that Hazel's presumption was a miscalculation. We seemed just as lost as before. Only now darkness was quickly enveloping the woodland.

"This is hopeless," I said in a frustrated tone. "It'll be pitch dark soon."

Hazel looked at me, visibly worried. "Well, I didn't think we would end up getting lost. Especially, on our first case together."

I looked at her with one eyebrow raised. "Our first case together? I didn't know we were a detective duo."

Hazel's face grew disappointed. "Sorry, Bel, I was just trying to make light of the situation."

We continued to walk in silence for a few minutes until Hazel tripped and almost fell over.

"Are you OK?" I asked.

"Yeah, my foot got caught on something."

Examining the ground closely, I made an interesting discovery: she had fallen over a dog leash. I picked it up and dangled in front of her.

"Case of the missing dog leash is solved," I said with a touch of levity.

Hazel's face lit up. "The plot thickens."

As soon as she said those words, I heard a noise in the distance.

"Can you hear that?" I asked.

Hazel listened intently. It was unmistakably the sound of a dog barking.

"Henry!" Hazel exclaimed. "But which way is he?"

Closing my eyes, I listened carefully to the barking to determine its direction. I opened my eyes then pointed. "That way," I said, with absolute confidence. "Onwards! The game's afoot."

Hazel and I jogged in the direction of Henry's barking. We soon had the dog in our sights. He was poised beside what looked like a pair of wellingtons. When we finally reached the dog, I gasped in shock.

The pair of wellingtons turned out to be Gregory – lying face down on the ground. Hazel's face became ghostly white.

"Is... he dead?" she asked.

I remained silent. *Was he dead?* Crouching down, I noticed a gruesome gash to the back of his head. A cragged rock with dried blood on it lay not far away. I checked his pulse. He was still alive. Yet it was clear he needed immediate medical attention.

"He's still breathing, but he needs an ambulance." I checked my phone. "No reception."

"Let's go back to the house and call there," Hazel suggested, her voice distraught. With this real-life situation very closely mirroring the mystery novels she was used to reading, she was probably more afraid of a would-be killer still lurking in the woods than Gregory's deteriorating health. She was right, however, an ambulance needed to be called from the house.

"Good idea. You go," I said to her. "I'll stay here until the medics arrive."

Hazel's face winced. "I don't think I can go back on my own, I'm scared. What if Jack's still around?"

I knew by her petrified eyes she wasn't willing to go. I walked over to Henry, who continued to bark, and tied the leash around his neck. Kneeling before him, I placed my hands on his wrinkled cheeks and stared into his droopy eyes.

"Hear me, boy. Your master needs you. I want you to take Hazel back to the house so she can call for help."

I couldn't believe I was talking to a dog like this.

Desperate times call for desperate measures!

Strangely, Henry ceased barking. His droopy eyes stared back into mine and he seemed to become quite serene. I stood up and led him to Hazel.

"Take this," I said to her, holding out the leash.

Hazel reluctantly took hold of the leash. I placed my hand on her shoulder.

"Take Henry with you. He'll be your guide. He'll protect you if you get into any trouble. I'm counting on you, Hazel. You have to do this. This man's life depends on it."

Hazel glanced at Gregory, then looked at me. She inhaled deeply and pursed her lips. "I'll do it, Bel. I won't let you down."

She turned and led Henry away. I watched them walk into the dark woods and disappear. I knelt beside Gregory who drifted in and out of consciousness. As I shifted him slightly to give his head more support, I noticed something protruding from his jacket pocket. I took it out to examine. It was a handwritten letter.

Dear Edith,

How've you been? Hope you haven't missed me much. I know we've been seeing less of each other thanks to that restraining order you took out on me. Dirty little trick! It won't keep us apart. It's just a silly piece of paper to me. A piece of paper that I burned a long time ago. I remember looking into them flames, and I thought of you.

Wherever you go, wherever you eat, wherever you sleep, wherever you write, I'll be there waiting for you. The final chapter in our saga will be me standing over your body, holding a bloody knife.

Sweet dreams,

JB

JB? That must stand for... *Jack Burley*. This was damning evidence of him being the assailant. Why had he left this letter in Gregory's pocket? It must be to send a message. A personal message to Edith. He wants her to know that he's here. Worse than that: he probably wants her to know that... *she may be next!*

*

Unsurprisingly, Mum was shocked when I told her about everything. We chatted on the phone until half past midnight. I assured her I was fine, having been escorted back to the house by police. Gregory had been taken to a hospital in Cambridge where he was being treated for head trauma but – thankfully – was in a stable condition. It was probably the longest phone conversation I had ever had with her. Mum was usually asleep by eight in the evening. Talking to me until this hour was clearly a sign she was worried. And who could blame her? The crazed stalker of Edith Ramsey had come to the sleepy village of Beaglesford and was now being hunted by police for suspected aggravated assault. It had all the makings of a mystery novel.

As I pondered the commercial potential of such a novel, I heard a loud crash followed by a heated commotion. As soon as I left my bedroom, the other class members began to emerge from theirs, each with the same look of perplexity on their faces. We listened. The commotion was coming from downstairs. We ran down the stairs and paused outside the library, where we could hear Edith's voice ranting and shrieking from inside. I opened the door and cautiously peered inside. Shirley was backed up against a bookcase pleading with Edith to calm down. Edith swayed back and forth with a bottle of Gordon's gin in one hand and a lit cigarette in the other. She was inebriated and in a belligerent state. A desk had been overturned on the floor.

"Edith, please calm down," Shirley pleaded. "I hate to see you like this!"

The class huddled together just inside the door and watched the argument like it was a theatrical performance.

"This is all your fault! You were supposed to make sure this never happened again!" Edith ranted.

"I'm so sorry, Edith, I have no idea how he found out about this place!" Shirley said, her eyes welling up with tears behind her large red spectacles.

"*I'm so sorry, Edith,*" said Edith, callously imitating Shirley's voice. "Will I ever be rid of that bloody lunatic! He follows me everywhere!" Edith smashed the bottle of gin on the floor. Shirley leapt in the air with fright.

Edith pointed her finger at her and snarled. "I'm not going to put up with this any longer! It was your job to make sure he never found out about this place. I trusted you and you've let me down! I am just fed up with your bloody excuses!" Shirley burst into tears.

Enough!

"Edith," I said in an assertive voice. "I think you should calm down!"

Turning to me, she shot me a gaze of contempt and said in a rasping voice: "Calm down? I'm sorry, are you the one being stalked by a bloody lunatic! You have no idea what I have to put up with! No idea at all. And you probably never will. None of you have what it takes to be successful!"

Aaron stepped forward. "That's enough. We didn't come here to witness this kind of behaviour!"

Edith was silent for a few moments, wobbling slightly on her feet. She took a drag of her cigarette and exhaled a thick cloud of smoke. She looked at Shirley, backed up against a bookcase in fear. Edith started laughing. Or rather, cackling. Cackling in a way that expressed an inner desperation that was driving her dependence on alcohol.

"You want to be writers, people?" Edith said to us in an exceedingly pompous tone of voice. "Learn from my trusted assistant here. She'll teach you all about being a writer. Am I right, Shirley?"

Shirley looked at her like a frightened dormouse, with tears streaming from her small eyes. Edith took another drag on her cigarette then left the room, marching past us like a prima donna. Jamelia walked over to Shirley to comfort her. Rita entered the library and looked dismayed at the sight of the broken glass.

"Oh my," she said. "What happened here?"

"Edith totally lost the plot," Robert informed her.

Shirley took off her glasses and wiped her eyes with a handkerchief.

"Are you okay?" Jamelia asked.

"Yes, yes," Shirley said, as she blew an excess amount of mucus into her hankie. "I'll be fine." Dabbing her tearful eyes with her hankie, she left the room abruptly.

The class were left standing around in shock and disbelief.

"This is serious shit," exclaimed Jamelia. "A stalker on the loose. When's he going to strike next?"

"Or *who's* he going to strike next?" said Hazel.

"Right," said Jamelia. "Who usually comes after the groundskeeper? Is it the maid?"

Rita glared at Jamelia.

"I'm sure he'll soon be apprehended by the police," I stated. "Then things will be back to normal. Let's hope."

Robert laughed.

"Back to normal?" Robert said mockingly. "What does that mean? Is it Edith downing one bottle of gin in a day rather than two?"

He shook his head while smiling callously at me. I had officially grown to hate his smile.

"Robert, why don't you just shut up?" Jamelia retorted.

"What?" Robert replied, raising his arms in feigned innocence. "Can't mystery writers have a sense of humour?"

4

Aren't Wolves Extinct in England?

The next morning, we waited like quiet obedient school-children at our writing desks in the library. Deep down, we all wondered how Edith would act today. Would she be distraught? Fearful? Apologetic? Or downright defiant? I felt it could well be the latter since she was clearly a head-strong woman with a larger-than-life personality.

Shirley walked into the library and made an announce-ment: "Good morning, class. My apologies for today, but Edith will not be joining us. She's feeling unwell and has decided to remain in bed."

"I knew it," Robert said under his breath. "Hangover."

I hushed him as Shirley continued.

"So, um, today... I will be teaching the class," she said.

Everyone looked at each other in amazement. Amazement that leaned towards major disappointment. Shirley teach the class?

"Are you kidding?" said Robert.

Shirley looked around the room with her timid eyes, not sure where to stand or what to do with her hands.

"Well," she mumbled. "I shall give it a try. After all, it's what Edith wants."

She sat down on the only empty chair in the room, looking like a witness who had taken the stand in a court-room. All five classmates stared at her as she mustered up the courage to look each of us in the eye. Her hands fidgeted on her lap.

"Well, from what I gather, today's class is about suspects. What is a suspect? A suspect is any person who may be guilty of a crime, such as murder," she stated like someone reading from a dictionary. "In mystery novels, it nearly always involves people who knew the victim and may have had a reason to kill them. There is usually more than one suspect in a novel, sometimes five or six, but never a huge number. In a mystery novel, we get to learn about each suspect, their relationship with the victim and what secrets they try to keep hidden. Each one of the suspects must have had a reason to kill the victim in order to make the story interesting and keep the reader guessing until the very end. Ultimately, it is up to the detective to determine who indeed is the real culprit."

Shirley spoke like she was reading from the blandest text-book on mystery fiction writing. She definitely knew her stuff, no doubt about that. But the entire morning session was just one long, boring, monologue. I couldn't bear another session in the afternoon, so I decided to steal away at the break and journey into the village. It was liberating to get away on my own. A feeling of claustrophobia about the writing course was beginning to kick in.

Truth be told, I had another motive for going into the village. I wanted to find out more about Jack Burley. Chances were, he'd left town since the police began looking for him but there was a slim possibility he had stayed somewhere in the village until recently. There was a B&B located on the village high street called the Birdwatcher's Inn, which I decided to make my first port of call. The building was postcard rustic, boasting a black-and-white, timber-framed exterior perched beneath a steeply pitched thatched roof. When I entered the reception, a wiry-framed middle-aged man sat on the stool behind the desk, speaking on the phone. He scribbled something down on a notepad, then jovially bade goodbye to the caller. He continued writing for a few moments, then looked up at me with his angular face.

"How may I help you?" he asked in a gravelly voice.

I asked him straight out if Jack Burley had stayed here at any point over the past few days. He frowned at my query.

"No, he didn't stay here," he replied, then narrowed his eyes. "The police have already been here to ask me that. Who exactly are you?"

"Um," I hesitated. "I'm a journalist."

"Oh," he said, with a touch of suspicion. "From what newspaper?"

"Um," I said, trying to think quickly. "The *Cambridge Express*."

"Ah," he said, squinting his hawk-like eyes. "Well, like I told the police, he was never here."

Smiling, I thanked him for his cooperation and quickly left the B&B. Outside on the high street I considered where I might go next. Surveying the small high street, I couldn't see any other B&B or hotel.

It's slim pickings when you're in the sticks!

Where else could I try? There was a butcher's across the way. An arts and crafts shop. The bookshop. A pharmacy. A post office. A vape shop (surprisingly in these parts) and, of course, the Greyhound Arms. The picture of the hound in the pub sign above the main entrance made me think of Henry.

It was unlikely that Jack had been back here since the night that Gregory was assaulted, but I thought I'd try my luck anyway and see what information I could dig up.

It was quite gloomy inside the pub during the day. A couple sitting at a table near the entrance glanced at me as I entered. Beneath their table, the eyes of an adorable Basset Hound stared up at me. They were large and solicitous, and made me feel welcome in this otherwise darkly uninviting realm. I approached the bar where the scrawny bartender polished the countertop with a not-so-clean-looking cloth.

"What can I get you?" he said in a husky voice.

"Um, I just need to ask a few questions, if that's alright?"

He looked at me and narrowed his eyes. "Questions about what?"

I repeated the ruse about me being a journalist, looking for information on Jack Burley. After I finished making my request, he stayed silent for a few moments as he rinsed the cloth in the sink. He whipped the damp cloth over one of his shoulders then leaned over the bar, to face me directly.

"You're no journalist," he declared. "You're one of those writers staying at Ainsley Manor. I remember you from a few nights ago. It was me and Mindy serving that night."

I gulped at his directness, then spoke with a slight quiver. "Yes, you're correct. I'm not a journalist. It's just... I wanted to get more information about this man. You know, to help Edith."

He smiled ever so slightly, which brought immediate relief to my embarrassment. "So, you fancy yourself a detective? Look, that fella you're askin' about is dangerous. I saw him the night he caused a scene in here and haven't seen him again. You're best to let the police handle it."

I was tempted to accept his words and leave the bar when my inner amateur detective prompted me to press on. "Did you happen by any chance to speak with him?"

"You mean before he caused all the fuss with ol' Gregory."

"Yes," I answered.

His eyes peered upwards momentarily, trying to remember the night in question. "Yeah, we spoke briefly." He took the cloth off his shoulder and started cleaning around the countertop again – the very same area he had already wiped down. After a few moments of silence, I further pressed him for information.

"What did you talk about?"

He shrugged. "Nothing. Only to say that he was in town for a few days."

"Did he say where he was staying?"

The barman squinted his eyes, recalling details from that night. "He said he was staying up near the church. No idea where he meant though – there are no places to stay up near the church. Didn't really take much notice of what he said until he smashed the glass on the floor. Bloody lunatic!" The fist that gripped the cloth tightened, squeezing the last drops of filthy water from it. "If he ever does show up here again, I'll show him the door faster than you can cry bloody murder, that's for sure. How's Edith anyway?"

Something rubbed up against my leg, which made me jump slightly. I looked down at my feet and there was the Basset Hound, staring at me with his adorable eyes. "Oh, she's fine," I said. "A little shaken by all of this but... she's staying strong."

The barman rinsed the cloth again, as I remained captive to the dog's solicitous stare. The man who owned the dog walked over.

"Come on, Stanley, stop annoying the young woman," he said, tugging the dog, making the poor canine yelp. As I watched the man drag the dog back to his table, I thanked the barman for his assistance. With fists clenched, he leaned on the bar and gave me a cold hard stare.

"Mind yourself, young lady," he said. "That fella's dangerous. Let the police handle it."

*

The police might well have been handling it, but all the mystery novels I'd ever read compelled me to think they could very well mishandle it. As I walked down the high street, I happened to bump into Hilda who was leaving the bookshop.

"Oh, hello again," she said. "How are you?"

"I'm good thanks."

"How's Edith? I was speaking to Mary this morning, the president of our book club. Her son's one of the bobbies here in the village and she told me what happened to Gregory. Poor man! For something like that to happen in a quiet place like this... Just goes to show that there's nowhere safe nowadays."

"Indeed," I said, as I cleared my throat.

"And that poor dog of his..." she continued.

"Henry?"

"Yes. I can only imagine what he's going through." Her eyes saddened, as if she was trying to empathise with Henry's state of mind in the wake of his master's assault.

"I'm sure he's fine. He's gone to stay with Gregory's nephew for a while, while his uncle recuperates."

She nodded. "Well, we all hope he fully recovers. An incident like that can have detrimental long-term consequences. He may become less adept at trailing people."

"Trailing people? I didn't know Gregory did things like that."

Hilda rolled her eyes. "I'm talking about Henry, my dear. He may have suffered trauma from witnessing the attack, which can impact a dog's personality. He could become depressed. I should know. My sister-in-law is an accredited dog behaviourist."

I was momentarily taken aback. She seemed more concerned for the dog than for the man lying in hospital. "That's an interesting perspective," I stated.

Hilda smiled. "I'd best be off, dear. I'm already late for our book club meeting. Tell Edith she's in our thoughts and prayers."

"I'll be sure to tell her," I said.

*

Walking onward down the high street, I wondered if Henry's welfare would be a discussion topic at Hilda's book club. I could imagine them sitting, like a coven, around a table in a teashop, obsessed by those awful animal-themed cosy mysteries. Detective cats and dogs! I cannot stand such drivel. Heaven knows I'm a devout animal lover, but mystery novels should be based on reality.

Leave sleuthing to the amateur humans!

As I turned the corner, a tabby cat purred at me from the open window of a little cottage. Smiling back, I gave him a wave. If I remembered correctly, I also said hello.

The wind was picking up as I arrived at the gate of the church. A large oak tree, centuries old, stood in the middle in the churchyard, surrounded by slanted old headstones, greening from decades of mould. There was a peculiar earthy smell in the air as I headed up the pathway, marvelling at the ancient monuments of death. Some of the gravestones dated back to the eighteenth century.

That's a long time to be dead. You think they have any living descendants?

Judging by the decayed states of their headstones, I presumed not. At least the weeds had been freshly cut around their resting places. Walking around the back of the church, I could see the surrounding woodland, spread out before me like an abyss of starkly standing columns of lumber. Where on earth could anyone stay around here?

"Excuse me?" a voice said behind me, causing me to almost leap out of my skin. Turning around, I was met with the scrutinising stare of an elderly vicar. "May I help you?"

Could he help me?

"Are there any places to stay around here?" I asked, with an air of obtuse naivety.

He looked around at the uninhabited landscape and shook his head slowly. "Not that I'm aware of. There's a B&B in the village but you need to go back onto the main street to get to there."

"I'm actually looking for a man," I said. He stared at me. "A man," I continued, "by the name of Jack Burley."

I gave a brief description of Jack, at which point his eyes narrowed, as if he recalled something.

"Yes, I remember him. I found him sleeping at the back of the church a few days ago. I politely asked him to leave, which made him get very upset. He became increasingly irate, so I threatened to call the police if he didn't leave. He hurled abuse at me, then stormed out of the church."

"Well, that man happens to be dangerously obsessed with Edith Ramsey," I informed him, "which is why he came to town. You know Edith?"

He frowned, pursing his lips. "Yes, I know of her. Can't say I'm surprised. Murder-mystery literature is a thoroughly vain pastime. If people read spiritual books more, there would be less obsessed people in the world."

A sudden, strong gust of wind howled through the air, causing me to shiver.

"It's only fiction," I said, rubbing my arms.

"Fiction is something I don't have time for," he said. "If you'll excuse me, I have parishioners to attend to. Good day." He walked back towards the church, leaving me alone to ponder the great expanse of woodland that stood before me. Where, indeed, could anyone stay out there? The answer was probably anywhere, especially if you want to hide and not to be found.

*

Exploring the woodland seemed like a daunting task, especially after my previous escapade with Hazel, but I wasn't going to allow my hesitancy to rob me of a chance to engage in some amateur detecting.

You mean some amateur meddling!
Why do you want to find this guy?
It's not your case!
You haven't been hired to investigate!
Leave it to the police!

As I walked into the woods, the wind howled again, accentuating my sense of foreboding. Was I making the right choice?

I explored the woods for what felt like hours but encountered nothing worth investigating. The sound of the dry forest floor crunched under my feet as I trekked up an elevated slope. The piney odour from the surrounding trees brought back childhood memories of Mum and I going for a weekend ramble through the local woods. I remember on one occasion we got separated. I cried helplessly until I was found by a couple out walking their collie. They shouted out for my mum. Eventually, she came running through the trees, having followed their shouting. She picked me up and hugged me tight and warned me never to wander off again on my own. She had so much energy back in those days. It's always pained me to think of the vitality she lost because of her condition.

Looking up, I could see blue patches breaking through the stubborn overcast sky. I was starting to enjoy my solitary walk. That is... until I heard what sounded like a *growl!*

Where did that come from? Another growl! What was that?

It certainly wasn't the wind. I looked around. Something ran towards me at a furious speed... something that was big... that was bad... something that was... a wolf! A *wolf!* Petrified, I screamed at the top of my voice.

"Help! Wolf!" I cried. "Help me! Wolf!"

The wolf stopped suddenly a few feet from where I stood, snarling at me with his gruesome teeth showing. My legs trembled with fear – fear that I'd never felt before.

Aren't wolves extinct in England? Surely, they are extinct!

I prayed the beast wasn't hungry. Perhaps he'd had a few rabbits this morning? Perhaps he saw me as a territorial intruder rather than food? If I backed away slowly, maybe he wouldn't follow me? But I was too terrified to move. Then... *I heard a whistle?*

Where did that come from? Could it be... Jack?

I heard another *whistle*. Does Jack own a wolf? That indeed would be one for the books. Finally, I heard a woman's voice.

"Charlie! Charlie, where are you, boy?"

A petite woman wearing a red windbreaker appeared among the trees behind the wolf. She stepped over a loose log and strolled into the small clearing where I stood stiff with fright, facing the drooling carnivore.

"Charlie! Come here, boy!"

As I watched as she wrapped her arms around the wolf's neck, a rush of tremendous relief flooded my body.

"I'm sorry, he must have given you such a fright. Are you okay?"

I nodded my head, then gulped. "Yes, I think I am. It's just that... well, I've never seen a real wolf before. I thought he was going..."

Before I could finish the sentence, she started laughing.

"Charlie's not a wolf. He's a Tamaskan."

"Oh, I see," I said, feeling completely foolish. "Tamaskan. Oh, yes, I've heard of that breed. He looks very... wolflike."

She smiled. "I let him off the leash for a few seconds and he got away from me. He gets so excited when he's outdoors. Almost ransacked someone's tent back there." She bent down and hugged the canine again who reciprocated by licking the woman's face.

"A tent?"

"Yes, maybe about a kilometre back in that direction," she said, pointing behind her.

"Did you happen to see the owner?"

She shrugged her shoulders. "Didn't seem like there was anyone there. Anyway, I'd best be off. Need to feed the wolf," she laughed. "See you around," she said chirpily, as she led Charlie away.

As they left the clearing, the Tamaskan looked back, and shot a predatory stare at me. After a few moments, they disappeared into the trees.

Breathing a sigh of relief, I headed in the direction of the tent. The blue patches in the sky had now vanished behind a thick layer of dark grey cloud which canopied the entire woodland. I checked my phone. It was almost half four in the evening and my phone battery was almost dead. Today's class must now be over.

I wondered what the rest of the group thought about Shirley's teaching skills. Truth be told, she was a bore. And very undramatic, compared to Edith. No doubt Robert would have an opinion. This masterclass was nothing like I'd imagined it would be. It was bordering on disaster, given all the drama that had happened so far. What did the others really think? Were they disappointed? Disillusioned? Dismayed? More importantly, what did they think of Edith? She was certainly a surprise: daring, theatrical, provocative, controversial, even callous – at least towards Shirley. And then there was her drinking problem.

You should never meet your heroes.

Well, she is just human. And she probably has to deal with a lot of pressures because of her career, not least being hounded by a maniacal stalker.

Just ahead, a glimpse of an army-green, dome-shaped tent, situated in the middle of a clearing. My heart rate elevated as I approached it. Is this where Jack had been sleeping? Was I being a complete idiot coming out here on my own? Too late now.

Crouching down behind a bush, I picked up a few loose stones and tossed them one by one at the tent. Nothing. I threw another handful of stones at it, still no movement.

I cautiously approached the front of the tent.

"Hello? Is anyone inside?"

No response. I crept right up to the tent door and took a deep breath. I pulled down the zip, which unleashed a very musty smell. Inside, clothes were scattered everywhere, cans of tinned food, eating utensils, and a newspaper. Reaching in, I picked up the newspaper and looked at the front page: it was dated yesterday. Someone was definitely staying here. There was a black coat rolled up into a ball just inside the tent door. It looked exactly like the black donkey jacket worn by Jack in the pub. Underneath the jacket was an old brown leather satchel. I unfastened the leather strap and examined the contents: there was a tattered paperback version of *Shedunnit*. Opening it, I saw it was autographed by Edith and addressed to Jack! A folded news article, used as a book-mark. I unfolded the article: it was about Edith's legal case against Jack's harassment. I read the page it marked – where Lady Buchan is stabbed to death in the rose garden. One of Jack's favourite scenes.

Further down in the bag was a brochure for the Cosy Mystery Masterclass and a crumpled map of Cambridgeshire. But this brochure was sent only to the winners of the writing competition. Did he know one of the winners? Opening up the map, I noticed that Beaglesford was circled in red. Clearly, Jack had done his research.

Suddenly, a branch snapped behind me. Frozen in my crouched position, I felt a pang of intense dread. Then... there was a voice:

"Who the bloody hell are you?"

It was a voice I had heard once before. Laying down the contents of the leather bag on the floor, I turned slowly around to face a person that I didn't really want to face at all. There he stood, tall, sweaty and menacing, carrying a bundle of small logs under his arm – the one and only Jack Burley. His eyes squinted as soon he saw my face.

"I know you," he said. "You're one of them writers staying at the manor house." He dropped his logs. "Bloody bitch, I'll teach you to snoop through my things!" With a menacing look on his face, he began to approach me.

I sprinted from the scene, leaping over a large tree stump into the woodland. I sprinted as fast as I could, rushing through fallen branches, loose logs and lumpy piles of foliage. Miraculously, I never lost my footing. Finally, I had to stop to catch my breath. I couldn't continue. I bent over, panting and perspiring and looked behind me. For a few seconds I couldn't see anyone. Then, galloping at a ferocious speed, Jack leapt over a large moss-covered log, barrelling towards me. The look of aggressive determination in his face petrified me. *He was coming for me!* I had to keep running.

Just keep running and don't look back!

Dashing through the maze of towering trees, I was overwrought with panic and exhaustion. How long had I been running? I could barely continue. I was dehydrated. I needed water. My heart thumped in my chest like a rapid drumbeat. Fearing the absolute worst, I turned around and surveyed my surroundings. No Jack in sight. Was I in the clear? Had I lost him? All I had to do now was get back to the house. Gazing around at the endless sea of trees, though, it seemed evident that I was completely lost. *You're not out of the woods yet!* Yes, yes, indeed, how do I get out of these woods?

Looking down at my feet, my canvas shoes were a mess. Clearly, not the best footwear for hiking. Or indeed, for being chased through the woods by a maniac. Perhaps he was still out there. Stalking me among the trees. What should I do?

Best to hide, at least until you're sure he's no longer out there!

Hide, yes, but where? Not far from where I stood, I could hear a noise. I listened carefully. A stream? I jogged towards the sound and found myself skidding down a slope. I collapsed onto my knees at the bank of the brook. Placing my hands in the cold, clear water, I cupped them and brought water to my parched lips. The natural water tasted amazingly pure and satisfying. I splashed water over my face, closed my eyes, and breathed in the air.

"Where are you?" bellowed an angry voice from very nearby.

The sound of Jack's voice struck terror in my heart. I crawled back against the slope and laid low, scratching my hand on a thick briar patch.

Ouch!

"Where are you, girl!" bellowed the angry voice again.

My eyes were drawn to the top of the slope where the voice had come from.

"Bloody bitch, where are you!"

He came into my view, standing just along the bank, looking around like a ravenous hunter. Could he see me? The sound of my rapidly beating heart resounded in my ears. Staring up at him, I waited for his eyes to wander to where I lay. Not a single muscle did I move. Like a hound that lost its scent, he disappeared from view, going back the way he came. I dared not move.

I lay still for about an hour. Twilight receded in the sky making way for the dusk to settle in. Slowly, and very cautiously, I sat up on my knees, brushing the leaves from my clothes. The darkening sky brought out my worst fears. Was poor Mum going to read about me being missing in the news? I could visualise the headlines: *Amateur Detective goes Missing in the Woods Trying to Track Down Dangerous Stalker.* Amateur detective? I was barely an amateur detective *writer.* I was out of my depth.

You're way out of your depth! You should have listened to your inner voice. Now look at you! Alone and scared, being hunted like an animal.

I had two choices: give in to fear and hide like a frightened rabbit until I was caught, or get to my feet like a fighter and find a way out of there. I chose the latter. These woods would not be the last of Belinda Boothby!

Rising to my feet with a newfound sense of confidence, I marched along the stream. Surely, I could see the church tower at some point? I felt like screaming for help but that could alert Jack to my whereabouts. I couldn't risk that. I pulled my phone out of my pocket. The battery was dead.

But wait... what's that? Sounds like... whistling.

I peered around the tree and saw a tall, elderly man, carrying a walking stick in the near distance. He whistled again. A golden retriever appeared and barked towards the man. The man lumbered towards the dog and began patting him on the head.

I cleared my throat. "Hey, over here."

The man glanced around, looking startled. "Over here," I said in a fatigued voice.

"Are you alright?"

I looked up at him and nodded. "I'm alright," I said in a hoarse voice. "Just got... lost in the woods."

The retriever stood behind the man, panting with his tongue hanging out. He looked concerned as well. The elderly man leaned on his stick and stretched out his hand to pick me up.

I took his hand, and he pulled me up. What a relief it was to be in his strong grip. "You look like you've been in the wars."

I brushed myself off. "I certainly feel that way."

"It can be dangerous walking out here alone at this time."

I looked at him blankly, not wanting to acknowledge the obviousness of his sentiment.

"So, what's your name, young lady?"

"Belinda."

He nodded and smiled. "I'm Roland. I know these woods like the back of my hand. This way, then."

*

It was almost 10 pm when I got back to the house. I was shocked to discover that I had been reported missing to the police. Everyone, it seemed, had been extremely worried over my disappearance.

Everyone except for Robert. I remember his face being wholly unimpressed as I sat in the living room, surrounded by all the houseguests listening with bated breath to the narrow escape I'd had with Jack Burley in the woods.

A local police constable later came to the house to take

a statement. He assured me that they would do everything to apprehend Jack and asked if I needed medical assistance, seeing as my hand was badly scratched. I told him I would be fine after a hot bath and a cup of tea.

After a late-night supper, I retired to my room and soaked in the tub for an hour. I thought about the adventure I'd just had.

Adventure? You mean the ordeal! You could have been killed! You had a very lucky escape. Maybe next time...

I submerged myself under bathwater to drown out my worrisome thoughts. I was alive. I had survived. That was enough for now. I unplugged my phone from its charger to call Mum. As the phone rang, I wondered if I should tell her about today? I didn't want to upset her. All I wanted was to hear her voice, since I missed her. She was in bed but we spoke for well over an hour. I didn't mention my ordeal in the woods. Afterwards, I rubbed ointment on my injured hand then settled down to sleep.

*

A chink of light filtered into my bedroom as the door slowly opened. In my semi-sleep state, I could still discern a dark figure walk across the floor and stand over my bed. Who was this figure? Could it be... *Jack?* The presence of a possible intruder made me fully awake. My hand frantically searched for the switch of the bedside lamp. As soon as I switched it on, my panic turned to perplexity: Edith was standing there. She pulled a chair up beside my bed and sat down. Her unannounced presence in my room felt very strange. I sat up in bed, as my eyes adjusted to the light.

"What time is it?" I asked.

"It's past midnight," she said, as she leaned towards me and placed her hand on my hand. I now felt very uneasy. What was she doing here?

"They caught him," she said, almost in a whispering voice.

"Caught who?" I asked.

"Jack. They've taken him into custody." She smiled.

"Jack's been caught?" I said. "How?"

"The police found the tent you described. He was inside sleeping. It's over. And it's all thanks to you."

She patted me on the hand. If I didn't know any better, I'd have thought she was on the verge of crying.

"I hate that man," she confessed. "He's made me feel like a hunted animal for so long." Her voice began quivering. "I know I'm probably not the person you expected before you came on this course. For that, I do apologise. I have just..." she paused for a few moments, as if to hold back the tears, "... so many things on my plate. You have no idea."

I found myself patting her hand back, compelled to comfort her. In that strange moment, she reminded me of Mum.

She smiled appreciatively. "You're a very brave girl. To go out there on your own and risk your life. You're a hero."

"I'm not a hero. Just a survivor."

"Yes, indeed you are. Anyway, it's late. I just wanted to check in on you." She rose to her feet and placed the chair back in the corner.

"I hope you'll attend tomorrow's class," she said.

"Yes, indeed," I said, "as long as Shirley's not teaching it."

She chuckled. "No way. I won't put you through that torment again. Good night, dear."

"Good night."

She left the room quietly.

Shouldn't you keep your door locked, in case of any more intruders? Yes, of course. I got out of bed and locked the door then settled back under the covers. I felt restless after Edith's midnight visit and struggled to get back to sleep. What could I do?

Just think of Shirley teaching the class, you'll be nodding off in no time!

5

Miss Marple, Make Way for Belinda Boothby

My hand was still quite sore the next morning, with a yellowish-green scab now surrounding the scratch. I rubbed some more lotion on it, got dressed quickly, and headed downstairs. When I entered the library, Robert, Jamelia, Aaron and Hazel were sitting at their desks. Edith was standing beside her desk, next to Shirley. Everybody was dead silent, staring at me. All of a sudden, Edith started clapping. Seconds later, the entire class started clapping.

"Class," Edith announced, with her hand held out towards me. "This is what an amateur detective looks like." She continued clapping. I felt very awkward. I needed to sit down.

"Please Belinda," Edith said, "have a seat."

Taking a seat, I smiled awkwardly at everyone as the applause died down.

"Miss Marple, make way for Belinda Boothby," Edith announced. "Today is a special day, people. We'll be going into the village to play a detective game. Shirley, in her infinite wisdom and familiarly with the detective mystery genre, has placed clues around the village for us to find in order to solve a murder. Don't worry, this is not one of those wedding party games. This is a very sophisticated mystery, whereby we will learn to sharpen our sleuthing skills and understand that true detecting involves meticulous planning, the careful gathering and scrutiny of evidence, deductive thinking and a serious commitment to truth and justice. Today will be one of the most important and hopefully fun-filled days of the writing course. Today we become detectives. We will learn how to think, feel and act like a sleuth and to understand what goes into catching a killer. But, before all that, let's spend a little time discussing yesterday's extraordinary events, with our true in-house detective, Belinda Boothby."

True in-house detective? What was she talking about? I wasn't in any mood to discuss what happened yesterday.

Edith turned to me, with outstretched arms. "Tell us, how did you find his tent?"

"His tent?" I asked.

"Yes," answered Edith. "Jack's secret hideout. How did you locate it?"

Was this a cross-examination or something? "I... I'm not sure how I discovered it," I said. "I guess it was just... luck."

"Luck!" Edith bellowed. "There is no room for luck in a detective's world. Am I right, Shirley?"

Shirley, who stood with a slumped posture behind Edith, straightened up and spoke in her usual soft, timid voice: "You're quite right, Edith. Detectives rely on the practical application of logical thinking and analysis to solve mysteries. Luck is as foreign to them as..."

"Yes, yes," Edith said, abruptly interrupting Shirley. "We get the picture. So, Belinda, tell us exactly how you came to discover the tent. Tell us your thinking, your analysis, your chain of evidence that led you to find the tent. We're all dying to learn about your methodology."

I sat in silence for a few moments. The class stared at me, anticipating some great revelation. I looked down at my feet and pictured myself running through the leaves with Jack hot on my heels. A strong sense of anxiety overcame me as I remembered the chase. Closing my eyes, I tried controlling my breathing.

It's over now. You're back safely at the house. Jack's been caught. You're no longer in danger.

Opening my eyes, I could feel everyone staring at me, waiting for me to explain how great a detective I am. But I wasn't a great detective. I ran through the woods like a helpless, frightened animal, hunted by a deranged stalker. Should I tell them how scared I was?

"Um," I struggled to think back to the time just before I discovered the tent. "There was a wolf."

"A wolf?" asked Jamelia. "A real wolf?"

"No," I said, "not a real wolf. It was um..." I couldn't remember the name of that dog breed! Think, Belinda!

"Wolf, as in, a metaphor for something dangerous?" asked Aaron.

"A metaphor for Jack," proffered Hazel.

I shook my head. "No, an animal that looked like a wolf, um, it was..."

"Maybe she got a tipoff from Red Riding Hood about the guy's hideout," quipped Robert, which made the others laugh. I looked at him, slouched back in his chair, with a condescending smirk.

"I'm sorry," I said. "I can't do this." I stood up and left the room.

*

Sitting on the bench by the herb garden, I nursed a cup of tea. At the end of the garden, two rabbits sprinted across the lawn, disappearing beneath a bush. *They must feel safer now that Henry's gone away for a few days.*

"Fancy some company?"

I turned to find Jamelia standing beside the bench. She had crept up on me as quietly as a cat.

"Jamelia, you frightened me," I said, placing my hand on my chest.

She sat down next to me. "Sorry to sneak up on you. You seemed very upset in class so I thought you could do with a friend."

Jamelia was indeed very friendly, but I didn't consider us friends. Of all the houseguests, she was particularly hard to read. She wasn't an open book like Hazel. Jamelia was confident and bubbly on the outside, but I got the feeling she kept a lot of things bottled up inside. Like most of us, she probably had her fair share of dark secrets. She looked directly at me, with her compelling eyes. They were deep and curious, and seemed quite capable of reading my vulnerable state of mind.

"It must have been terrifying what you went through," she said. "But we all think you're really brave. Jack's now caught and going to prison."

I pictured Jack behind bars, sitting at a small wobbly desk, writing letters to Edith.

"Well, let's hope he gets sent to prison," I said. "He'll have to be put on trial first. Or perhaps be examined by a psychiatrist to see if he's fit to stand trial."

"Yeah, well, whether they send him to prison or a

nuthouse, let's hope he'll be put away for a long time." Jamelia sighed, then looked at my hand. "What happened to your hand?"

"Scratched it on some briars yesterday," I said, examining my hand, which was visibly on the mend. "While hiding out."

"War wounds, right?" she said smiling.

I smiled back. "Something like that."

Jamelia inhaled deeply through her nose, taking in the wonderful blend of herbs in the air. "Smells great here. Hey, you on for the murder-mystery game later? Should be fun."

I took a long sip of tea. "I don't think I'll go. I need to rest."

"Suit yourself. You've already had your adventure. I'm going to get a coffee and a bun. You want anything?"

"No, I'm fine," I replied.

"Alright, then," she said, as she stood up. "See you later... hero!" She winked and smiled at me, then strolled back toward the house.

Hero? Me? I didn't think so.

Don't be so modest. It was because of your misadventure that Jack was apprehended.

Maybe I am a hero, I thought. A hero whose tragic flaw is her unfailing sense of modesty.

*

In the drawing room, I wrote about my experience in the woods. It was bringing back a lot of anxiety. But perhaps that it was a good thing. Writing about things can help alleviate anxiety rather than leave it buried inside. I had so far filled up three pages of my notebook. As I turned a new page, Hazel entered the room.

"Hey, Bel, how are you?" she said in her usual chirpy manner.

"Hey, Hazel, I'm fine. Just doing a bit of writing."

She sat down on the sofa next to me. "What are you writing about?"

Placing my pen in the spine, I closed the notebook and placed it on the table. Rubbing my eyes, I sighed deeply. "It's nothing. I just tried to write about yesterday."

"Your brush with death. It must have been very scary. Alone in the woods, all by yourself, being chased by a madman. It's exactly the kind of stuff that you read about in mystery books. You're so lucky!"

I frowned at her. "Lucky? What do you mean?"

She grinned. "Sorry, I just meant, to go through an adventure like that, must be great for inspiration. I wish I could have an adventure like you did. Then I'd be able to write better."

Her words annoyed me. She really had no idea what I'd been through. Was this all a game to her?

"Hazel," I began, "it wasn't an adventure. It was a traumatic ordeal. I was terrified. And still am. I'm trying to put my feelings into words to help me to cope. So, I don't appreciate you putting a light-hearted spin on the matter."

She winced.

"Sorry, Bel. It must have been awful for you. I can't imagine." She glanced at the notebook on the table. "Perhaps when you finish writing about it, I could read it? Might help me really understand what you went through?"

I sighed. "Yes, why not? Maybe you can give me some feedback on my writing style."

"It would be my pleasure," Hazel said. "Who knows? This could be the beginning of a new writing partnership."

"Yes, indeed, who knows?"

There were a few moments of silence. Hazel turned her head toward me, staring at me over her spectacles, which had slipped down her nose.

"I'm glad you're safe, Bel. Of all the people staying in this house, you're the last I would want to see anything bad happen to."

"Thanks Hazel, you're a good friend. Although, I'm sure not everyone was glad about my safe return," I said.

"What do you mean?"

"Robert," I said. "He clearly didn't give a monkey's about my welfare, judging by his comment this morning."

Hazel nodded in agreement.

"Yes, well, that's Robert for you. He's doesn't care about anyone but himself. He tried to make us bet if you'd make it back alive."

"What?" I exclaimed.

"Yes," she answered. "I told him I wouldn't be involved. Fortunately, no one else wanted to bet either. He's just a nasty person."

Nasty person? That's putting it mildly. And to think I thought he was charming...

"The guy is such a..." I began.

"The guy is such a what?" said Robert's voice.

Standing in the doorway, he stared at me. How long had he been there? He swaggered into the room, hands in pockets, and stood in front of us. Behind him, the fox's head observed Robert's cocky stance, while Hazel shifted in her seat, looking slightly uncomfortable.

"Well?" he asked arrogantly with raised eyebrows.

"Well what?" I asked. "You were trying to bet on me yesterday."

"Yes," he admitted. "I was trying to lighten the mood. Is that a crime?"

"Not a crime," I stated confidently. "It's just another example of you trying to be the group provocateur."

"Provocateur?" he repeated. "What the hell is that meant to mean?"

"It means," Hazel spoke up, "you seem to enjoy trying to shock others."

"Well, well, well," he said haughtily. "That's quite an insight. The two of you make quite the team when it comes to judging others. Maybe you should take a look at yourselves. You're a pathetic pair of Holmes and Watson wannabes."

"We're just saying what's on everyone's minds. No need to get so defensive," said Hazel.

Robert took his hands out of his pockets and grimaced slightly, annoyed by Hazel's remark. "How would you know what's on everyone's mind? You have the social intelligence of someone half your age."

"Hey, screw you. I'm not a child," Hazel shouted.

"Ha," Robert scoffed. "Could've fooled me."

Hazel took off her glasses as her eyes filled up with tears.

"Hazel," I said, putting my hand on her shoulder. "Ignore him."

She began to sob heavily, then got up from the sofa and ran out of the room. Robert stood in front of me with a look of satisfaction on his face.

"That was out of line."

He rolled his eyes and sat down on the sofa, replacing Hazel. He leaned back on the cushions.

"She needs to grow up. You know it. I know it. The whole class knows it. She's the typical bookworm who'll never fully live in the real world."

I looked at him, reclining there, scratching one of his armpits, yawning. Now I wanted to tell him what I really thought of him.

Don't hold back! Let him have it!

"I'll refrain from using harsh words," I started, "but it seems like your whole personality is a façade. The way you make inappropriate jokes, offhand remarks, and thoughtless judgements about others. You want to come across as someone who lacks empathy and compassion, trying desperately to be the token sociopath of the group. Really though, *you're* a child. A child who's afraid of letting someone get close to you. I'm sure Rita will find this out for herself."

He stopped scratching, straightened up on the sofa and gave me a cold, hard stare. I had definitely got under his skin. He leaned in towards me and spoke in a whispered tone.

"I think people who indulge in pop psychology should have their stomachs cut open and their livers removed."

While his breath had a minty-fresh scent to it, his words filled me with repulsion. Leaning back, he smiled.

"How's that for sociopathy?" he said.

He stood up from the sofa and began to walk toward the door. Just before he left, he stopped and turned toward me.

"Oh, and whatever you imagine is going on between me and Rita, try not to fantasise too much over it. I'm sure there are plenty of village lads living around here that would be desperate enough to date you."

He left the room with the same swagger as when he had entered. His words had stung me.

What a total creep!

The fox's head glared at me from above the mantlepiece. I think it agreed with my opinion of Robert.

*

"Hazel?" I said in a gentle voice.

I knocked on her door again. No answer. I opened the door slightly and peered in. Hazel was lying face down on her bed.

"Hazel," I said in a whispered tone, while knocking lightly on the open door. "It's me. I've brought you tea."

She turned her head on her pillow to face me. Her eyes were reddishly teary.

"Can I come in?" I asked.

She sat up on her bed and nodded. Closing the door behind me, I tiptoed towards her bed and laid the cup of tea on her bedside table. Without her glasses, she looked younger and more childlike, and her morose expression made me feel quite sad.

"How are you feeling?"

She shrugged, as she picked up the tea and took a tentative drink. She put the cup back down on the locker, then wiped her eyes on her sleeve.

"Sometimes, I feel so... worthless," she began. "Like, no one likes me... I hate feeling like this."

I placed my hand gently on her hand, which lightly clasped the edge of the bed.

"Hazel, everyone here likes you. Trust me. There's only one person who wants to make you feel bad. He wants to make everyone feel bad."

I felt her hand squeeze the edge of the bed, as her face grimaced with anger.

"Robert!" she fumed. "I hate him. I really, really hate him. I just want to..." She grabbed a pillow and put it against her face, into which she growled in frustrated rage.

"Hazel, I understand. I feel the same way." I gently placed my hand on the pillow, which enticed her to lower it from her face. "You remember the lesson that Edith taught us? About using the person you hate most in life as the basis for the victim in your novel? Well, this is an opportunity to utilise that lesson."

She pursed her lips, as her eyes drifted to the ceiling, contemplating my words. "Yes," she said, with a touch of renewed enthusiasm. "I could think of many ways of killing Robert. So many ways indeed. I could write a hundred stories about that." Clearly the thought of killing Robert brought a sense of glee to her heart. Her face seemed much happier all of a sudden.

I smiled at her. "Well then, all you need to do is work on turning your murderous rage into your source of inspiration. You'll be a bestselling novelist in no time."

She smiled back at me. Someone knocked on the door.

"Come in," Hazel said.

The door opened and Rita popped her head in.

"The gang's leaving now. They're going into the village to play the murder-mystery game."

"Oh," I said, nodding my head. "I won't be joining them. I'm going to take a nap. I feel exhausted."

"I see," said Rita. "No worries. Hazel, will you be going?"

Hazel looked at me with resolute determination. She wasn't going to let Robert's words ruin her evening. She put on her glasses and replied to Rita in a militant voice: "I'll be down in one minute." I smiled again. It was so wonderful to see her not letting Robert get her down. She leapt out of the bed and put on her shoes.

"Are you sure you won't come, Bel?" she asked.

"No," I replied, as I stood up from the bed and headed to the door. "Like I said, my feet are too sore." I stepped outside and waited with Rita in the hallway. Hazel left her room, closing the door behind her. "Okay then," she said. "I'll see you later." She trotted down the stairs, shouting back, "I'll bring you back the murder weapon!"

Rita and I looked at each other and chortled.

*

It was pitch dark outside my window when I woke from my nap. That annoying owl outside had begun its hooting. I rose from bed, slipped on a light sweater, and left my room. It was eerily quiet in the hallway. The others must have returned hours ago. I wondered who won the game?

I crept down the stairs. Darkness and quiet filled the kitchen, as I stole to the door that led to the back garden. I turned the key in the door and stepped outside. The ground was cold beneath my feet as I walked out onto the lawn.

I followed the hooting to the large sycamore tree next to the coach house. Staring up into the darkness of its branches, it was difficult to pinpoint the exact position of the owl. Picking up a handful of loose stones from the ground, I fired them sporadically into the tree. The hooting ceased.

Standing beneath the tree, I could hear only the still quiet of night. What a beautiful sound! So peaceful. So tranquil. So...

"What are you doing here?"

Jumping with fright, I landed on a sharp loose chipping that caused me to yelp with pain. *Ouch!* I turned around and stood aghast, looking at what first appeared to be a ghost. But it was no ghost. It was Gregory, wearing a dressing gown, with a white bandage wrapped around his head.

"Gregory," I said in a trembling voice, "what... what... what are you doing here? I thought you were in the hospital?"

He took a deep breath as he wobbled slightly on his feet. "I was discharged this evening. What are you doing out here so late?"

Bending my left knee to rub my sole with my hand, I explained to him about the noisy owl, and the measures I took to scare it away. He listened to me with a tired concern. It was late, or perhaps he had taken sedatives for his head injury? He looked upward into the dark abyss of the sycamore's branches then winced, clasping his bandaged head with his hand.

"Are you alright?" I asked.

"Yes," he said, visibly in pain. "Just my head is still quite sore."

"Can I get you anything?"

"No, no, I'll be fine. I'll fix myself a hot brandy before I go back to bed."

He continued to massage his head with his hand.

"Well, at least they caught the man responsible for assaulting you," I said, wanting to brighten up his mood.

He looked at me and narrowed his eyes. "I sincerely doubt that."

"Why do you say that?"

He placed both his hands in his dressing gown pockets, while his face became solemn. "I never saw my assailant.

Someone attacked from me behind. It's all... very fuzzy. I can remember bits... like a pair of clogs."

"A pair of clogs?" I repeated.

"Yes, I was walking Henry home from the pub that night, when he ran off before I could put the leash on him. He ran right into the woods. I called out after him but he didn't return. I searched for my whistle in my jacket but couldn't find it, so I went after him. Finally, I heard him barking. I followed the sound until I found him, sitting down chewing on a bone. Just as I was about to give him a hug, I felt a mighty blow to the back of my head, then I hit the ground hard. I remember lying there, flat on my face, and seeing a pair of clogs, worn by the person who hit me. Navy in colour, if I remember. Judging by their size, they might have belonged to a woman. Before I could look up to see my assailant, I got another blow to my head. Next thing I remember is waking up in hospital."

What a strange tale. "Who do you think was it?"

He raised his eyebrows. "Heaven knows! Not that big fella I met in the pub. Those shoes wouldn't have fit him!"

No, indeed not. Could it be possible that Gregory's mind was playing tricks? After all, he did receive two massive blows to his head, which may have skewed his ability to recollect that night's sequence of events accurately.

He looked upward again into the great sycamore above him. "Let's hope that owl doesn't return. I can hear it from my lodgings. We're all in need of a good night's sleep."

He smiled at me, then walked back to the coach house.

I lingered beneath the sycamore for a few moments, as I contemplated Gregory's words. Could a woman have attacked him? If so, who was she? Perhaps Jack had an accomplice? It was too late to think about these things. And my feet were too cold. Turning to go back inside, I jumped again with fright. It was... Edith, standing on the lawn, completely quiet and motionless. Her long, white nightie, which flowed in the strong breeze, coupled with her white nightcap, made her look like an apparition. I walked right up to her and inspected her closely. Her eyes were open but were completely vacant. Her lips began moving. She was whispering something, but it wasn't clear. I moved in closer to listen.

"She writes everything. She writes everything. She writes everything."

I couldn't understand what these words meant but they sounded eerie. She finished whispering, then lumbered back inside the house.

This masterclass gets more mysterious by the day.

The wind became gustier as I lingered outside. Perhaps the wind will scare away the owl if he starts hooting again. One can only hope. My feet were now stone cold, so I headed back inside.

6

No Plan is Ever Perfect

"Who among us is a murderer? Who has it in them to take another life? Who among us is not who they say they are? Who here has already fingered their victim and awaits the right time to commit... *murder* most foul?"

Edith was in full theatrical mode as she paced around the class, delivering these murder-themed rhetorical questions in her operatic voice. Shirley sat in on the class today, quietly taking notes in the corner. Sitting opposite me was Robert whose eyes stared at me intently, while spinning his pen between his fingers with annoying consistency. Despite feeling uncomfortable, I stared back at him. I wanted him to know that his Jack-the-Ripper-inspired threat to me yesterday would not daunt me. I refused to let him get under my skin. Edith stopped pacing and stood right between myself and Robert and delivered her final rhetorical question.

"Indeed, what does it take to be a killer?"

Her eyes scanned each of us as she stood in the centre of the class. There was silence for a few moments until it was broken by the one voice I wasn't in the mood to hear.

"Patience," said Robert flatly.

"Patience?" asked Edith.

"Patience to plan everything carefully and execute it without flaw," replied Robert whose eyes had now fixed upon Edith's.

Edith looked at Robert and pursed her lips. "I see," she said. "So, pre-meditated murder you mean?"

Robert sat up in his chair, clenching his pen firmly. "Is there another kind?"

"There are crimes of passion," Edith answered calmly.

Robert's face became determined. "Let your passion be murder, I say. Plan everything in perfect detail and you're sure to get away with it."

It was time to intervene. "No plan is ever perfect," I stated confidently.

Robert's eyes locked with mine.

"Not if it's done by an imperfect person," was his cold response.

Ouch! Direct hit. Time to respond in kind.

"And you're a perfect person?" I replied. I could tell everyone was watching us.

"I believe I could murder perfectly. Leaving not a single clue or any trail of evidence behind."

I noticed a flaw in his "perfect" thinking.

Time to exploit this flaw and bring this wannabe Patrick Bateman down!

"But how will you gain the notoriety you so desperately crave, if you get away with murder?" I stated objectively.

Robert's face winced ever so slightly. "Who says I want notoriety?"

I shrugged. "Everything you say and do says you want it. The way you try to be the shock jock of the group. It's obvious you want attention. Robert the well-bred boy-next-door sociopath. Being an anonymous killer goes against the image you try to project. Sooner or later you'd want people to know that you murdered someone."

Robert sat in silence for a few moments, staring at me. A stare which, admittedly, did frighten me but, nevertheless, I held without flinching.

"You don't know a bloody thing about me," he retorted. "Maybe I would want people to know, eventually," he admitted, "but after I was gone. My complicity would be a prize for posterity, something that the future would acknowledge as having eluded the best minds of the day."

I smiled ever so slightly: "Then you admit that your perfect plan would eventually not be perfect."

Robert exhaled impatiently and cast his eyes down to his feet. I had broken his stare, which I took as a little victory.

"Why does murder have to be perfect?" queried Aaron.

There was a brief moment of silence, while everyone pondered his question.

"Because it's a test," said Robert.

"Murder's a test?" replied Aaron. "A test of what?"

"A test of character, of wits, of intellect, of steel..." Robert answered.

"Of evil," said Hazel.

Robert shrugged. "Only the herd thinks in terms of good and evil. A true villain knows that murder is an art and every murderer an artist, who is above and beyond the norms that lesser mortals are bound to. A murdered body is the canvas for the villain to show his true genius to the world. It's the window to his tortured soul."

Edith raised her eyebrows. "Hm, that's a very aesthetic opinion of murder."

"Aesthetic?" intervened Jamelia. "The lad's talking rubbish. Murder's not an art. It's a crime, perpetrated by someone who's either mentally disturbed or doesn't know right from wrong."

"Hear! Hear!" said Hazel triumphantly.

Robert looked straight at Jamelia. "You think like a child."

"Child? Excuse me? I've probably seen more bad shit in my life than you have, you spoilt twat. Have you ever witnessed a murder?"

Robert sat back in his chair and stared at Jamelia for a few moments. "Maybe I have."

"Or maybe you're just full of shit," retorted Jamelia.

Robert smiled and spun his pen in his hand. Something inside compelled me to respond.

"How would you murder someone, Robert? Since you're so passionate about the artistic merits of murder, why don't you enlighten us on how you would do it?" I asked.

He looked at me with a raised eyebrow. "It would depend on the person. Whether they deserve to go quick, like with a gunshot. Or slowly, like being disembowelled and having their organs kept in glass jars." He smiled at me. How I hated that smile!

"Well, you may well be a successful murderer one day, but a successful crime writer? People want to read about how the murder is solved and the murderer brought to justice by a great detective."

Boom! Knocked that smile right off his smug face.

He shifted in his chair and leaned over his desk, looking at me intently. "There are many people out there fed up with the tired, old, run-of-the-mill hero detective drivel. There is a huge appetite for darker themes. My readers will want to celebrate the Machiavellian majesty of the deviant personality because, deep down, they know that detectives are total bores!"

Jamelia laughed. "Man, Rita is one lucky lady to have you in her life. Total psycho!"

Robert frowned. "What are you talking about? There's nothing going on between us."

"Yeah, sure there isn't," Jamelia muttered.

"Are you spying on us or something?" Robert fired back at her.

"Spying on you?" Jamelia laughed. "In your dreams. I'd rather watch paint dry!"

Edith clapped her hands. "Okay, okay, class, let's refocus on the mystery novel," she said diplomatically. "I think we're getting way off the point here. While the murderer is usually revealed at the end, in the denouement, his or her story, including the relationship with the victim and motive for killing, must be made clear throughout the novel. To be sure, there will be many red herrings along the way, to cast our suspicion on other characters, but the murderer is there from the beginning, as it were, right under our very noses. Usually, the person... who we least expect." She looked at me directly. She continued. "Take, for instance, my novel *Shedunnit*. It looks like the person who killed Lady Buchan is the gardener, since he was last seen in the rose garden. But we all know it was Mr Granger, the man who she had been secretly blackmailing."

The class looked at one another, bewildered.

Jamelia spoke up: "Mr Granger?"

"Yes," Edith replied, turning to look at Jamelia. "You've read my bestseller?"

Jamelia narrowed her eyes. "Yes, I have read it."

"Then you know that Mr Granger is the murderer," Edith robustly declared.

Again, the class expressed confused expressions.

Jamelia sat up in her chair. "Ah no, Mr Granger is arrested for the murder of Lady Buchan. But he's later released. The real murderer turns out to be Alice Boyd, Lady Buchan's spoilt niece. How could you not know that?"

Edith's face grimaced with indignation: "You're a bloody idiot!" she blurted out. "Mr Granger is the murderer! Everyone knows that!"

The group were shocked. I looked at Hazel. She looked back at me, wide-eyed. Had Edith forgotten her own novel?

Jamelia sat up. "How dare you call me an idiot! Who the hell do you think you're talking to... you... you... *pathetic ol' drunk!*"

Edith took a step back, her mouth wide open.

"You don't even know the plot of your own novel!" Jamelia continued. "What the hell kind of novelist are you?"

She rose from her chair, with her tablet firmly in her clasped hands and stormed out of the room.

Edith's mouth remained wide open. "Well, I never... that girl clearly hasn't read my..." Shirley tiptoed up to Edith's ear and whispered into it. The outrage slowly recoiled from Edith's face as Shirley finished and returned to her chair.

Standing alone in the middle of the class, Edith looked at our faces with a confounded expression, then cleared her throat emphatically.

"Um, well, what can I say? I seem to have made a mistake," she said shakily. "Ahem, where is my mind today? I was referring to an early draft of my book. Yes, yes, of course, Alice Boyd, as Jamelia quite rightly said, was the killer. Thank you, Shirley for reminding me." Edith swallowed hard, looking embarrassed. "Excuse me, um... Take five, class."

Edith left the room abruptly. Shirley looked at us, smiled politely, before following Edith out of the library. The class were left sitting in silence. A silence, inevitably, broken by Robert's impetuous directness.

"Bloody hell, she can't even remember her own works. She's probably gone to drown her sorrows again! This masterclass sucks. It's more an amateur-class being run by a raving wino. I mean, where's the interactive discussions about story arcs, or the secrets of great writing techniques that were on the brochure. This is the worst thing I've ever done. Someone needs to get her to rehab."

The class remained silent, mulling over Robert's diatribe.

Aaron straightened up in his chair and addressed everyone with a look of solemnity. "I have to say, I agree with Rob. This course is a major disappointment. I mean, the classes are basic, they're poorly planned, everything is all over the place. Edith seems just... unfocused or distracted. Like she doesn't really want to do this writing course. I mean, I wonder why she organised it in the first place?"

"This is probably just a contractual obligation for her," Robert stated flatly. "She doesn't give two hoots about our writing careers."

"To be fair," Hazel began timidly, "Edith has had to deal with a lot of stress so far, with that stalker and everything. And who nearly killed Belinda."

Robert cast his eyes on me. "Ah, yes, that's the highlight of the week so far."

I couldn't hold back. "You really are a spoilt little brat."

"At least I'm going places."

"Yes, places your parents have paid for," I retaliated.

Robert pointed his finger at me. "You know what you are?"

"No, Rob, tell me. What am I?" I said defiantly.

"I'll tell you what you are," he said. "You're a..."

"Class, excuse me!" It was the shrill voice of Shirley. The class looked towards the doorway of the library where she stood. "We will have afternoon tea in the garden today. The weather is splendid, so please make your way outside. Rita will serve tea and scones in fifteen minutes."

She vanished from the doorway. Robert and I stared at each other. Was he going to finish the sentence he had begun before Shirley's announcement? What was he going to say I was? Surprisingly, Robert stood up, picked up his pen and notebook, and looked at the class.

"Well, I do fancy a cuppa. Beats being in here bickering with you lot." He strolled out of the room.

Aaron stood up from his chair. "This'll be a writing course none of us are going to forget. See you outside."

Hazel and I watched him leave the room then looked at each other. He was right – we were going to remember all of this for a long time to come. She closed her laptop and stood up.

"You coming, Bel?"

"Yes, I'll be right there."

Hazel left the library, leaving me reflecting on Edith's blunder. Was it really stress that made her forget the denouement of her own bestselling novel? Although she was still one of the bestselling mystery writers of modern times, Edith was getting older. She had lost that natural vivacity of her early years, which I remember from interviews she did when she first became a success. Add in the dependence on drink. She needed an intervention by people who cared for her. But all she had was Shirley, who clearly lacked the confidence to intervene.

That said, none of this justified her rudeness to Jamelia. Poor girl! She must have been mortified by Edith's remark. I needed to check up on her.

*

I knocked on Jamelia's bedroom door and waited. "Jamelia? Jamelia? Are you in there? It's me, Belinda."

After a few moments, she opened the door. She looked extremely sullen.

"Are you alright?"

She sighed. "Yeah, just tired. Tired of this whole week."

"Can I come in?"

She shrugged and held her door open. Her room had a very fresh, sweet-smelling scent to it. There was a bunch of freshly picked roses standing in a glass of water on her desk.

"These from the garden?" I asked, as she closed the door.

"Yeah, roses are my favourite."

"Look, Jamelia, Edith was way out of line with what she said to you. She should apologise."

"That ol' bat better watch herself. I never let anyone speak to me like that. She's lucky I didn't give her a slap. If she wasn't so old... Raving ol' drunk is what she is."

I remained silent for a few moments, allowing her anger to settle in the air.

"I, um, totally understand your anger. I'd be angry too."

"Oh yeah," she said. "What would you do?"

I took a step back from her. Her closeness was slightly intimidating. "I would talk to her. Tell her how I feel. Over a cup of tea."

She laughed. "Over a cup of tea! You're such a square, Belinda!"

Square? Admittedly, I was taken aback by her comment. "What would you do then?"

"Me? I'd make sure she ends up like one of the victims in her books. Maybe like Lady Buchan. Sneak up behind her and put a knife in her back!" She made a stabbing motion in the air with her hand. "That'd teach her."

I knew she was angry, so I chose to ignore her threat. She was clearly speaking out of character. At least, I hoped she was.

"Jamelia, I like you. You're a nice person and it's the second-last day. So, let's go outside and enjoy the nice weather. And, if it's not too square of me to suggest this, you can have a cup of tea and a scone."

She smiled. "Yeah, alright. Why not? Second-last day and all. Let me just powder my face."

I left, looking forward to the afternoon tea and scones.

*

Write in one sentence how you would commit the perfect murder.

"You've all been given the same assignment," Shirley declared. "But you must all come up with your own individual answer."

There was blank space beneath the statement, where we would have to write our name and our answer. We looked at each other, amazed by the assignment. Shirley was smiling broadly.

"Well, enjoy the rest of your day," she said chirpily. "See you bright and early tomorrow." She turned and shuffled back to the house.

We were left speechless as we sat in our chairs, looking at the cards each of us had been given. What kind of assignment was this? I looked over at Hazel whose eyes were fixed on her card. Aaron and Jamelia were immersed in their cards as well. What exactly were they thinking? Robert slipped his card back inside the envelope. He reclined in his seat and started whistling. This assignment clearly didn't mean much to him.

Trying my best to ignore his whistling, I picked up my scone and ate it. It was perfectly baked. As I savoured the taste, I wondered if Shirley had heard the news about Jack's release. More importantly, had Edith heard the news? How would the rest of this day play out? Tonight would be the final night of the masterclass – would I sleep soundly knowing the news? Would the others?

Robert's whistling was getting on my nerves. Resisting the urge to tell him to shut up, I decided to go back inside the house. Picking up my assignment card, I excused myself from the table.

*

Edith didn't return to teach the class that day. No doubt because of the news of Jack's release. And perhaps also because of her embarrassing blunder. After afternoon tea, we waited in the library until Shirley popped in to apologise for Edith's absence, claiming she had a headache. None of us bought it. Shirley also told us that Jack had been transferred to London, assuring us that we had nothing to worry about. The police had everything under control. I didn't believe her. Shirley encouraged us to spend the rest of the day thinking about the assignment. After she left, we discussed the assignment for a while, but deep down I couldn't stop thinking about Jack. Excusing myself from the discussion, I went outside into the back garden and walked inside the labyrinth, trying to let the news of Jack's transfer to London calm me down. But this news did not quell my fears. As I reached the centre, I had a very strong feeling we would hear from him again.

From the centre, I took in the surrounding view, admiring the tranquillity of the countryside. Then... my eyes landed on Edith. She was sitting alone on the bench inside the herb garden. I navigated out of the labyrinth and walked towards where Edith was sitting. I waved at Edith to get her attention. She didn't respond. She sat completely silent, wearing sunglasses, reading a book. There was an empty glass on a stand beside her. I called out her name.

"Edith?"

She ignored me.

I stopped in my tracks, acknowledging her desire not to be disturbed, then walked back towards the house. Who could blame her for not wanting to talk with anyone? She must be completely distraught about the news of Jack's release. I felt immensely bad for her.

*

From my bedroom window, I stared towards the group of cypress trees behind which Edith sat in solitude. Her life was a tragic memoir in the making. Would there be a happy ending for her? I hoped so. With any luck, Jack would slip up soon and be sent to prison, giving Edith the freedom she deserved.

Closing my curtains, I turned my attention to the envelope that Shirley had handed to each of us earlier in the day. I took the card out of the envelope, placed it in front of me, and mulled over the calligraphic typescript:

Write in one sentence how you would commit the perfect murder.

Those words seemed all the more ominous in the wake of Jack's release. Nevertheless, this assignment was part of our writing course. Perhaps the most important part. This is what I had signed up for. Despite all the drama and danger, I still wanted to be a mystery writer. I still wanted to give this masterclass my best shot. Winning this assignment could enhance my chances of being a successful mystery writer and earn praise from Edith Ramsey. That would look great on my CV.

Praise for the perfect murder on your CV?

Maybe not on my CV. But nevertheless, I wanted to impress her. The only question was: *How exactly would I commit the perfect murder?*

The question was perplexing. Nothing came to mind. At least, nothing immediately. What was Edith looking for when she created this assignment? Something original? Something ingenious? Something...

... she could use in her next novel! Perhaps old Edith is running dry on ideas, too much gin in the blood has blunted her creativity!

Poised with my pen, my hand hovered over the card, awaiting instruction from my murder-mystery-obsessed mind. How would I commit the perfect murder? Nothing came. I could imagine the others getting on with the assignment. Surely, it was going to be a breeze for Robert, who must have a whole multitude of mind-bending, twisty scenarios. Should I go to him for advice?

You must be joking, right?

I rested my hand on the table and stared at the card. Did I even *want* to devise a way of committing the perfect murder? The perfect murder implies that no one is ever caught, which means the detective never solves the crime. Did I really want to devise a scenario where the crime goes unsolved? That, to me, defeats the whole point of mystery fiction.

The mystery must be solved! Otherwise, why read mysteries?

Suddenly, I had a rush of inspiration. Picking up my pen, I wrote down the following words on the card:

> To attempt to commit the perfect murder is to commit the perfect fallacy, since the perfect crime relies, not on the perfection of the criminal's method, but on the imperfections of the criminal investigation, which lacks the one thing that makes mystery fiction worth reading: the great detective.

This was probably not what Edith was looking for, but I thought I would be a little different, since I imagined the other four class members coming up with various murder scenarios. Leaning back in my chair, I felt satisfied with what I had written. If nothing else, I had taken a solid ideological stance, which could be summed up in one simple dictum:

The detective rules!

The bell rang loudly from the hall downstairs, followed by Rita's voice: "Dinner is served."

*

Roast pheasant! With porcini mushrooms and bread sauce. I had never eaten pheasant before. As Simon carved, Robert inhaled the aromatic vapours of the meat, looking pleasantly satisfied.

"My word," he said, "we eat like kings tonight. Well done, Simon, this looks delish."

Simon winked at Robert. "Cheers, mate!"

Rita popped the cork from a bottle of red, then moved around the table, filling up everyone's glass. "This is Simon's last time in the house," she announced, as she filled up Robert's glass. "He officially finishes here tonight."

Simon flung his apron over his shoulder. "That's right. Last day on the job for me. Been a pleasure to serve you."

Hazel smiled. "It's been a pleasure to eat your meals. Thanks for not poisoning any of us!"

Simon smiled. "The night's still young."

The group laughed.

Robert raised his wine glass: "Here's to the cook! The man with access to all the knives!"

Everyone raised their glass and toasted Simon.

Simon gave a pretentious bow. "Thanks for that," he said. "You've been a nice bunch. See you around."

Jamelia poked at the crispy edge of her meat with a fork. "Did someone shoot this?" she asked.

"No, it volunteered itself freely for consumption," replied Robert.

Jamelia ignored him: "I don't want to promote hunting and that kind of thing. Is there something else to eat?"

"Of course, there is," Robert said. "There's plenty of baked potatoes and mushrooms."

"Unfortunately, there is no veggie option tonight," Rita informed Jamelia. "Sorry."

Jamelia pursed her lips. "I'll just have the mushrooms."

Robert cut into his meat and ate a mouthful of pheasant, chewing with exaggerated relish, whilst eyeing Jamelia. "Mm, this meat is amazing!"

Jamelia looked at him with contempt. Shirley entered the room and stood at the end of the table, in front of the stag's head. From where I sat, it looked like her head had grown a set of enormous antlers.

"Well, I hope everyone is having a very pheasant evening," she said.

Robert laughed derisively. Shirley blushed, realising her pun. She cleared her throat.

"Edith has retired to her room for the evening. As you can imagine, she has a lot on her plate. She will see you all bright and early for tomorrow's final class, where you will submit your assignments. For now, I just wanted to let you know about the prize for whoever comes up with the best answer."

We looked at each other, surprised. *There was a prize?*

Shirley placed her hands on the back of a chair. "The winner of the assignment will have the chance-of-a-lifetime opportunity to pitch their idea for a mystery novel to a big-name publisher."

There was a gasp of astonishment from everyone at the table. Hazel's mouth hung open.

"Which big-name publisher?" Jamelia asked.

"The very publisher who publishes Edith's novels."

Wow, pitching an idea to Edith's publisher. The stakes of winning just went through the roof!

Everyone at the table looked excited.

"Well, enjoy your roast dinner." Shirley said, walking towards the door. "Oh, before I forget. Rita, can you please make sure the back door in the kitchen is locked tonight. There's probably nothing to worry about, but just for Edith's peace of mind, can you please double-check every door and window downstairs is locked."

Rita nodded. "Of course, Shirley. I do every night."

Shirley smiled awkwardly at us then left the room.

We looked at one another like we were, each of us, a murder suspect in a mystery novel. The prize for the assignment had focused us all. I now *really* wanted to win this assignment. But was my answer good enough? Was it too wordy? What had the others written? As I examined the faces of everyone else at the table, I noticed the atmosphere had changed. Suddenly, we were like five strangers, now in direct competition with each other, suspicious of each other's writing talents. Everyone wanted the prize. The question was: how far were each of us willing to go to get it?

*

It was strangely quiet as I lay in bed that night. Not a peep could be heard from the owl. Perhaps the wind from last night had frightened it away. And yet, I couldn't sleep a wink. Two things kept bugging me: Jack Burley and the assignment. Where was Jack now?

Was he back in London, plotting his next move against Edith? Or was he somewhere... *closer*? The police would be on the lookout in case he returned to Beaglesford. But the police are not perfect when it comes to preventing crime. Especially, village police.

Then there was the assignment. Did my answer stand a chance of winning? I felt it was the most accurate representation of my inner thought. Unlike modern commercial writers, I didn't want to concoct some cheap, guessable locked-room mystery just for the sake of revealing some tantalising twist. I wanted to give a statement that was true to my heart. And true to my love of mystery novels.

There was a *smash* outside my door.

What on earth was that?

Trying to remain calm, I got out of bed and slipped on my sweater. Very slowly, I opened my door and peered out. Although it was dark, I could see that the glass peacock had fallen on the floor, and this time it had smashed into pieces. I looked the other way and spotted the back of Edith, clad in her ghostly white nightie and cap, lumbering into her bedroom.

Another night. Another sleepwalking incident.

The door closed behind her. Then there was another noise. Robert's bedroom door opened. I withdrew my head back inside my door, leaving just an inch to peer out. He tiptoed across the hallway to Rita's room and knocked lightly on her door. Rita answered and welcomed Robert inside.

What about the broken glass?

It was late, I knew, but I couldn't ignore the broken glass

in the hallway. What if someone walked on it in their bare feet, as could easily happen if Edith went sleepwalking again? Quietly, I tiptoed downstairs.

I took the dustpan and brush from a cabinet beneath the kitchen sink. On my way out, I noticed the living room light was on. Creeping up to the door, I opened it ever so slightly and saw that Aaron was inside, talking on his phone. Leaning in, I listened carefully:

"Yeah, they're all in bed asleep," he said, in a whispering voice. "Come tomorrow, they're gonna get the surprise of their lives... yeah, don't worry, by the time they find out, I'll be long gone."

My heart raced. What was that about?

From the sounds of it, you're going to find out tomorrow.

Conscious of the late hour, I tiptoed back upstairs with the brush and dustpan in hand.

7

Are We Suspects?

After a restless night, I picked up my assignment card and made my way down. Our final day. When I reached the bottom of the stairs, I was surprised to find the other four class members standing outside the library door.

"Why are you all out here?" I asked.

Jamelia looked irritated. "We're waiting for Shirley to get the keys from Rita. Apparently, Edith's gone AWOL."

"AWOL?" I asked, astonished.

"Yeah, probably gone on one final bender," said Robert, who leaned against the wall.

"Ah, you brought your card," said Hazel.

I self-consciously held it behind my back. Surely they had all brought their cards too?

Shirley shuffled into the hallway holding a set of keys. She stooped down at the door and tried to insert one of the brass keys into the lock. She fumbled, and dropped them on the floor. Flustered by her clumsiness, she picked up the set and tried a second time... alas, the keys fell from her hands again. "Fiddlesticks!" she muttered to herself, as she bent over to pick them up again.

Robert stood out from the wall and sneered. "Third time lucky, Shirley. You can do it."

Shirley, whose sheer lack of self-confidence was not in any way improved by Robert's sarcasm, managed to open the door on her third attempt. We entered the library and took a seat at our usual desks.

"I'm sure Edith will join you in a while, I'll just um... try her mobile again," Shirley said. "Before I go, could I ask you to give me your assignment cards?"

Each class member produced their assignment cards and placed them on their desks. Shirley collected them one by one, then left the library. After a few moments of awkward silence, I decided to speak up.

"How did everyone sleep last night?"

All eyes focused on me.

"Badly," said Aaron. "Didn't sleep a wink. Kept hearing these creaking sounds outside my door."

"Yeah, me too," confirmed Jamelia. "Like a ghost or something."

"Ghost?" exclaimed Robert. "You seriously believe in ghosts?"

"No," stated Jamelia. "I only said it sounded like a ghost."

"I heard noises too," added Hazel. "Maybe it was the wind."

"There was no wind last night," said Aaron. "It was perfectly calm."

"What about you?" Robert asked me, in a slightly accusatory manner. "How did *you* sleep?"

"Oh," I said, as I sat up in my chair. "Like a log."

I smiled at Robert who squinted back at me. The class returned to silence. Robert spun his pen in his hand. I willed him to drop it, just this once.

The silence in the library was shattered by a bloodcurdling *scream*!

"That sounds like *Rita*," said Jamelia.

Robert immediately leapt out of his seat and rushed out of the library. Seconds later, we followed him. We rushed through the kitchen and out the back door which was wide open. Rita was standing in the centre of the labyrinth, with her hands over her mouth. Robert leapt over the hedge walls, towards the centre. When we arrived at the centre, we stood aghast. It was like a scene straight out of a mystery novel. Edith lay face down in her white nightie and cap, with a kitchen knife lodged deeply in her back, a scarlet patch of blood spreading across her body. Her head was turned to one side, revealing her porcelain white face. Was this another game? Aaron knelt beside her and placed two fingers to her neck. He looked at us in horror.

"She's dead."

We stood in mutual shock within the labyrinth. Above us, dark grey clouds had gathered in the sky, accompanied by a blistering, cold gust of wind. Rita sobbed in Robert's arms. Aaron rose to his feet and shook his head at the tragic scene. Jamelia stared at Edith's body in disbelief. Hazel and I looked at each other, astonished. *Was this really happening?* I looked back towards the house. Standing at a window was Shirley, who gazed at the scene with a completely frozen expression. I looked at the corpse and wondered how long Edith had lain there.

*

That evening, I observed the scene from my bedroom window. Edith's body was removed by a coroner and police erected tape around the labyrinth. Two forensic investigators scoured the back garden, searching for evidence. There were countless other police personnel present in the garden at various times, talking to each other, taking notes. It all felt so surreal. Each of the house guests had been questioned by the police throughout the day. I knew the police were only doing their job, but their hard-line questioning made me feel like I was in some way responsible for what happened. Like I was not telling them the whole truth or deliberately withholding information. Deep down, I felt numb. I had yet to fully process the death of Edith Ramsey.

No... the *murder* of Edith Ramsey. *This was a real-life murder investigation.*

I picked up my phone and contemplated calling Mum, but hesitated. How exactly would I break this to her? Then there was a knock at my door. Relieved to be interrupted, I hopped out of my chair and opened it. It was Rita.

"The police want to speak to all the residents of the manor house in the drawing room in fifteen minutes," she said with blunt urgency.

"They want to speak to us again?" I asked. "I thought they finished questioning us?"

She looked exhausted. "That's what I was told. Please be on time."

She left abruptly and walked down the hallway towards Hazel's door. I closed my door quietly and sat on my bed. More questioning? How much more could I take? I had told them everything already. At least, I thought I had.

*

"We're doing everything we can to find Edith's killer and bring them to justice. We know this must be a very difficult time for each of you."

Detective Chief Inspector Wallace addressed the entire household in the drawing room. Standing at about five foot five inches tall, he was a portly man, mainly bald, apart from the hair that grew at the sides of his head, and he sported a very bushy moustache that just fell short of being a full-on handlebar. Every now and again, his cheek would twitch, indicating he had a facial tic. Behind him stood DCI Brice, a much taller and leaner chap, with a handsome, chiselled face, despite a prominent scar on his left cheek.

"What do you mean by serious developments?" Jamelia asked.

DCI Wallace grimaced slightly. "Well, there is a slight possibility that the killer could return to the scene of the crime. But this would be very unusual. Nevertheless, DCI Brice will be staying here tonight, just as a precautionary measure. As you know, we have questioned each of you and are satisfied that none of you is a person of interest. We are currently looking for one suspect and one suspect only. We presently do not know their whereabouts but are following a number of leads."

"You're talking about Jack?" Hazel proffered.

"Yes, the suspect is Jack Burley," DCI Brice confirmed.

"Are there any witnesses?" I asked

DCI Wallace looked at me, with narrowed eyes. "We've not been able to find any eye-witnesses to the murder, I'm afraid. But, as I said, we are following a number of promising leads."

"Then," I continued, "why are you certain that Jack Burley is the culprit, since you just used the word 'criminal'?"

His eyes fixed on me again. "We are not certain about who the murderer is but right now he is our main suspect."

"Are we allowed to leave the house?" Aaron asked.

DCI Wallace adjusted his stance. "Erm, we strongly advise everyone to remain here for the time being. For your own safety. Just until we've apprehended Mr Burley."

"What about dinner?" Hazel said. "We no longer have a cook."

DCI Wallace looked around the room with a confused expression. "Dinner? Eh…"

Rita cleared her throat. "I can do the cooking."

"I can help as well," said Shirley.

DCI Wallace nodded. "Alright then, that settles the question of dinner."

Just to let you know that this case is sure to be very high profile, given that the victim is a renowned author. Indeed, I should say, a renowned crime fiction author. We expect that there will be a number of reporters looking for an interview, so we advise you not to speak to anyone outside your immediate family. This would be the best approach to safeguard your own privacy and the details of this serious investigation. I would be most grateful for your cooperation in this matter. Are there any questions?" He looked at each of us with an intense scrutinising stare, as if to discourage us from asking any follow-up questions.

Robert, clearly needing to get some attention spoke up: "I'd like to know one thing, detective: do you think all this has the makings of a bestselling novel?"

DCI Wallace pursed his lips, and ignored him.

*

After the meeting, Hazel and I sat in the living room, side by side, each holding a cup of strong tea.

"I can't believe she's gone," Hazel said morosely. "On the very last day of the writing course. This is like something..."

"From a mystery novel," I stated flatly.

She nodded, then took a sip of her tea.

"I agree that this is all very unreal, but this is the situation that we are in," I said. "We need to carefully consider all the facts of the case before we jump to any firm conclusion. I agree that Jack is the most likely suspect, considering his antics over the past few days, but there are other factors to consider that should not be overlooked."

"Bel, what are you talking about? We're not detectives. This is bloody serious!" Hazel retorted; she was clearly not interested in amateur sleuthing. "That poor woman is gone. I can't get the image of her lying dead on the ground out of my mind. I'm going to be traumatised forever! I want to go home!"

She began to sob. Suddenly, I felt like sobbing too. She was right. That poor woman was dead. Murdered in cold blood. The image of Edith's cold, lifeless body, lying face down, with a knife lodged deep in her back, made me feel sick to my stomach. I felt it was my job to make Hazel feel better. I placed my hand gently on her hand.

"Hazel, we'll get through this. Together."

She looked at me, as she struggled to smile. "I hope so, Bel. I've never been in this kind of situation before. It's not like in novels, where the excitement begins when a body is discovered. This just feels..."

"Too real," I suggested.

She nodded in agreement. We both sipped our tea in

silence. The box for "Cluedo" rested on the table in front of us. Suddenly I remembered the missing dagger piece and how ironic its absence seemed in the wake of Edith's murder.

"What did your mum say about all this?" Hazel asked.

"I haven't told her yet. Didn't want to upset her."

"She's going to find out anyway. It's already in the news. Come tomorrow it'll be all over the front pages."

"Yes, I'll ring her. How about you? How did your parents react?"

Hazel looked at me, blinking repeatedly. "They're in shock. They want me to come home as soon as possible. Why can't we go home today?"

I looked at Hazel who seemed to be on the verge of a breakdown. "They probably think it's unsafe for us to leave the house? If Jack is still out there? I'm sure he'll be apprehended soon and we can then leave."

"But you're not convinced Jack is the murderer?"

I sighed. "It's not that I don't think he murdered Edith. He is the most likely suspect, given his recent behaviour. But the fact that there are no eye-witnesses to the murder makes it difficult to rule out other suspects completely."

Hazel warily looked around. "Who else do you think could have murdered Edith?"

I shrugged my shoulders and remained silent. I didn't have an answer. I looked at my watch.

"I think it's time I called Mum. Will you be okay?"

Hazel looked at me and swallowed hard. "I'll be fine, Bel. Don't worry about me."

*

Mum had been trying to ring me throughout the day, leaving panicky text messages. The story had clearly made the news. Within a second of her phone ringing, she answered.

"Belinda?"

"Hey, Mum."

"Where have you been? Been worried sick about you."

"Been a little busy, Mum, sorry," were the only words I could think of.

"Is it true?"

"What's that?"

"Edith Ramsey. Is she... dead?"

"Yes."

"Murdered?"

"Yes."

"At the country house?"

"Yes."

The phone went dead silent.

"Dear God, Belinda!" she exclaimed. "You need to get out of there now! What if the killer returns to finish you all off?"

"Mum, please don't be so dramatic," I said. "The police are here. We're in no immediate danger."

There were a few moments of silence from the other end.

"I'm coming to get you," she said bluntly.

"Coming where?" I asked.

"To Beaglesford. I'll drive up."

"Mum don't be silly," I said, taken aback. "You can't drive long distances. It's not safe. Remember when you drove to Liverpool?"

"Then I'll take the train," she stated.

I took a deep breath. "Mum, I didn't call you earlier because I didn't want to stress you out. Now you're talking about driving here, which will make you exhausted."

"Belinda, a mother should be by her daughter's side if she's in trouble!" Mum's voice was determined. Suddenly, I felt tearful.

"Belinda? Belinda, are you there?"

I cleared my throat. "Yes, Mum, I'm here. Look, it's very kind of you to offer to come here. Let's sleep on it and see what happens tomorrow. I have a good feeling they'll catch Jack Burley soon."

"Jack Burley? Is that who killed Edith?"

"The police believe so. So, you've nothing to worry about. They're out looking for him right now."

Mum yawned. "Oh Belinda, I'm so tired. Sorry – all this worry has worn me down."

"I understand, Mum, please get some rest."

"Will do," she said as she yawned again. "Let's speak in the morning?"

"Yes, Mum. Talk to you in the morning."

"Goodnight, Belinda. Stay safe, love. Don't answer the door to any strangers!"

"I won't, Mum. Goodnight."

I felt like weeping as I placed my phone on my bedside table. Poor Mum! She must be so worried about me. I really hoped she wouldn't try to travel tomorrow. I could already see raindrops accumulating on the bedroom window. Bad weather combined with the stress of travel would not be good for her condition. I needed to go home, to see her. When would it be safe to leave? I lay down and stared at the ceiling. It was so silent in the house. A sudden, strong gust of wind roared fiercely outside, whipping the rain harder against the window. It was going to be a rough night. I wondered where Jack Burley was right now.

*

I lay there, restless, listening to the rain beat against the window. My mind wouldn't calm down – so much for an early night! I slipped on my shoes and made my way downstairs. The door to the living room was slightly ajar, and I could hear people conversing at a subdued volume. I entered the room to find Jamelia, Hazel and Aaron sitting inside, huddled together around the table with the board games.

"Hey Bel. What's up?" Jamelia asked.

I closed the door behind me. "Hey. Nothing really. Been lying in bed, unable to sleep. So many things going through my mind."

"Join the club," said Aaron. "We've been going over details of Edith's murder. Trying to make sense of it all."

I dragged a chair to the table and sat down. "Details?" I asked.

"Yes," said Hazel. "Like how Jamelia saw Gregory outside last night with a gun."

"A gun?" I said, shocked.

"Yeah, saw him walking around the back from my window. He was carrying a big gun, like a rifle or something."

"What time was this?" I asked.

"Around two in the morning," she said. "I got up to go to the loo."

"Why would he be out there at such a late hour?"

"Maybe he heard something," Hazel suggested. "Like when Jack broke into the property. Scary to think he was here last night. We're lucky that we're still alive."

"It hasn't been established he was here last night," I stated. "There's no evidence of a break-in."

Jamelia leaned forward, placing her hand under her chin. "He must have broken in. How else did he get the kitchen knife he used to kill Edith?"

I shrugged my shoulders. "I've no idea. But all the doors and windows were locked last night. Rita double-checked everywhere, remember?"

Hazel raised her hands. "Then how do you explain what happened?"

Looking at the Cluedo box on the table, I shook my head. "Honestly, I can't say."

Aaron stared down at the floor, ruminating in his thoughts. What was he thinking?

"Did you see or hear anything last night, Aaron?" I asked.

"Me?" he said, raising his head towards me. He seemed quite surprised by my question. "No. I was in bed by eleven. Slept like a log throughout the night."

"You were in bed by eleven?" I asked.

"Yeah, pretty much."

"You didn't go downstairs later?"

He scratched his head, looking slightly befuddled by my line of questioning. "No," he said, unconvincingly. "Didn't leave my room at all. What about you? Did you notice anything?"

I remained silent for a few moments, thinking of the smashed peacock. "Yes, I did, as a matter of fact."

They looked at me intensely.

"I saw Edith on the upstairs landing. She was sleep-walking. It must have been... between one and two."

"Sleepwalking?" Hazel exclaimed. "I didn't know she was a sleepwalker."

"Yeah, she is," Jamelia confirmed. "Saw her myself two nights ago. She was wandering around upstairs in her night clothes." She smiled. "When I first saw her in her white dress and hat, honestly, I thought it was Ebenezer Scrooge or something." She laughed briefly. "Sorry," she said, as her face became serious. "I shouldn't be making jokes at a time like this."

"Her sleepwalking doesn't surprise me," Aaron flatly stated. "Given that she drinks alcohol and takes Zopiclone."

"Zopiclone?" Jamelia said.

"It's a sleeping pill," he said.

"How did you know she takes it?" I asked.

Aaron glanced momentarily towards the door, as he expected someone to walk in at any second. "I found Edith asleep in the library a few nights back. The bottle of pills was on a table beside her. It looked like she had taken it with her gin. She was snoring quite heavily."

I pondered Aaron's revelation. Drinking alcohol with medication would almost certainly exacerbate any side effects.

"Maybe she climbed out her window while she was sleep-walking?" Jamelia suggested. "That's how she ended up outside."

"Climbed out the window?" exclaimed Hazel. "Then she would have fallen onto the patio and broken her legs or her neck. How would she have made it to the labyrinth?"

"She was dragged?"

Hazel narrowed her eyes, clearly not impressed by Jamelia's theory.

I pictured Edith's body in the labyrinth, her porcelain white face, her white nightclothes. Almost angelic.

"Falling from a second-storey window is not consistent

with the state of Edith's body," I said academically. "She had no visible signs of injuries on her face, legs or arms."

Hazel smiled slightly. She was visibly impressed with my assessment of Edith's corpse.

"Wait a second," Aaron said, clasping his hands together. "Rita said that Edith's window was locked when she entered her room today. She couldn't have climbed out."

That settled the "Edith falling out of the window" theory. However, my mind was still fixed on the image of Edith's body. Something had occurred to me.

"I just realised something," I said.

"What?" said Jamelia.

I pictured the blood-soaked back of her nightie, where the knife had been lodged. "If I remember correctly, the buttons of her nightdress were on her back, just above the knife entry."

They gave me a perplexed look.

"Meaning?" Jamelia said.

"Her nightdress was on back to front," I stated.

Hazel nodded, then asked: "So what's your deduction?"

I looked at her and clenched my jaw. I didn't have a deduction. "Nothing. Just pointing out a peculiarity."

Aaron leaned back in his chair and placed his joined hands beneath his chin. "She probably put it on back to front by mistake. Can happen if you drink alcohol before going to bed."

That was a plausible explanation.

Jamelia yawned and stretched her arms. "I think it's time I went to bed. All this talk of sleepwalking has made me sleepy."

"Me too," said Hazel. "I'm so glad the police are staying here tonight."

Jamelia's suddenly face lit up. "Ooh DCI Brice! He's fit, isn't he? Even with that scar, he's a hunk."

Hazel smiled. "He is very handsome."

"Try not to get too excited, girls," Aaron remarked, as he stood up to leave the room.

"You coming, Bel?" Hazel asked.

"Not just yet. I think I'm going to stay here for a while."

"Suit yourself," said Hazel. "Goodnight."

As the three of them headed out the room, Jamelia stalled at the door. She waited a few moments, for the others to be out of sight, then turned to me.

"Listen Bel," she said, in a low volume. "I hope you didn't take that thing I said about Edith seriously? You know, yesterday, about killing her with a knife?" She made a stabbing gesture the air with her hand. "I didn't mean that to be taken seriously, you know that, yeah?"

"Of course," I said, frowning. "You were just letting off steam. I hadn't really given it a second thought."

She stared at me for a few moments. I felt the need to swallow. After a few tense moments, she beamed. "Great, glad we cleared that up. Catch you later!"

"Yeah, later," I said, allowing myself to swallow. Was she worried that I could finger her as a suspect? Although I didn't know her that well, I couldn't picture her as someone capable of murder. Then again, she was angry with Edith the day before she died. Could that have driven her to murder her? Deep down, it didn't seem enough.

And what about Aaron's phone conversation in the living room? He'd *lied* about being downstairs last night. His behaviour seemed more suspicious than Jamelia's. He was clearly hiding something. But could he be a murderer? I couldn't imagine him doing something as dreadful as killing someone.

Yet, how well did I know him? How well did I know any of my classmates? And where was Robert this evening?

Why was Gregory out at such a late hour last night, carrying a gun? Had he seen or heard something? Or someone? Did the police know he had been out walking with a gun? I needed to find out more. It was late but not too late to pay him a visit.

*

It was dismally wet and windy as I walked briskly across the garden, passing the police tape that surrounded the labyrinth. Arriving at the coach house, I banged loudly on the door above the howling wind. Despite the lights being on downstairs, there was no response. I banged on the door again and waited. Still no response. I walked to the downstairs window and peered in.

Gregory was asleep in an armchair, no longer bandaged, with an empty bottle of booze by his side. A hunting rifle hung on the living room wall behind where he sat. I was about to knock on the window, when a hand grabbed my shoulder. Jumping with fright, I turned to see DCI Brice, standing under an umbrella. He looked very annoyed.

"What the bloody hell are you doing out here?" he bellowed, as the rain lashed against his brolly.

Good question. What was I doing here, at this time, getting soaked to the bone?

"I... I... I wanted to see how Gregory was doing. Was... worried about him."

His face flinched. "Get inside!" he ordered. "You'll catch your death out here!"

Good advice. We both could catch our death out here.

*

DCI Brice sat next to me at the kitchen table, with two cups of tea. I ran my hair through a towel, then picked up the warm cuppa.

"So, you want to tell me what you were doing outside?" he asked in a calmer manner.

I took a sip of tea. Impressively, he had used the right amount of sugar and milk. "I was, um, worried about Gregory. Just wondered how he was doing, since Edith's death."

"I see," he said. "You were just checking up on him?"

"Yes," I said.

"It must be tough on all of you, what happened here last night. How are you feeling yourself?"

I took a moment to gather my thoughts. "I'm... shocked. Can't believe it's happened."

He folded his arms and leaned back in his chair. "A woman who writes murder mysteries, gets murdered. It *is* almost unbelievable."

I stayed silent and rubbed the scratch on my hand. The scab was now quite itchy.

"It's a case of life imitating art, isn't it?" he said, observing me scratch my hand.

I straightened up in my chair. "It seems to me that it's a case of a famous person being murdered by a dangerous and violent stalker. Someone that you're here to protect us from."

"Ah yes, Jack Burley," he said. "He seems like the most likely suspect."

His tone was very blasé. Suddenly, I realised there may have been another reason why the detective was staying over at the house. Jack Burley may well have been the prime suspect but perhaps the police had not ruled out the residents of the house. After all, we did come here to learn about murder – albeit as a fictional theme. But what if the police suspected one of us of taking our subject matter too seriously? I looked at the detective whose eyes had wandered to the wooden plaque on the wall. Immediately, I thought of Simon.

"Have you interviewed Simon?" I asked.

"Simon?" he said, redirecting his eyes toward me.

"Yes, he did the cooking for the house guests. He lives a short drive away."

The detective nodded his head. "Yeah, we've spoken to him. He's in York with his wife, visiting his folks. He has an alibi."

That ruled out the cook as a suspect. I thought about other details of Edith's murder. "What about the knife?"

"The knife?"

"Yes, the one used to kill Edith. Did you find any prints on it?"

The detective yawned and stretched his arms out on the table, joining his hands together. "Nope. Handle was wiped clean."

"Oh, I see," I said, disappointed by his answer. "Then may I ask another question?"

"Yeah, go on," he answered.

"Are we *suspects*?"

He looked me squarely in the eye. "Suspects? You?" He then smiled. "Come on, do you really think any of you has it in you to commit murder?"

I looked again at the wooden plaque. "No," I answered him unconfidently. "I suppose not."

"Don't worry about it," he said in a disingenuous manner that did make me worry. "We'll have Jack Burley caught in no time. Then you can all go home. Just like a happy ending in a book."

He smiled broadly. The scar under his left cheek became more prominent when he smiled.

"Yes, of course," I said. "Just like in a book."

*

I sat in bed with my notebook on my lap, as the rain lashed against the window outside like lead pellets. There was no way my brain was going to let me sleep tonight. I had drawn a bubble diagram of potential suspects in Edith's murder case. In the centre bubble, I wrote "Jack Burley", the most likely suspect. Orbiting the centre, I entered the names of the other possible, yet unlikely suspects.

Jamelia – she had threatened to kill Edith after she was insulted by her in class. The reference she made to the murder victim in Edith's novel *Shedunnit* raised the question whether her words were just a coincidence, or a chilling warning. In all likelihood, she was being facetious. After all, Jack Burley referenced the same scene from *Shedunnit* on the first night we met him in the pub. But I couldn't entirely rule her out as a suspect.

Aaron – he was a curious case. His phone conversation in the living room on the night of the murder did raise suspicions, or at very least, some serious questions. Who was he talking to? What exactly did he mean when he said we were about to get the surprise of our lives and, when we did, he'd be long gone? Did he know something was about to happen to Edith? And if he planned to leave, why was he still here? Aaron certainly was a mysterious, quiet fellow. But it was too early to tell if there was something much darker beneath his quietness.

Robert – I entered his name in the second-largest bubble, closest to Jack Burley. He was definitely one to watch. Was it all posturing and bravado, or something more sinister in his character? He was with Rita the night Edith was killed. He therefore had access to the keys of the door that led to the back garden. Could Rita be involved too? Was she an accomplice? Or was Robert just using her?

Then there was Shirley – she had taken a lot of stick from Edith throughout the week. The two of them seemed like the classic odd couple, with poor Shirley often on the receiving end of Edith's tantrums. But a murderer? It was hard to think of her as anything but a pushover. I wondered if on some level she was relieved that Edith was dead.

The rain continued to lash against the window. I yawned and placed my notes on the bedside table. This bubble diagram wasn't going to solve the mystery anytime soon.

What about Hazel? You haven't included her in the diagram!

Indeed, what about Hazel? She wasn't the murderer, I knew that much. She just didn't have it in her. She didn't even have it in her to be a red herring.

8

Hello, Ladies.
Remember Me?

What a nightmare!

"It's bucketing out there," Hazel lamented as we stood in the living room the next morning, gazing at the torrential rain outside the window. She wandered over to the table where the games were stacked and picked up the Cluedo box.

"Fancy a game, Bel?" she asked timidly.

"No, Hazel, I am definitely not in the mood for that game," I answered assertively.

"How about Connect Four?"

"No," I said. "I'm not in the mood for any game."

Hazel slumped onto the couch. "What are we going to do then?"

I looked at her momentarily. I knew by her glum face that she wanted to talk – but I was in no mood for talking. "I suppose... we will just have to wait this out."

Through the window, I stared into the gloomy, overcast sky. It was a fitting analogy of how I felt inside. It seemed that the heavens were angry – if not furious, in fact – over the heinous crime that had been committed on these grounds.

Hazel sighed aloud. "Bel, how long do we have to stay here? Jack could come back at any moment."

I turned towards her, as she slumped on the sofa with her hands in her pockets. "Detective Brice is staying here. I'm sure we're in good hands."

"Well, I still don't feel safe. What if Jack kills him as well? Then who'll defend us?"

I rolled my eyes. Honestly, I felt that her excessive worry was unbecoming of someone who deep down wanted to be a detective. How would she hack it if *she* was put in charge of a murder investigation? The door suddenly swung open. Jamelia entered the room, holding her tablet.

"Hey guys, check this out," she said, walking toward the table, while her eyes remained glued to her tablet screen. "You need to see these headlines. Edith's death is all over the internet."

Hazel and I scuttled over to where Jamelia stood and gaped at her screen.

"Look at this," she said, as she trawled through some of the media headlines.

"Queen of the cosies dead!" ran the *Daily Mail's* headline.

"Edith Ramsey slain!" The *Daily Express*.

"Mystery author murdered in cold blood," in the *Metro*.

"Murder in the labyrinth: Who killed Edith Ramsey?" An editorial in *The Guardian*.

"Hack stabbed in the back!" *The Sun* was the most dramatic, with a dagger as a substitute for the exclamation mark.

Finally, Jamelia browsed to a local news outlet, *The Cambridge News*, which ran with the headline: "Murder Comes to Beaglesford: Award-winning author found dead at local manor house."

Jamelia tapped the screen of her tablet. "This is serious shit. I mean, this is mega!" We looked at each other, amazed that we were at the centre of a true-life crime investigation that was causing a media sensation. As Hazel and Jamelia were glued to the screen, I felt the need to stretch my legs. I found myself under the stern gaze of Lord Ainsley.

"Blimey!" exclaimed Hazel. "Are we gonna be in the news?"

"Let's hope so," said Jamelia, who was curiously upbeat. "Have you seen the cars outside the gate?"

"No," said Hazel. "Who are they?"

"Local press, is my guess. I can see them from my window. Belinda, you seen 'em?"

"Yes," I said, leaning on the mantlepiece. "There's only a few cars out there."

Jamelia lowered her tablet to her waist. "Yeah, for now, but this place will be swamped with journos over the next few days."

"You mean this is going to be... *a media frenzy!*" Hazel sounded almost ecstatic.

Jamelia's face lit up with a delighted smile. "Yup, it's gonna be a total field day!"

As the two of them became excited by the prospect of media attention, I looked up at Lord Ainsley and empathised with his glare. It seemed inevitable that was going to be the case: a famous writer, hounded by a deranged stalker, found murdered with a knife in her back during a country house writing course, only a day after giving an assignment to five young hopefuls to plan the perfect murder. Who wouldn't make a juicy story out of that? And that would mean they would be interested in us.

There was a light knock on the open living room door, followed by Shirley entering the room.

"Hello, everyone. How are we all doing today?"

"We're alright," replied Jamelia. "How are you doing, Shirley?"

Shirley looked down at her feet, as the weight of the world seemed to weigh heavily on her slumped shoulders. "Oh, I'm OK, I think. Been difficult to sleep... The weather is just awful."

"Horrendous!" Hazel asserted.

"Yes, well, given the circumstances I think it would be best if we arranged an activity for this evening. To keep our spirits up."

"An activity?" I asked.

"Yes," Shirley said, glancing at me. "How about charades in the drawing room at eight?"

Jamelia and Hazel both smiled. "Yeah, that sounds great."

Shirley smiled awkwardly at us. "Well, looking forward to seeing you all later." She shuffled out of the room.

Jamelia looked at me. "Poor woman, all this must be tough on her."

Looking up at Lord Ainsley, I sighed. "This is tough on us all, Jamelia."

*

To kill time, I went to the library with my notebook and pen. I looked at the six writing desks, positioned in a circle. It was chillingly poignant to observe the empty seats, especially where Edith used to sit – although, truth be told, she did more standing than sitting during her classes. I chose my usual seat and sat in silence for a few moments. No longer filled with Edith's thundering, theatrical voice and dynamic presence, the library seemed like a cold, desolate mausoleum, filled with the mustiness of ageing books and manuscripts.

As I opened my notebook, I heard something from the back of the library. Something that sounded like... *weeping*. I stole along the corridor that ran down the side of the bookcases towards the rear. I found Rita sitting on a stool, with her face in her hands, sobbing. She looked up at me, embarrassed.

"Is everything okay?" I asked.

She wiped her eyes on the sleeve of her sweater. It was the first time I'd seen her in casual clothes.

"I'm fine," she said, as she took out a handkerchief and blew her nose. She clearly was not fine.

Kneeling beside her, I asked "What's wrong?"

"Nothing's wrong. It's just... Rob. He's been really mean to me," she sobbed.

I placed my hand gently on her shoulder. "What happened? You can tell me."

Rita's eyes looked into mine, scrutinising me to see if I could be trusted. She looked at her hands as she squeezed the hanky tight.

"Well," she started, "we had an argument. He got really angry."

I adjusted my position - kneeling was uncomfortable. "Why was he angry?"

"I lied to the police. When they questioned me, they asked if I saw anyone or noticed anything after I had gone to bed. I said I didn't. Truth is... Robert was with me. But he made me promise not to say anything."

"Why did he not want you to tell them he was with you?"

"Because he's embarrassed to be with me. He says he doesn't want our relationship to be a matter of official record, because I'm... only a *maid*." She sobbed into her hands, using the hanky to mop up the tears.

"Oh," I said. "That's... awful."

She blew her nose profusely. "He said his parents are old-fashioned and wouldn't approve of him dating someone who's..."

"Someone who's?" I asked.

"Someone who's *common*." She placed the hanky under her runny nose.

"So, you lied about Robert being with you the night Edith was killed?"

She nodded. "I said I was alone all night. I told Robert I wanted to go back and tell the police the truth. I mean, what's the difference now? Edith can't say anything. But he totally flew off the handle, saying that if I change my story now, it'd make us both look guilty."

I patted her on the back as I contemplated her words. "You said Edith can't say anything. What do you mean?"

She sat up on the stool. "She caught me and Rob in the library one evening. She got livid and said she was going to report me to my employer because I shouldn't be having relationships with house guests. It's against company rules. She was really mean about it. I could have lost my job... but I guess they won't find out now."

"Oh," I said. "I see." Rita could have lost her job if Edith reported her. Would that be reason enough to kill her?

Sounds like motive to me.

Yes, indeed, but to believe Rita would resort to murder over the prospect of unemployment was a stretch too far for the imagination. She was a good-natured person, who didn't fit the profile of a cold-blooded killer, unlike...

Bang. A book had fallen to the floor at the other end of the bookcase. Standing beside the book was Robert. Had he done that on purpose?

"Everything alright, Rita?" he said in a patronising tone.

Rita wiped her nose and looked up at Robert with fear in her eyes. Without saying a word, she got up from the stool and walked past him, leaving the library. I rose to my feet and stared at Robert. He walked towards me and stopped only a few inches from my face.

"Playing the detective again, are we?"

"Just comforting someone in need," I replied.

He leaned in closer, putting his face right into mine. I was tempted to recoil.

Hold your ground. Don't back down.

"In real life there are no amateur sleuths, only nosy-parkers. And nosy-parkers all end up the same way," he said, showing his teeth.

I held my ground, not backing down. "Enlighten me, Rob. How do they end up?"

He stared at me in silence. Neither he nor I flinched during the intense standoff. Eventually, rather than answering my question, he walked away.

You can breathe again! The psycho's gone.

I collected my pen and notebook. So much for trying to take my mind off things. I decided to return to my bedroom. When I got to the upstairs landing, I observed the empty wooden stand, where the glass peacock once stood intact. I remembered Edith sleepwalking. Just then, Shirley came out of her bedroom, holding a stack of books. She passed me in a very hurried manner, almost knocking me over, and proceeded down the stairs. Incensed, I was about to shout after her, when I noticed something on the floor: a card, which I picked up. On first inspection, I realised it was Robert's perfect murder assignment card. Did Shirley drop this by mistake or was it for me? My heart stopped as soon as I read what was written on it. Warily looking around, I quickly entered my bedroom.

Sitting down at my desk, I read the card again. This was an intriguing development. Someone knocked on the door. Expecting it to be Shirley, I slipped the card into my notebook and got up to open the door. Hazel stood there, looking quite bored.

"Hazel. Everything okay?"

"Yeah," she said, "what are you up to?"

"Nothing much," I said, as I shot a wary glance towards my notebook. "You want to come in?"

"Sure."

I invited her to sit on my chair at the desk. I picked up my notebook and pondered what to do.

"Hazel, I have something I need to show you. But first you must promise not to tell anyone."

Her eyes narrowed. "What is it, Bel?"

I opened the notebook and took out the card. "Shirley dropped this outside. It's one of the assignment cards."

"You mean the perfect murder assignment?"

"Yes, and you'll never believe who it belongs to."

"Who?" she asked, her bespectacled face looked like a bewildered owl.

Without answering her, I handed her the card. Her eyes widened and she let out a slight gasp.

"Write in one sentence how you would commit the perfect murder: Kill the teacher and frame her stalker.

Signed Rob the lady killer, with a smiley face winking." She looked at me amazed. "Why would he write that?"

Gazing out the window, I observed the incessant downpour. The gloom outside seemed endless but nevertheless brought a sobering clarity to my thinking. "Maybe he thinks this is his time."

"His time for what?"

I turned to Hazel. "His time to shine. Murder for him is an art. 'The body is a canvas to express a killer's genius,' remember him saying that? What if he planned all this from the beginning? His twisted imagination, his dark, cynical humour, his shameless lack of empathy which he loves to show off. Perhaps it's not all posturing on his part. Perhaps he's not a wannabe at all. Perhaps, he really is..."

"Really is what?" Hazel exclaimed.

I paced up and down the room, thinking deeply. Was I getting carried away? Was my mystery-obsessed mind leading me down fanciful avenues? I needed to think everything through before I answered Hazel's question. Could this masterclass have been an opportunity for Robert to stage an actual murder? I should show the card to the police.

Hazel leaned back in the chair, placing her hands behind her head, observing me pace. She probably thought I was overthinking. She knew that Robert and I didn't get along.

"If Robert killed Edith," she said reflectively, "then how do you explain Jack's behaviour?"

I stopped pacing. "If Jack really did murder Edith in the back garden with a knife from the kitchen here, how would he have locked the kitchen door after he took the knife?"

Hazel raised her hands. "Maybe he locked the door from the outside?"

"But the kitchen door was locked from the inside.

Remember? Rita had locked up the night before. The next morning, she gave the set of keys to Shirley, to open the library door."

Hazel's eyes wandered to the ceiling as she reflected on the puzzle. "Maybe Jack snuck into the house days before he committed the murder, without anyone noticing, and made a copy of the key, before returning the original?"

"Or maybe Robert lured Jack to this village to frame him for the murder? After all, he did say how a kitchen knife would make a better murder weapon than a butter knife."

Hazel raised her eyebrows. It was clear she thought my idea was farfetched. It sounded more like something out of a...

Mystery novel... yes, yes, we know!

"It doesn't add up for me, Bel. I do think Robert is a nasty piece of work... but a murderer? I'm not convinced."

I sighed. Her reasoning was correct. There wasn't really any hard evidence to point to Robert being the murderer, despite his assignment card. On the other hand, Jack Burley had threatened to kill Edith in the letter found in Gregory's pocket, coupled with having a history of harassment against her. If I was to play the odds, I would have to put my money on Jack. But I wasn't entirely convinced he was the culprit.

"Hey, Bel?"

"What?"

She pointed at her wristwatch. "It's time."

I looked at her, confused. "Time for what?"

"Charades."

"Oh yes, of course. Completely slipped my mind."

*

"Book title."

"Two words."

"Second word."

Jamelia stood next to Hazel and began pointing at her repeatedly.

"Friend," said Aaron.

Jamelia shook her head, as she continued pointing at Hazel.

"Librarian," I said.

Jamelia shook her head again.

"I'm a library assistant," Hazel corrected me.

Jamelia began pointing her finger in an up-and-down movement at Hazel.

"Small?" suggested Aaron.

"Hey," said Hazel. "I'm slightly below-average height for a girl."

Jamelia stood on her toes, pointing directly at Hazel again.

"Oh," I said. "Girl."

Jamelia pointed straight at me and smiled. She returned to the top of the drawing room, standing beneath the fox head, raising her index finger.

"First word," said all the players, which presently included myself, Jamelia, Hazel, Aaron, Shirley and – surprisingly – DCI Brice. Missing were Robert and Rita, which did concern me. Jamelia stood next to Shirley and pointed at her. She then stood in front of her and gestured, as if to say: "where did she go?" It was then I knew the obvious answer.

"*Gone Girl.*"

She looked at me and clapped. "Nice one, Bel. You're up now."

Suddenly, I regretted getting the correct answer. I was

in no mood to perform a charade in front of people. The theme of the evening's game was mystery books, which, on any other occasion would have been great fun, but felt a little unseemly in the wake of Edith's death. Taking a stand in front of the small audience, I turned my back to think of a book title. The fox's head glared at me from above. Refusing to be put off by its snarling leer, I stared back hard. Then I had an idea. Turning around to face the eager players, I unfolded my hands to gesture opening a book.

"Book title," everyone chanted.

"Five words."

"First word."

"The."

Struggling to think of how to convey the second word, I thought for a few moments, then started clawing the air with my hands, trying to imitate a set of paws.

"Climbing?" said Aaron.

I shook my head and started clawing the air.

"Scratching," said Hazel. "The scratching?"

Jamelia snickered at Hazel's guess. I ceased clawing the air and thought for another few moments. I was going to have to humiliate myself if I wanted to them to guess the book title I chose. Falling to my knees, I held my hands limply in front of my chest and stuck my tongue out, panting loudly. Everyone laughed. It was very humiliating.

"Dog," shouted DCI Brice.

Rising back to my feet, I pointed at the detective and waved my hands frantically to compel him to elaborate on his answer.

"Puppy?" he said.

I rolled my eyes, then continued waving my hands.

"Something to do with a dog?" proffered Jamelia. "A Rottweiler?"

"A Labrador?" said Hazel.

"A bulldog?" said Aaron.

All wrong! I fumed in silence. I looked at the blank faces in front of me. I dropped on all fours and began to howl in silence.

"A wolf," cried Shirley. I nodded at her to indicate that she was close.

"The boy who cried wolf," shouted Hazel.

Shaking my head at Hazel's second impertinent guess, I crawled frantically around in circles on the floor, howling in silence.

"The wolf that couldn't howl?" joked Jamelia, which made everyone laugh. I rose again to my feet, feeling frustrated.

"Can I ask, is this one of those werewolf mystery books?" said Aaron.

I calmly shook my head to answer no to Aaron's question. I held five fingers in the air again.

"Fifth word."

"First syllable."

This was going to be tough. I gently tugged my ear lobe.

"Sounds like."

I placed both my hands over my face in such a way that revealed only my eyes.

"Eyes," Aaron said. "Seeing. Staring. Looking."

"Mask," said Jamelia.

Immediately, I pointed at her.

"Sounds like mask," she said. "Flask? Cask? Task?" She continued to guess. Then finally: "Bask?"

I nodded, happily smiling at her.

"Bask?" she repeated, looking completely confounded. "The something like a dog, something, something, Bask, something... wow, this is a real puzzler." Everyone giggled at her glib attitude. She was right, however. I totally sucked at charades. I felt like giving up. I had already embarrassed myself, which I presume is the real point of these games.

"The Hound of the Baskervilles," uttered a voice from the drawing room doorway. Robert, casually leaning against the doorframe. Breathing a sigh of relief, I finally spoke: "Yes. That's correct. I guess you're up next, Rob."

Gladly, I walked back to my seat. He took his place at the top of the room, beneath the fox head, and stared at each of us. He then focused his stare on me. He knew what I was thinking.

Where was Rita?

He ceremoniously unfolded his hands in front the group, who responded in unison.

"Book title."

"Five words. First word. The. Second word..."

Robert placed his index to his lips, as if to hush us all.

"Quiet?" said Aaron.

"Silence," said Jamelia.

Robert nodded.

"*The Silence of the Lambs*," said DCI Brice. Robert applauded him then bowed to the room. "Your turn mate," he said to the detective.

The detective rose from his chair and walked to the top of the room, while Robert sat next to me. I looked at him, curious as to why he sat next to me. He looked at me and smiled.

"Well, didn't expect to stand here," the detective said nervously. "Usually, I'm just an observer."

"Get on with it!" jeered Jamelia.

The detective chuckled. "Yes, yes, okay then. A book, hmmm." He closed his eyes and stood in silence for a few moments. Reopening his eyes, he nodded, indicating he had thought of something.

"Book title," chanted the class like clockwork. Then everyone gasped when the detective held up nine fingers. "Nine words," everyone exclaimed. "First word. The. Second word..."

The detective scratched his head in an exaggerated manner, looking puzzled.

"Thinking," said Aaron.

"Head lice," teased Robert.

The detective continued to shake his head.

"Curious?" said Hazel. The detective nodded frantically at Hazel.

"*The Curious Incident of the Dog in the Night-Time*," blurted Shirley, pouncing on Hazel's correct guess. The detective smiled at Shirley, bowing gracefully at her. Shirley, looking both ecstatic at guessing the correct answer and embarrassed that she would now have to perform in front of everyone, rose from her seat and stood beneath the fox's head. She blushed like a crimson rose, then cleared her throat and looked at each of us timidly. She performed the hand gesture for book title, then indicated two words.

"First word," everyone chanted.

Shirley began to flap her hands, like a bird of some kind and move about in circles. It looked absolutely ridiculous. Truth be told, she reminded me of an ostrich, but I didn't want to guess that in case she'd take it personally.

"Headless chicken," said Robert.

"Chicken run," suggested Aaron.

"Penguin detective?" added Jamelia. They were being unnecessarily mean.

Shirley continued to flap her arms and prance around in circles, causing everyone to laugh at her. What was she trying to do? I was about to intervene and advise Shirley to choose a different charade when the lights suddenly went out. The dark room was filled with intense silence.

"What the hell is going on?" said Jamelia's voice.

"Everybody relax," said the orderly voice of DCI Brice. "It's just a blackout. Probably the weather. Remain calm and stay where you are. I'm going to call the station to see if I can get more information." The dark outline of DCI Brice left the drawing room, leaving us alone.

Shirley cleared her throat. "Um, I better go and see if I can do anything," she said. "Be back in a jiffy."

"Well, I guess another game of charades is out," said Robert. "Anyone know any games we can play in the dark?"

"Oh no, this isn't good," said Hazel in a perturbed voice.

"What's wrong?" asked Jamelia.

"In situations like this, when the lights come back, someone is always found... *murdered*."

"Calm down, Hazel," I said. "This isn't a murder-mystery novel."

"Well, it's been exactly like one so far," quipped Robert.

Point taken. However, there was a more pressing issue that needed to be addressed.

"Where's Rita?" I asked Robert straight out.

His dark outline shrugged. "How should I know?"

"You were with her last," I asserted.

"No, I wasn't. Where's the evidence to support that?"

"Evidence?" I asked.

Suddenly, we heard a *scream*.

"Sounds like Rita!" shouted Jamelia. Everyone scrambled out of the drawing room and down the stairs.

At the foot of the stairs, we heard another *scream*.

"That's from the kitchen," Hazel yelled. All of us dashed towards the kitchen. We barged through the kitchen door, where we could hear Rita whimpering somewhere in the dark.

"Rita?" Robert shouted out.

"Over here!" replied her timid voice, which came from a dark corner. We rushed over to her and found her slumped on the floor.

"Rita, what's wrong? What happened?" I asked.

"He's here," she whispered.

"What? Who's here?" said Aaron.

"He... he... has a knife," she said in a more elevated tone.

"Who are you talking about?" Hazel asked.

"*Behind you!*" Rita shouted.

We turned around. A large black shape approached us. Hazel grabbed my arm as the dark shape passed a shaft of moonlight coming through the window, which partially illuminated his face.

"Hello, ladies. Remember me?" said a familiar voice. A voice that struck terror into our hearts.

Hazel's hand squeezed harder on my arm. "Oh my God, it's..."

"*Jack!*" I shouted. We ran toward the back door. Aaron frantically tried to open the door, but it was locked.

"The key. The key. Where's the bloody key?" Aaron cried.

Rita searched her pockets and took out a set of keys. With quivering hands, she tried to unlock the door but couldn't find the right key.

"Hurry!" shouted Hazel. "We're all going to die!"

As soon as the door opened, an exodus of petrified amateur mystery writers – and Rita – poured into the back garden. We sprinted towards the end of the garden. Halfway there, Hazel slipped and fell, landing in a filthy puddle. She shouted at the top of her voice: "*Oh no!!! Help me! Don't leave me!*" Her terrified voice made me stop in my tracks. I rushed back to where she lay and knelt beside her.

"Come on," I panted. "Get up! We need to get out of here!"

Unfortunately, she was struggling to breathe.

"I'm... I'm... having an asthma attack. My... my... inhaler... it's in my room."

I looked back at the house, knowing that she couldn't go any further without her inhaler. Above the rooftop, the moon lingered like a great bright pearl in the black sky, and provided a decent bit of visibility. Strangely, I couldn't see Jack anywhere. That meant only one thing: *he was still inside the house.*

"Bel, where are you?" shouted Jamelia.

"I'm back here with Hazel," I shouted back. "She's having an asthma attack." Jamelia and Aaron appeared at my side.

"Is she alright?" Jamelia asked.

"We need to get her inhaler. It's in her bedroom."

"But Jack is back there. How do we get it?"

I thought for a few moments. Then it struck me. "Gregory! He owns a gun!"

"Good idea," said Jamelia. "We'll go. You stay with Hazel." Jamelia and Aaron sprinted towards the coach house. I looked down at Hazel and held both her hands. "You're going to be okay, Hazel. I promise." I could hear her wheezing getting worse.

A bone-chilling *scream* came from the house. An upstairs window slid open, followed by Shirley's voice: "Help me! Help me!" My heart stopped as I watched her climb out the window and clamber up a drainpipe towards the roof. Her rotund figure wobbled side to side as she climbed upward.

Jack suddenly appeared at the same window, shouting after Shirley: "Where do you think you're going, you ol' hag!"

By some miracle, Shirley climbed onto the rooftop, then began crawling at a snail's pace up the sloping slate roof towards the chimney. My heart pounded in my chest.

Where on earth was DCI Brice?

Jack mounted the drainpipe, which began rattling under the weight of his powerful build. He quickly reached the rooftop and pursued Shirley. Within seconds he'd caught Shirley by her ankle.

"Bloody bitch!" he shouted at her. "Think you can fool me!" Grabbing her by the hair, it looked as if he was going to throw her off the rooftop: "Now let's see if you can fly!" Not wanting to see the outcome, I closed my eyes.

Kaboom!

A thunderous, deafening sound rang out, which caused myself and Hazel to jolt with fright.

"What the hell was that?" Hazel exclaimed.

I opened my eyes. Gregory was standing in the garden in his dressing gown, aiming his rifle at the roof. Jamelia and Aaron stood a cautious distance behind him.

"Let her go!" Gregory bellowed. "Or the next shot will be straight at your head!"

Shirley broke free from Jack and scurried away on her hands and knees. Jack crawled after her, grabbing her by the foot again. Shirley struggled to break away from Jack's grip and her shoe slipped off, toppled down the roof, and fell to the ground below. As she tried to crawl away, Jack leapt on top of her and began choking her with his bare hands.

Kaboom!

Gregory fired his gun again. Jack clutched his shoulder, letting out an agonising groan. The gunshot had wounded him, allowing Shirley to break from his grip and crawl away. Jack fell onto his back, then rolled off the rooftop. Hazel and I gasped in shock as we saw him drop to the ground, accompanied by a horrible thump. There was a deathly silence for a few moments afterwards.

Was he dead?

Shirley whimpered from the rooftop. "Help me! Someone, please help me!" She was clinging to the chimney like her life depended on it. Releasing Hazel's hand, I rushed over to where Jack lay on the patio. Sprawled on his back, his eyes were wide open while blood poured profusely from the back of his head. His mouth opened as he struggled to speak. Gregory stood over him, clutching his gun in case Jack rose again. Jack didn't move except for his mouth, which muttered something. Gregory squatted down to try to listen, while the blood gathered around his feet.

"What's that you say?" Gregory said to Jack.

Jack's lips moved repeatedly but it wasn't clear what he was saying. Gregory leaned in very close, placing his ear up to Jack's mouth. After a few moments, Gregory leaned back, looking puzzled.

"What is it?" I asked.

He shook his head. "He needs an ambulance."

"I'll call one," said Aaron, taking out his phone.

Shirley shouted for help again from the rooftop.

Jamelia started running towards the coach house.

"Where are you going?" I shouted after her.

"Going to get a ladder," she shouted back. Within a few moments, she disappeared into the dark. My thoughts refocused on Hazel. Through the back door, I entered the kitchen. Still pitch dark inside, I searched the drawers for a torch. Just a BBQ fire lighter, that would have to do. Pushing the button, it produced a modest flame, revealing a grim discovery. DCI Brice was sprawled on the floor. I knelt beside him to examine him. He was still breathing but unconscious.

What should I do? Get the inhaler? Help Hazel or help DCI Brice? An ambulance is on the way.

I made my decision. Leaving DCI Brice on the floor, I ran up the stairs, squeezing my finger hard on the lighter trigger to keep the flame alive. After a quick search of Hazel's drawers, I found the inhaler and bolted out the door.

*

On the patio, Aaron stood at the end of a ladder, holding it steady as Jamelia climbed up to the roof, to rescue Shirley. A few feet away from the ladder, Gregory stood next to Jack, holding his gun by his side. His face was filled with dismay as he stared at the ground. I looked at Jack, who lay completely still in a murky pool of his own blood.

"Is he dead?" I asked.

Gregory continued staring at the ground. He didn't answer me. I was about to repeat my question when I heard Hazel coughing in the distance. I sprinted to her. Her eyes were closed and her breathing very laboured when I got to her. Falling on the muddy grass beside her, I repeatedly shook her: "Hazel! Hazel! Wake up! Hazel, can you hear me?" She opened her eyes and tilted her head upward. Putting the inhaler to her lips, I sprayed two puffs into her mouth. Her breathing improved almost immediately. She sat up on the grass.

"How are you feeling?" I asked.

She raised both her hands, which were covered in mud. "Look at me, I'm a mess."

I hugged her tightly, which made her cough. "I'm really glad you're okay."

"Thanks, Bel. I owe you. Again." I handed her the inhaler which she used a few more times. She looked at the house.

"Is Jack gone?"

"Yeah, he's gone."

"So, he got away?"

"No," I said. "He's... dead. He fell off the roof."

Hazel looked at me, amazed.

"Then it's over. We're no longer in danger."

"So, it would seem," I said.

"I hate to say this, Bel," she started.

"I know Hazel. I know. Just like an ending in a mystery novel."

9

Trapped in this Bloody House

"What a relief! Finally, we can close this chapter in our lives and get on with living." Jamelia stretched her arms behind her head. It was afternoon and the power was back on in the house. The police had questioned us into the late hours of the night, so we had risen late in the day.

Aaron joined Jamelia at the window.

"Look at all that police tape," Aaron said. "They've probably used up all the tape in the village."

Jamelia grabbed her foot with one of her hands and stretched her calf muscle. "Some scene, yeah? Like something out a movie. It was such a pretty, picture-perfect garden only a few days ago."

Aaron nodded. "What was once Eden has now become the Land of Nod."

Jamelia smiled, releasing her foot back onto the floor. "Wow, that's so poetic! You might be the next great bard."

Aaron smiled. "Actually, I have published a book of poetry. During my undergrad. I can give you a copy when we get back to our lives."

"Signed?" Jamelia asked.

"Of course."

Jamelia placed her hand on Aaron's shoulder as they both gazed out the window. They had become close throughout the week. I wondered if romance was blossoming between them.

Hazel topped up her glass with orange juice. Her plate was filled with the crusts left over from her toast. "I really hope we get to go home today," Hazel said. "This place is getting really claustrophobic."

Jamelia turned towards Hazel. "I'm sure they'll let us leave today. After spending all bloody night answering their questions. Geez, the way they spoke to us, you'd swear *we* were the bad guys."

I picked up the teapot and poured myself a half-cup of tea. Hazel pushed the bowl of sugar towards me.

"I'm sure they're just trying to be thorough," I said, dipping my spoon in the sugar bowl.

Jamelia sighed. "Well, I think their questioning caused me more stress than climbing up onto a roof to save Shirley."

"You were quite the cool cat," Aaron said, "the way you went up that ladder without the slightest bit of fear."

Jamelia shrugged, raising her hands in a showy manner. "What can I say? I've got nine lives. Unlike... you know who?"

The room went quiet for a few moments, as we silently recalled Jack's fatal fall.

Jamelia grabbed her other foot and stretched her calf. "Shirley was so petrified, poor woman, the way she was clinging on to the chimney."

"Where is she, anyway?" asked Hazel. "Haven't seen or heard her all day."

Jamelia placed her hands on her hips and began rotating her head, to exercise her neck. "I think she might be with Gregory. She said she was going to pay him a visit, because he was feeling down."

"What happened to DCI Brice?" asked Hazel.

"He was taken to hospital last night," said Aaron. "He's on the mend, I heard."

"Poor guy," said Jamelia. "I think I'll take him flowers as soon as we can leave the house."

I drank my lukewarm tea as I reflected on the events of the night before. "I wonder what Jack said to Gregory?"

"What do you mean?" said Jamelia, as she progressed to touching her toes with admirable agility.

I held my cup in both hands, swirling the tea. "He said something into Gregory's ear before he died."

"Yeah, I remember that," said Aaron, as he wandered away from Jamelia and stood beneath the fox's head.

"Probably gibberish," Jamelia said. "He had just cracked his head open on the patio. People tend to speak gibberish when half their brain is spilling out their head."

It was a gruesome way to put it, but it was possibly true. "Yes," I said. "It was probably gibberish."

Jamelia stretched again, then said: "Time to hit the shower. See you later." She left the room with a bounce in her step. I lingered on her words for a few moments. Deep down, I wasn't convinced it was gibberish, recalling how Gregory's face reacted to his words. Jack, I suspected, had said something meaningful but I had no idea what it was. But there was one way to find out.

*

As soon as I opened the back door, a bitter gust of wind blew in my face, spraying the cold rain right into my eyes. I wiped my face on my coat sleeve as I stepped out onto the patio. Carefully, I navigated around the police tape erected around the spot where Jack fell to his death and made my way down the garden path towards the coach house.

Arriving on the porch, I made a fist to knock on Gregory's door, when suddenly...

Kaboom!

My eardrums rattled.

That sounded like a gunshot!

I knocked on the door again, this time with frantic urgency. No response. I walked to the living room window and peered in. The hairs on the nape of my neck stood up. I couldn't believe it! Gregory was slumped in an armchair with his head hanging to one side. His rifle was on the floor beside his chair. The sound of something smashing came from the back of the house. *What could that be?* I dashed around the side and found the kitchen door to the coach house wide open. Next to the door, a potted plant was smashed on the ground, having seemingly toppled off an adjacent ledge. I looked around but there was no one in sight.

Despite the dread I felt, I entered the kitchen and made my way towards the living room. In the living room, I gasped: Gregory sitting lifelessly in his armchair, with a single bullet-hole in his forehead. There was a strong smell of gunpowder in the air. A thin stream of smoke billowed from the barrel of the rifle on the floor. Beside the armchair was a small table with an empty glass and a note. I picked up the note and read it:

```
I never meant to take that man's life.
Although he was a bad apple, I never
meant to kill him. May God forgive me!
Please take care of my beloved dog Harry.
```

A suicide note? I felt the barrel of the rifle. It was still warm. I laid the note back down on the table and observed the grim scene. None of this made sense. I thought about the smashed potted plant outside the back door. Did somebody flee the scene before I arrived? If so, who? Was it Shirley? Or someone else? So many questions... I ran outside and called the police.

*

Edith dead. Jack dead. Gregory dead. Three deaths in three days. How did all this come to pass? There were so many question marks surrounding the circumstances in which they died, it was causing me a lot of anxiety.

Whoever said a sleuth's life would be easy?

As I sat alone in the drawing room, wondering how real detectives deal with all the horrible things they witness from day to day, someone knocked on the door.

"Come in," I said, sitting up in my chair.

The bald, round, moustachioed head of DCI Wallace popped in the door and smiled vacuously.

"Evenin' Miss Boothby," he said formally, as his portly figure shuffled over to a chair opposite me. "Mind if I take a seat?"

"Sure," I nodded.

He sat down and produced a rather tattered pocket-sized notebook and a small pencil that looked to have been worn down to its stub after prolonged use.

Very old-school, this detective!

He sifted through a few pages of the notebook until he found a blank page, then scribbled a few words.

"So, you discovered the body of Gregory Bramble at what time, you say?" he asked without looking at me.

"Um, it must have been just after two."

"And you heard the gun blast?"

"Yes," I said. "I was about to knock on the front door when I heard it. It was so loud. I still have a little bit of ringing in my ear."

"What was the reason you had gone to visit him?" the detective asked, as he scribbled in his notebook.

"I just, um, wanted to know how he was doing. Considering what had happened the night before. He was a very nice man, very... upright," I said, as a lump formed in my throat. Gregory was indeed a very nice man. Such a sad, tragic way for him to die!

DCI Wallace looked at me, stroking his bushy moustache. "The two of you were close then?"

I looked down at my feet. "I wouldn't say close. But we shared a few genteel conversations. He very much loved his dog."

"Ah yes," said the detective, "his dog Harry. Poor boy, he'll be without his master."

"Harry?" I said, raising my eyebrows. "You mean Henry?"

He looked at me and narrowed his eyes. "Come again?"

"Henry," I repeated. "His dog was called Henry."

The detective's face grimaced slightly. He reached into his pants pocket and took out Gregory's suicide note. "That's not what it says here. Look, quite clearly, he says please take care of my beloved dog Harry."

I read the note in his hand. *My word, he was right.* I hadn't realised the first time I read it but the note did say Harry.

"No," I said, amazed. "That's a mistake. His dog's name was definitely Henry. I wonder why he wrote Harry."

The detective's rotund face frowned. "Are you sure about that?"

"Quite sure," I said.

He looked at the note again and pursed his lips. "Strange then he would have made a mistake like that. Or maybe, Harry was a nickname. Doesn't make any sense, I admit. But who knows what goes through a man's mind when he's about to blow his brains out?"

I looked at the detective and frowned. I really didn't approve of his insensitive comment. He crumpled up the note and stuffed it carelessly back inside his pocket.

"Well," he said, "it remains a mystery. God rest his soul. Anyway, that's all the questions I have for now, my dear. How are you feeling otherwise?"

I sighed. "I'm alright. Considering."

"Good, good," he said indifferently, as he closed his small notebook. "We'll be holding a meeting here later this evening. Just to update everyone on the investigation into Edith's murder and any other business. We appreciate all of your continued cooperation."

The chair creaked loudly as he stood up. I had one question yet to ask.

"What about Shirley?"

"Shirley? What about Shirley?" he said.

"I believe she was with Gregory before he took his life."

His cheek twitched. "I have interviewed her. She said he was very depressed when she went to visit him but he was definitely alive when she left."

I mulled over his words. "When I went around the back of the house the kitchen door was wide open and a potted plant was smashed in pieces on the ground. It almost seemed like someone had left there in a hurry."

He nodded his head and stroked his moustache. "Yes, yes, probably the wind that knocked the plant over. The weather's been very bad recently. I presumed Shirley hadn't closed the kitchen door fully after she left."

I pursed my lips. "Yes, that does make sense. I suppose." I wasn't at all convinced by the detective's assumptions. I was sure that a person knocked that plant over, rather than the wind.

The detective swayed his head side to side, as if to exercise it, then shuffled out of the room. After he left, I sat alone, pondering Gregory's suicide note. Why did he refer to his dog as Harry? It was hard to believe that was a mistake.

A typo in a suicide note?

He loved Henry dearly, so it seemed unlikely he mistook his name. So why did the note say Harry? Unless...

It was written by someone else!

*

Upstairs on the landing it was dead quiet. It seemed everyone was quietly resting in their bedrooms, counting down the hours until we were free to go home. It was obvious that none of us would be in a hurry to embark on another writing course any time soon. Our dream opportunity had turned into the ultimate nightmare; we were now trapped inside what the media had dubbed a "real-life murder-mystery mansion". As I stood outside my bedroom door, I thought about Hazel and her asthma attack from last night. Curious to know how she was doing today, I decided to knock on her door.

"Enter at your own peril," replied her high-pitched voice from the other side.

I opened her door and entered. Hazel was lying on the floor on her back.

"Hazel, what's wrong?"

"Nothing," she replied. "I'm just doing some thinking. Lying like this helps me put things in perspective."

I smiled. "Oh, I see," I said. "How very... stoic."

She sat up on the floor and stretched her back. "I was doing a bit of writing earlier," she said, pointing to her desk, where I could see a Word document on her laptop screen.

I walked over to the laptop and read a few paragraphs from the document. It described, in very fine detail, the time we found Gregory lying in the woods, severely injured with a head wound. I was surprised at the level of objectivity with which she documented the events. It depicted the facts of that day with exceptional clarity and vivid detail. She clearly had a gift for literary realism. I checked the word count at the bottom corner of the document. She had almost written 10,000 words.

"Hazel," I said in a puzzled manner. "What exactly are you writing?"

She quickly got to her feet and stood beside me. "It's a first-hand account of our experiences over the past few days."

"Are you planning to publish it?"

"Not really. I don't know what I'm going to do with it. I just thought it would be important to keep a record of everything that's happened so far. Heaven knows, we're gonna face questions once we leave here. Even if you go online, there's already loads of stories and conspiracy theories about who killed Edith. I figured, someone's got to keep a true account."

I stared at her for a few moments then smiled. I was truly impressed with her. "Brilliant idea!"

Her eyes widened. "You think so?"

"Of course," I said. "One of the most important things

about being a detective is keeping a true, accurate account of everything. You know, Robert wasn't far off the point when he referred to you as Watson."

She giggled. "I guess that would make you..."

"Yes, yes," I said, "let's not get carried away. I have far to go before I could be compared to the great Holmes."

I continued to peruse the Word document which depicted the day Gregory went missing. "I remember this day began with Henry barking non-stop in the garden."

"Yes," said Hazel. "I remember. Quite annoying it was."

"It's funny, you know I've read Gregory's suicide note."

"It was humorous?"

"No, indeed," I said. "It's just that... he mentioned his dog in it. He referred to him as Harry."

Hazel's mouth opened wide, looking perplexed. "Harry?"

I nodded at her. "Evidently, a typo in the note. According to Detective Wallace, at least. But I'm sceptical."

I began to pace up and down the room, ruminating in my thoughts. Hazel's eyes followed my feet.

"What are you thinking, Bel?"

I paused and looked out her window, where I could see the coach house. Placing my index finger on my lower lip, I began to summarise my sceptical thoughts to her: "Gregory was about five foot eight inches tall. At best. Not an exceedingly tall man. The average length of a hunting rifle is around forty inches. It would be extremely difficult, almost impossible, for someone of his height to put the barrel of a rifle to his forehead and pull the trigger. It doesn't seem possible. Added to that, before he shoots himself, he writes a note in which he gets the name of his beloved bloodhound wrong. It just boggles the mind."

Hazel stared at me, almost incredulous.

"I hope you're following my train of thought, Hazel?"

She shrugged her shoulders. "Sure, Bel, I hear you. But there's one thing I don't get."

"What's that?" I asked.

"Why would he shoot himself over killing a psycho like Jack Burley? If he killed someone innocent by mistake, I could understand. But to shoot himself over a deranged killer – that seems a little over-the-top."

I looked at her and sighed. "I fully agree with your assessment, Hazel. My point is I don't think he did kill himself. It's quite possible Gregory was *murdered*."

Hazel's mouth widened even further, to the point where I could clearly see her tonsils. "Murdered?" she gasped.

"I'm afraid so," I confirmed. "It's getting to be quite a common occurrence in this house."

"But who... who would have..."

I placed my hand on her shoulder before she finished her question. "I'm not sure. But I think Shirley can shed some light on it. She was possibly the last person to be with Gregory before he died."

Hazel pushed her glasses up her nose and blinked incredulously. "Shirley," she said to herself. "You need to be careful, Bel. Who knows what's going to happen next? Any one of us could be the next victim."

I patted her supportively on the shoulder. "Don't worry, Hazel. I'm sure you'll be okay. After all, someone must live to write about the tale."

*

Once I left Hazel's room, I walked straight to Shirley's bedroom door and knocked. There was no response.

"Shirley, Shirley, it's Belinda. Are you in there?"

Still no response. I decided to look downstairs.

In the downstairs hallway, I noticed that the library door was closed. I could hear noise from inside. Placing my ear to the door, I could hear someone humming. I considered knocking but curiosity got the better of me, so I opened the door very gently. I tiptoed inside and crept along the rows of bookcases until I saw Shirley sitting by herself at a desk towards the rear of the library, humming a tune to herself. I hid behind a bookcase and peered through a gap between two books. Shirley was tearing out pages from a book, one by one, and letting each page fall to the floor. It was a very strange scene. Then she spoke to herself.

"Goodbye Edith, you'll be missed by so many, I'm sure. If only they knew the secret you took to your grave."

Secret? What was she talking about? As I adjusted my standing position, there was a *bang*. Shirley jolted with fright and rose out of her chair.

"Who's there? Hello, is someone there?"

Looking down, I realised I had kicked the steel step. I tiptoed around to another bookcase. Shirley walked down the aisle where the kick step was and examined it. Crouching in the next aisle, I stayed completely still, waiting to see her reaction.

"Is there someone there?" she asked.

As she began to walk towards the aisle where I lay hidden, I crawled into the next one. I could see Shirley's movements through the bookshelves. She stopped at the place where I had previously lay hidden, and sniffed the air. It seemed as if she was trying to pick up a scent. Perhaps she could smell my perfume?

Quietly, I moved along the bookcases, hoping she would lose my scent. Shirley walked along, peering down each aisle.

"Who's there, I say? Where are you hiding?" she said in a confident voice.

I gulped as she approached the final bookcase aisle. What would I say when she saw me?

Think fast, Bel!

A bell rang loudly from outside the library.

"Could everyone please make their way to the drawing room," bellowed Rita's voice above the resounding clamour. "Detective Wallace wishes to speak with us. Please make your way to the drawing room now. Tea will be served."

Shirley stopped in her tracks. Once the bell stopped ringing, she sniffed the air again. "Must be losing it," she said to herself then walked to the library door. Her eyes darted around the room one last time, before she left the library.

Once she had gone, I breathed a sigh of relief. Curious about her strange behaviour, I walked to where Shirley had been sitting. I observed the torn pages scattered on the floor, then picked up the book from which they had been ripped. Astonishingly, it was a copy of Edith's novel *The Final Draft*. Why was Shirley tearing the pages out of it? Next to the torn novel, were the perfect murder assignment cards that she had collected from us. I quickly checked through the names on each card and found the one with Robert's name on it. It read:

Write in one sentence how you would commit the perfect murder.

*Since practice makes perfect, to commit the
perfect murder I would have to kill many
times over.
Signed Rob ;-)*

This was a completely different sentence from the version
that I had found earlier. Why did Robert complete two
cards? Unable to form a conclusion, I placed the card back
among the others and made my way to the drawing room.

*

DCI Wallace's cheek twitched repeatedly as he stood in
front of us in the drawing room, flicking through pages of
his mini notebook. Eventually he folded up his notebook
and put it in the pocket of his tweed blazer. He stroked his
moustache, then cleared his throat.

"Right, so, firstly an update on the weather. According
to the most recent report from the Met Office, the worst
of the stormy weather has passed. Should be looking to see
clearer skies in the next few days."

There was a collective sigh of relief from everyone in the
drawing room.

"Unfortunately," the detective continued, "due to the
adverse weather conditions, the local train station has been
closed. Also, access to the M11 has been cut off by several
trees that have fallen on the roadside, due to gale force
winds. And all accommodation in the village has been
taken up by the media. So, all in all, I'm sorry to say that,
for the moment..."

"We're trapped in this bloody house!" exclaimed Jamelia.

The detective eyeballed Jamelia, before nodding his head

in agreement. "Yes, that seems to be the case. But I am optimistic that the situation will be resolved within the next few days. We've been in touch with the National Trust who own the property and have made them aware of the situation. They are happy for each of you to remain in the house free of charge, until it is safe to leave."

"Do the media want to interview us?" Hazel asked.

The detective's cheek twitched emphatically. "We've had several briefings with the press about the situation. We've asked them to respect your privacy at this time and not to try to enter the grounds as the investigation into Edith's death is ongoing."

Immediately, everyone became alarmed. Hazel and I shot perplexed glances at one another.

"Ongoing?" Aaron said. "What does that mean?"

DCI Wallace stroked his moustache, growing slightly uncomfortable with the rising murmuring in the room. "All I meant is that we are tying up loose ends. That's all. Just routine stuff we need to wrap up."

Rita raised her hand. "Um, excuse me. What about our safety here in the house? The police detective who was assigned here is still in hospital."

"That's correct," confirmed the detective. "DCI Brice is recovering in hospital after sustaining a head injury. I'm happy to say he's doing well but has to remain in hospital for observation. Since the prime suspect in Edith's death is now dead, I don't see that there's a substantial risk to the safety of the present occupants of the house." He pointed his hand toward Shirley, who sat slouched in a chair, staring dewy-eyed into space. "Miss Shirley Atkins will be the main point of contact if anyone needs anything. She has also kindly volunteered to help with household duties and eating arrangements. If anyone wants to discuss anything confidentially, I have left a few of my cards on the table in front of you. I know each of you want to return to your families as soon as possible, so, rest assured, we are doing everything to accommodate that. Any questions?"

The room remained silent. But the collective feeling of frustration was palpable. The detective smiled at us from under his bushy moustache. "Well, that's all I have to say for now. I'll be in touch. Shirley, may we speak outside for a minute?"

Shirley rose lazily from her chair, nodding her head, and accompanied the detective out of the drawing room. We remained sitting in silence, awkwardly exchanging looks. It was obvious that none of us was looking forward to the prospect of enduring each other's company for another few days.

10

It's Turning into Quite a Thriller

The tenth day inside this house! I'd hoped this would be the last. The morning sky looked gloomy but the rain had ceased and the wind had abated. Honestly, I felt like staying in bed rather than risk witnessing more calamity, but my stomach was rumbling. I needed some breakfast but we wouldn't be getting any more of Simon's delicious fry-ups. Fortunately, I was in the mood for a simple bowl of porridge with raisins.

As I stood in the upstairs landing, locking my bedroom door, a drop of water landed on my head. Looking up, I could see that the ceiling had a minor leak.

Typical old house!

Presumably, this would have been a job for Gregory when he was around. But who would deal with the maintenance of the house in his absence? Should I tell Shirley? Another drop hit my head. I was getting wet standing here. Better head downstairs.

I had almost made it to the kitchen when I heard a heated commotion from the living room. I could hear Jamelia's voice.

"I'm going to kill that bastard!"

Pausing at the kitchen door, I wondered whether I should get involved. Hadn't I been involved in enough things so far? Why not switch off and let things take care of themselves? And yet... is that how a detective would think? *Supposing Holmes decided to switch off and play his Stradivarius every time someone came to him for help. Think of Victorian London's crime rate!*

Tentatively, I knocked on the living room door and entered. Aaron, Jamelia and Rita were standing by the mantelpiece, directly under Lord Ainsley's gaze.

"What's the matter?" I asked.

Jamelia held out a folded piece of paper. "Look at this! That sick twat slipped this under my door last night."

I took the piece of paper and unfolded it. It was a note with the words

you're next i-)

written on it. I recognised the handwriting, but I didn't want to say it out loud. I calmly handed the note back to her.

"Who do you think wrote it?" I asked.

Jamelia clenched her jaw. "I think it's bloody obvious. It was that narcissistic mummy's boy Robert. Who else could it have been? This type of shit is right up his attention-seeking alley."

"I'm not sure it was Rob," Rita quietly stated. "He was with me all night."

Jamelia sighed in deep frustration. "Were you awake all night, Rita?"

"No, of course not," she said.

"Well then, how do you know he didn't get up in the middle of the night and slip this under my door?"

Rita bowed her head, passively reflecting on Jamelia's question. "I just know he didn't. I would have sensed it if he got up. Like when..." She abruptly stopped her sentence and shot me a cursory glance.

"Like when what?" Jamelia fired.

Rita shook her head. "Nothing. Look, I'm not defending Rob. I'm just..."

"Screwing him!" Jamelia said harshly.

Rita blushed. She looked directly at Jamelia, with a deep-set frown. "How dare you speak to me like that! Just because I'm the maid, doesn't mean you can talk down to me. Who do you think you are?"

Jamelia squared up to Rita. "I'm the one who's going to teach that twisted boyfriend of yours the lesson he deserves. He's seriously messin' with the wrong person!" Jamelia raised her hand to Rita's head and made a gun gesture. Rita swiped Jamelia's hand away.

For several seconds, there was a tense standoff between the two, which I feared was about to explode into blows. Fortunately, Aaron stood between them, before things escalated.

"Alright, alright. Calm down both of you. We don't know for a fact this was Robert. I mean... anyone could have written this."

"Yes, exactly," Rita said defiantly.

Unfortunately, I knew otherwise. It was undoubtedly Robert's handwriting, since I had read his perfect murder assignment cards. But *they* didn't know that. It was time to be diplomatic.

"Why don't we discuss this as a group, in the presence

of Shirley. Since she has been put in charge by the police detective, she can perhaps deliberate."

Jamelia scowled at me. "Shirley? Yeah right, she couldn't deliberate if her life depended on it."

I maintained a calm demeanour. "Well, why don't we try, and see how it goes. I'll inform Shirley and we can discuss this incident as a group."

"What?" retorted Jamelia. "You mean, with Robert present as well?"

"Yes," I said. "I think it would be better to deal with this as a group rather than accusing people when they're not present, which could quickly descend into anarchy. Don't get me wrong, whoever wrote that note, clearly overstepped the mark. At this moment in time, this kind of behaviour cannot be tolerated. But I feel we should discuss it as a group and whoever did this should come clean and apologise for causing you offence."

Jamelia rolled her eyes. "Honestly, Belinda, if they ever need a new chief at the UN, they should call on you."

I didn't react to her sardonic comment, since I had an ulterior motive for holding a group meeting. Discussing the note in front of everyone would give me the perfect opportunity to examine everyone's reaction. Specifically, I wanted to see Robert's and Shirley's reactions.

*

The Montblanc pen spun effortlessly in Robert's hand as Shirley explained the purpose of the group meeting to all the house residents. This was the first time we had been together in the library since Edith's death, which undoubtedly made the occasion a poignant one for all in attendance.

I had successfully persuaded Shirley to host the meeting, insinuating that it would give us the opportunity to detect Robert's culpability. What I didn't tell her was that I was also interested in *her* demeanour.

Shirley addressed the group.

"Well, um, we had an incident last night. A note was slipped under Jamelia's door. This would have been at around..." she looked at Jamelia.

"Around 3 am," Jamelia asserted. "Someone knocked on my door and ran away. Someone of a cowardly and sneaky nature," she said, shooting an accusatory stare at Robert. Robert frowned at her.

"Okay then," Shirley said. "Does anyone have anything they want to share with the group? Does someone want to, um, put Jamelia's anxieties to rest and own up to what they did."

The group remained in compete silence, yet, almost unanimously, they stared at Robert. Robert remained completely calm, as the Montblanc flipped fluently between his fingers.

Shirley cleared her throat. "Well, um, I examined the handwriting of the note and have compared it to the cards you submitted for the perfect murder assignment. It is quite clear that, um, the handwriting, um... how should I put it... well, having examined them all, I find that there is a clear correlation between the note that was slipped under Jamelia's door and one of the cards."

Everyone waited with bated breath for Shirley to voice her conclusion.

She straightened up in her chair. "Specifically, the card that the handwriting matched belonged to... *Robert*."

Immediately, the Montblanc stopped spinning in his

fingers. Robert's face contorted with disbelief: "That's bullshit!" he rasped.

The group's collective gaze focused intently on Robert.

Jamelia sneered at Robert's innocence. "It's obvious you're the culprit, Rob. Be a man and fess up!"

Robert glared at Jamelia, "Go to hell!"

"You first!" retaliated Jamelia.

"This is complete crap," declared Robert. "Why would I waste my time passing a stupid note like that under your door in the middle of the night. Where's the motive?"

Jamelia rolled her eyes. "Motive? Please, this isn't a courtroom. You heard what Shirley said. The handwriting's yours. You're trying in your own pathetic little way to exploit my fears. And, I can add, failing at it! A note like this isn't going to scare me!"

"Well, good for you," Robert said. "So, what's the big deal then, if you're not scared?"

"The point is, mate," Aaron intervened, "you've been trying to wind people up in this house since the beginning. Now you're trying to wind Jamelia up after all the shit that's happened. Personally, I think it's sick to play a prank like this in the wake of Edith's and Gregory's deaths. I think you should apologise."

Jamelia nodded in agreement with Aaron.

Robert sat forward in his chair, narrowing his eyes at Aaron. "Is that what you think, Aaron, is it? Well, let me be clear and tell you that I couldn't give two hoots what you think! It's quite clear you've wanted to bed Jamelia from the start. And this is yet another lame attempt at getting her to like you."

Jamelia's face contorted with annoyance. "Rob, you're such a prat!"

"You shut up!" Rob shouted at Jamelia, firing his Montblanc pen across the room in anger. Hazel looked extremely uncomfortable, sitting between Jamelia and Robert. She looked at me with a very concerned expression.

Aaron raised his hand towards Robert as if to try to appease his rage. "Take it easy, mate! That's uncalled for!"

Unfortunately, Aaron's gesture merely aggravated Robert further. He rose from his chair and addressed Aaron provocatively.

"Or what, mate? What are you going to do about it?"

Aaron rose from his chair, rising to the challenge that Robert posed. Shirley winced as she witnessed the two young, athletically built men squaring up to each other. Suddenly, I regretted arranging this meeting.

This was a bad idea! So much for ulterior motives!

Robert lunged at Aaron, getting him into a headlock. Aaron struggled in Robert's grip and drove him into a bookcase but failed to escape Robert's headlock. Robert started punching Aaron in the head. Aaron squirmed and writhed until his head was freed from Robert's arm, then countered with a barrage of punches into Robert's face. Robert fell back onto the floor. Aaron jumped upon him and continued his relentless campaign of punches. Jamelia, Rita and I took hold of the enraged Aaron and pulled him off of Robert. Shirley fled the room, squealing in terror. Hazel took cover under her desk.

Robert rose from the floor with a bloody nose. A distressed Rita offered him a handkerchief which he took. The two fighters stared at each other.

"You want some more, mate?" Aaron said.

Robert placed Rita's handkerchief to his nose and shook

his head. He had had enough. It seemed. He extended his hand towards Aaron, offering to shake hands.

"Put it there, mate," he said in a nasal voice.

Aaron stared at Robert, analysing his gesture with scepticism. After a few moments he extended his hand. They shook. Suddenly, I felt relieved. That is, *until I looked at Robert's eyes.* He wasn't seeking reconciliation. He was still angry. This wasn't over. This was just...

Bam!

Robert struck Aaron with a sucker punch in the face, while their hands were still connected. Aaron fell back against a bookcase, knocking several shelves of old books to the floor. Jamelia, Rita and I ran to take cover behind the desk where Hazel was hiding. Robert lunged at Aaron, delivering several more punches until Aaron picked up one of the books – a big, bulky hardback – and whacked Robert in the face. Robert immediately fell back onto the floor, completely dazed. Aaron walked over to where Robert lay and raised the hardback over his head...

"Enough! Enough already!" said Rita, standing beside me. She rushed over to stand in front of Aaron, to plead mercy for the sake of Robert. Aaron stared at her for a few moments, then lowered the book in his hands. Rita crouched beside Robert and helped him to his feet. Robert glared at Aaron, then cast his gaze at everyone standing in the room. He had been humiliated. He pushed Rita's arms from him then stormed out of the library. A few moments later, a dejected-looking Rita left the library. Jamelia stood by Aaron, whose right eye was visibly swollen from the fight.

"Are you alright?" she asked.

Aaron shook his head.

"Come on, let's get you to a seat," Jamelia said as she guided him to a chair.

"You need some ice," Hazel said.

"I'll get some," I offered.

"No," said Jamelia. "I'll do it. Come on, Aaron, let's go to the kitchen instead. I'll make you a tea while you're there." She placed her arm around his shoulder and helped him up again. She escorted him out of the library, leaving myself and Hazel standing by ourselves.

Hazel walked over to where Aaron had left his hard-cover book. She picked it up and read the cover. "*Wuthering Heights*," she said, then looked at me. "Whoever said reading was a harmless pastime?"

*

Hazel and I sat on the bench in the herb garden, each with our hands in our pockets, musing on the heated events of the past few hours. "How long do you think Robert will have to stay in his room?" Hazel asked.

"However long DCI Wallace decides," I replied.

"Will the detective be staying here tonight then?" Hazel asked.

"I presume he will."

DCI Wallace had arrived on the scene an hour after the fight and decided that the best way to preserve the peace was to confine Robert to his room. It would inevitably mean that the detective would have to stay here overnight, to keep an eye on things.

Hazel sniffled, then took out a tissue and blew her nose into it. "Bel? Can I ask you a question?"

"Yes, do."

"Have you known people like Robert before?"

I looked at her as she crushed up her tissue and put it inside her pocket. "You mean spoilt, attention-seeking, borderline-narcissistic personality types?" I stated quite rapidly.

She gulped at my overextended use of adjectives. "Yes, something like that. I've known one or two myself. I always wondered... why do they always have to push people's buttons?"

It was a profound question in its simplicity. I sighed heavily.

"I guess they need to feel that others acknowledge their existence. They need to get under their skin, or otherwise they might feel invisible."

Hazel looked at me as I stared up at the partly cloudy sky. "Hopefully, with him locked in his bedroom, there'll be no more incidents."

My gaze remained fixed on two drifting clouds that, together, resembled a question mark. It was an appropriate analogy to what was running through my mind: *Who really slipped that note under Jamelia's door?*

"Personally, I don't believe Robert did it."

Hazel frowned at me. "Did what, Bel?"

I looked at her, raising my eyebrows. "I don't believe Robert slipped that note under Jamelia's door. Nor do I think he wrote it."

Hazel warily looked around. "Well, then, who do you think wrote it??"

Turning my gaze away from the sky, I looked down towards my feet and sighed. "I can only speculate. But I have my suspicions." It was then that I noticed something. I leaned forward on the bench and picked something off the grass. I held it close to my face.

"What is it, Bel?" asked Hazel.

"It's a button. Looks just like one of the buttons from Edith's nightie."

Hazel leaned in, squinting her eyes at my discovery. "You mean, the nightie she had on back to front the night she was killed?"

"Exactly that!" I said. "But how did it end up here?"

*

Hazel returned to her bedroom to write about today's events, while I decided to visit the library, which I was glad to find empty. The place was still a mess after the fight, with tables and chairs overturned and several books lying on the floor. I got to work tidying, placing each book in Dewey Decimal order back on the shelf. I strolled to the rear of the library to examine the desk where Shirley had been drinking Edith's gin. The desk now contained nothing but a pencil eraser and a few loose paper clips. Then, I heard the door open.

"Rita?" said Shirley's voice. "Rita, are you in here?"

I remained perfectly still and quiet. I could hear Shirley walk to the back of the library. Crouching down, I crawled around the side of a bookcase, shielding myself from Shirley's sight. She was walking towards the bookcase where I was hiding, when suddenly another voice entered the room.

"Miss Atkins, are you in here?"

It was DCI Wallace. Shirley stopped and turned around.

"Eh, yes, yes. I'm here, detective."

"Ah, Miss Atkins – you mind if I have a word in private?"

"Oh yes, of course," she replied timidly. "Eh, please call me Shirley."

"Shirley it is then," the detective said merrily, as he firmly shut the door.

I remained crouched behind the bookcase as I listened to their conversation.

"I have some rather bad news, I'm afraid to say," said the detective.

"Oh, what is it?" said Shirley.

"The toxicology report has come back from Edith's Ramsey's autopsy. There's evidence of a drug called Zopiclone in her blood at the time of her death. This drug is usually used for insomnia. In fact, the same drug was detected in Gregory's blood, which has led us to believe that someone may have drugged them."

"Drugged them?" squeaked Shirley.

"Yes, we believe so."

"But that's what Edith took as a sleeping pill. She took it regularly."

The detective cleared his throat. "The levels in her blood, and in Mr Bramble's blood, were twenty times the normal dose."

"Oh," said Shirley. "This isn't good."

"Furthermore," continued the detective, "we're finding it hard to link Edith's murder with Jack Burley. The evidence against him is entirely circumstantial. What's more, we have a witness who saw Mr Burley leaving a pub about two miles north of Beaglesford, around the time of Edith's death. So, it looks like he couldn't have done it. In fact, it looks like Edith and Gregory were killed by the same person, and that the killer is still very much at large."

"Oh dear!!!" rang out Shirley's shrill voice. "This is terrible news!! But... but... but he came here the next night. He tried to kill me."

"Who's that, my dear?"

"Jack Burley."

"Oh yes, of course. We're not exactly sure why he came here to try to kill you. Whatever the reason, he's dead now, so there's no need to panic, eh?"

Shirley began to sob.

"Now, now, there's no need to be upset," said the detective. "Come here, let me wipe away those tears."

Shirley continued to sob. "Oh detective, why did all this have to happen? I just wanted to plan the perfect masterclass. And now look what's happened."

I crept around the side of the bookcase to steal a glance at the pair. The detective held Shirley in his arms, stroking her frizzy hair.

"There, there, my dear. There, there. It's alright. The good detective is here. Nothing to worry about now."

Then the library door burst open, causing the couple to jolt with fright. It was Rita, looking visibly distraught.

"Detective?" she said in a panicked voice.

"Yes, what is it?" he replied, in a rather unnerved manner.

"It's Robert. He's no longer in his room. Can't find him anywhere."

"What do you mean you can't find him anywhere?" bellowed the detective. "He's supposed to be confined to his bedroom!"

Rita furrowed her brow. "I went to take him some tea and when I looked inside he wasn't there."

The detective looked incredulously at Shirley.

"Bloody young rogue!" he fumed. "Come on, let's see if we can find him."

All three stormed out of the library.

I was left alone in the library, astonished by the new

information I had overheard about Edith's and Gregory's deaths.

*

I relayed everything to Hazel once we were in the privacy of her bedroom later that evening. Unsurprisingly, she was shocked by the revelations.

"What are we going to do, Bel? We're all in grave danger if the killer is still out there!"

A pen hung precariously from her lips as she proclaimed her fears from her desk. At the time I entered her room, she seemed to have been writing in a notebook and transcribing the notes into the document saved on her laptop.

"You're not wrong, Hazel, but there is another, more worrying way to look at all this," I said, lying back on her bed.

"What's that, Bel?"

I flung my head back to look at the ceiling. "Now that Jack has been ruled out as Edith's killer... *all of us are possible suspects.*"

The pen fell from her mouth as she realised the implications of what I'd just said. "Do you think it could be Robert?"

I sat forward on her bed and put my head in my hands. "I'm not sure. I don't know what to believe. There are several possible suspects."

"Several?" Hazel repeated.

I closed my eyes thinking about the suspects I had in mind. "Jamelia's a suspect, since she threatened to kill Edith after she stormed out of class the day before Edith was killed."

Hazel's eyes widened in amazement. "She did?"

I nodded. "She was in a bad mood when she said it, so I didn't take her seriously. But her behaviour since then has got me wondering. Despite her upbeat attitude, she has quite a fiery temper and is prone to mood swings.

"Then there's Aaron: I overheard him on the phone the night Edith was killed. He said we would get the surprise of our lives the following day."

Hazel recoiled. "Who was he talking to?"

"No idea. But I'd be very interested to find out. Aaron is quite the man of mystery I have to say. I have a strong feeling he's hiding something from the group.

"Rita could be a suspect, too, since Edith had threatened to report her to her company for having a relationship with one of the houseguests. But I sincerely doubt Rita would murder Edith over that."

I locked my hands together as I thought about the final two suspects I had in mind.

"Shirley must be considered a suspect. Her recent behaviour has been questionable to say the least. She definitely had a motive, given Edith's constant demeaning attitude to her, which would have driven anyone over the edge.

"And, last but not least, is Robert: the upstart who has single-handedly thrown the entire house into chaos to prove to the world that he has as much cold-blooded intellectual superiority as Leopold and Loeb."

Hazel put the pen behind her ear and turned towards the table. "I better add these details to my account. It's turning into quite a thriller. Robert could be the killer..." She then paused and turned to me, with a worried expression. "It's frightening to think that a possible murderer is right next door to us."

"He's not next door."

She raised her eyebrows. "I thought he was confined there?"

I shrugged my shoulders. "Apparently, he's done a runner. He's not in his room. Nor is he anywhere in the house. The police are out looking for him."

"Well, where's he gone?"

I raised my hands. "Who knows? He could be anywhere. Although it'll be difficult to hide in a small village like Beaglesford, with the press everywhere."

Hazel frowned as she pondered everything I'd just related to her. "Gosh, with all these suspects, who do you really think is the killer?"

I looked at Hazel and narrowed my eyes. "Well, I think the answer's obvious."

She narrowed her eyes as well.

"It's you, Hazel."

She stared at me in disbelief as her mouth became wide open. I laughed. She quickly closed her mouth and sighed, realising that I was pulling her leg.

A bell rang loudly from downstairs.

"May I have everyone's attention," bellowed Rita. "Could all houseguests make their way to the drawing room for a brief meeting. I repeat, could everyone make their way to the drawing room. Tea will be served."

*

It was déjà vu inside the drawing room as DCI Wallace stood in front of the household, stroking his moustache, preparing to deliver yet another update. Robert was still AWOL and none of us, it seemed, knew his whereabouts.

"Um, some new and rather unseemly developments have come to light," he said in a subdued, solemn voice. "Robert Eccleston has left his room, despite being told by myself not to leave unless otherwise granted permission. We believe he has fled the grounds of Ainsley Manor and, well, could be anywhere." He looked around the room with a befuddled expression. "As you may have already been informed by Miss Atkins, we now believe Jack Burley was not the killer of Edith Ramsey. We also believe Mr Gregory Bramble's suicide was in fact... a *murder*."

The small gathering began murmuring among themselves.

"Who killed him then?" Jamelia demanded.

The detective cleared his throat. "We don't know who killed him. We do know that both victims had been drugged before they were killed. We now have a suspect in mind."

"Who is it?" shouted Aaron.

The detective looked at each of us squarely, before revealing: "*Robert Eccleston* is now the main suspect."

The group gasped in shock.

The detective continued. "After conducting a search of his room today, we found a bag of pills. We have now identified the pills as Zopiclone, which were used to drug Edith and Gregory before they were murdered."

Pandemonium erupted among the group. As far as I could tell, everyone was outraged.

"That slimy bastard!" Jamelia retorted.

"Total scumbag!" Aaron ranted.

Rita looked utterly dismayed, while Shirley, who sat beside her, shook her head in disbelief. Hazel and I, however, remained relatively calm.

The detective rubbed his eyes, looking very tired. "We have yet to inform the press about these latest developments.

We should like to apprehend Mr Eccleston first before a media circus explodes around his disappearance. We shall continue our search until the morning, after which time, whether we find him or not, we shall be releasing a statement to the press. That's all I have to say for now. If you'll excuse me, I have to get back to work."

Shirley stood up from her chair and accompanied DCI Wallace out the drawing room door. The group remained seated and proceeded to rant and rave about Robert's involvement in Edith's murder. Rather than join in, I sat in silence and gazed at the fox's head, whose frozen snarl seemed to say more about the unfolding situation than anyone else could.

*

Sitting at my desk that night, I spun a pen between my fingers, trying to emulate Robert's skill. Still, I couldn't master it. I opened a notebook and jotted down a few things about the day's shocking developments.

What a difference a day makes, I thought, as I wrote Robert's name in block capitals and drew a circle around it. On the circumference, I drew an arrow pointing to the words "prime suspect" to which I then added a question mark. Was Robert Edith's killer? I stopped writing and began tapping the pen on the paper, trying to motivate my deductive thinking process. If Edith was indeed drugged before she was killed, as the toxicology report suggests, someone must have dragged her from the house into the garden, where they then drove the knife into her back. Robert had access to the keys to the back door, since he spent the night with Rita, and also the physical capacity to drag an adult. But that left the mystery of Gregory's death. What reason did Robert have to kill Gregory? That was a question that was truly puzzling me.

Suddenly a stone hit my window. Followed by another. Then another. I turned the lights out so I could see clearly into the back garden. To my amazement, it was Robert.

What on earth was he doing out there?

He waved at me to come down. What should I do?

He could be a killer, like he's always boasted!

Indeed he could. But I wasn't convinced. My detective hat was overriding my natural fear.

Why not meet him? After all, only he could shed light on why he fled the house.

*

It was quite mild outside. The moon shone beautifully bright in the night sky, just like it did on the night Jack Burley fell to his death. Standing on the garden patio, however, I couldn't see any sign of Robert. Then, all of a sudden, I heard an emphatic "psssssst" that seemed to come from the sycamore tree next to the coach house. Cautiously, I walked towards the tree where I could see the dark outline of Robert, standing in the shadows. I halted a few metres from his dark shape and asked what he wanted.

"They think I murdered her," he said in a tremulous voice. "But I didn't. I had nothing to do with her death."

"Then why don't you come inside and you can tell all this to the detective. I'm sure we can sort this out."

His dark shape moved slightly closer, which almost caused me to step back. But I stayed put. "Are you mad?"

he said. "I'll be arrested and it'll be all over the tabloids. They'll rip me to shreds. I'm from a privileged background. They hate poshos."

I breathed in slowly, trying to sound calm. "Rob, the worst thing you could do right now is go on the run. The media will definitely paint you in a negative light if you don't cooperate."

"Cooperate with what? The police haven't a clue what they're doing. And that bitch has completely manipulated their investigation."

"Who do you mean?" I asked, as I took step closer towards his shape, genuinely interested in who he meant.

"That flake Shirley. Rita told me they found pills in my bedroom. That's bullshit. She planted it there."

"Why do you think that?" I asked as I took another step closer.

His dark shape shrugged. "Just a hunch. I don't trust her."

I moved closer again, just within one metre of where he stood. "I've just one question: Why me? Why did you want to speak with me?"

He walked towards me, until his face was illuminated by the moonlight. He looked desperate, anguished, in need of help. There were a few bruises around his mouth and nose from the fight he had with Aaron. His eyes however... they looked scared. Genuinely scared.

"Because you saw past my mask from the very beginning," he said. "Look, you may not like me. You may not care for my antics or my personality. But you're a natural detective. You won't give up until you get to the truth."

Suddenly a bright light shone all around us. "Who's out there?" bellowed a voice. I turned around and observed the portly figure of DCI Wallace coming towards me, waving a flashlight. "Who's there I say?"

"It's me," I replied. "Belinda Boothby."

The detective walked right up to me, blinding me with the light in his hand. I squinted my eyes and turned away from the brightness in the direction of where I spoke to Robert. But Robert was gone. Vanished into the night.

"What are you doing out here?" he demanded.

"Um, just doing some thinking. On my own."

He narrowed his eyes. "Thinking, eh?" he said condescendingly. "Come on. Back inside. You can do some thinking in the morning."

11

A Twist in the Plot

"Police now consider 25-year-old Robert Eccleston to be the prime suspect in the investigation of Edith Ramsey's murder. Mr Eccleston, of Hampstead Heath, was last seen at the Ainsley Manor House on Tuesday afternoon. Following an altercation with a fellow housemate, he fled the manor house, sparking a manhunt for his whereabouts. Police have released a photo of Mr Eccleston to the general public and said that they believe him to be unarmed yet dangerous. If any member of the public comes into contact with this man, they are urged not to approach him directly but instead to call the police.

"In other news, the government today has announced a new initiative to increase the use of wind energy in rural areas, blah, blah, blah..."

Jamelia crammed a large spoon of cornflakes into her mouth as she stared at her tablet beside her bowl on the kitchen table. "Can't believe it," she exclaimed with her mouth full, "it's all over the news. That boy's in deep shit!" She laughed with her mouth full.

I buttered a slice of toast in silence. I found Jamelia's pleasure about Robert's fugitive status very concerning.

"There can't be that many places to hide around here. How come the police haven't found him?" said Hazel who sat across the table from me.

"He's probably fled the village. Gone back to Mummy and Daddy in... where'd they say he lived?" Jamelia said, eating another spoonful of cornflakes.

"Hampstead Heath," I said.

"Isn't the train station still closed?" Hazel said.

Jamelia nodded while chewing. "Yeah, but being a rich kid, he could easily take an Uber all the way back to London."

I paused, buttering my toast, and thought for a few moments. Should I tell them I met Robert last night? Hazel I could trust with such information, but I was reluctant to tell Jamelia. Understandably, she detested Robert. I decided not to mention it.

Aaron entered the kitchen and took a seat opposite Jamelia. He poured himself a bowl of muesli. Hazel, Jamelia and myself gazed at the bruise on his right eye.

"Alright Aaron?" said Jamelia.

Aaron nodded his head. "I'm alright thanks. Had a good night's sleep."

"That's quite the shiner," Jamelia said.

"Yeah," Aaron said, gently touching the bruised area of his eye. "I'll live, I guess. Pass the milk."

Hazel passed Aaron the jug of milk, which he poured into his bowl of muesli. We ate our breakfast in silence for a while. Then, Jamelia started choking on her cereal.

"Are you alright?" Hazel asked.

Jamelia continued to cough harshly. I ran to the sink and poured a glass of cold water and handed it to Jamelia. She quickly drank the glass, which brought an end to her coughing fit. Picking up her tablet, she winced at the screen.

"What is it?" I asked.

She shook her head in disbelief. "You're not going to believe this."

"What?" asked Hazel.

"This site has done an exposé on us. Look!"

Hazel and I gathered around Jamelia's tablet. The tabloid website on her screen showed a detailed plan of Ainsley Manor House, revealing the layout of each room. Beneath the plan was a photograph of each of us, presented as a list of potential suspects, like a murder-mystery themed version of Big Brother. There was a one-line description about each of us next to our photos. Mine read: "Belinda Boothby, a twenty-six-year-old jobless wannabe-detective from Brighton, whose vain ambitions will more likely lead to the end of a dole queue than a detective agency." Dole queue? How dare they say that? I was really stung by their words. And the photo they had of me wasn't too flattering ether.

Equally cringeworthy is what they said about Hazel: "Hazel Griffin, the typical wallflower of the group, who probably has had more relationships with characters in mystery novels than in real life." I looked at Hazel, whose face became vexed.

Edith was cast as "an abusive and volatile alcoholic" who ended up murdered like a character in one of her own novels. Shirley was Edith's "spineless doormat". Rita was the "saucy maid from Essex" who was having a secret fling with the "posho, arch-villain Robert". Aaron was the quiet, understated member of the household, curiously labelled as the "George Harrison of the group". And then there was

Jamelia: she was characterised as "an athletic, ambitious go-getter" who had won a scholarship to RADA despite her adolescent battle with bulimia.

I looked at Jamelia, who frowned fiercely at the screen. "What the hell? How do they know about my past?"

I pursed my lips. "It's the press. They can dig up all sorts."

Jamelia grimaced at me. In hindsight, I should have chosen more supportive words. Hazel and I returned to our seats. Hazel looked decidedly glum as she poured a glass of OJ.

"I don't understand," Jamelia continued angrily. "How could they have found this out? Bloody leeches!" She banged the end of her spoon on the table.

"I think it's best not to read what they're saying about us," I said. "There's nothing we can do while we're in here. I'm sure it'll all blow over soon when Edith's murder is solved."

Jamelia shook her head defiantly. "You don't understand. Only my mum and sister knew about my bulimia. It was a tight-kept secret when I was going to school. I took time off to get better, telling all my friends I had glandular fever. None of them knew what I was going through. So, this doesn't make any sense. My family would never talk to the media. And I've never mentioned it to anyone outside my family, except..."

She paused abruptly, raising her head. Her eyes darted across the table.

"Except to you, Aaron."

Aaron looked up from his bowl of muesli and gulped down what was in his mouth. He looked at Jamelia, then cast his eyes down at his bowl. He remained conspicuously silent.

"Did you mention what I told you to anyone?" she asked. Aaron remained silent.

"You know the things I shared with you, I've never shared with anyone, except my mum and sister. You know that?"

Aaron nodded. "I know."

"So how do they know all this shit about us? About me?"

"The media have ways of finding out about things," said Hazel objectively. "That's their job. Unfortunately."

Jamelia raised her spoon in the air. "Yeah, I know that. But that doesn't explain how they knew about me!" she said forcefully, which caused Hazel to recoil in her chair. Jamelia flung her spoon on the floor. She then placed her head in her hands and started crying over her cereal.

Hazel and I looked at each other. We were both gutted for her. Aaron looked at me concernedly, then shut his eyes.

"Jamelia," he said, with his eyes closed. "It was me."

Jamelia slowly lifted her face from her hands, her eyes filled with tears.

"I told the press," he said.

The kitchen fell silent. Jamelia's face contorted, expressing a mixture of bewilderment and outrage.

Aaron threw his spoon into his bowl and sat back in his chair. "I told the press about you. I told them about everything. Look, I'm really sorry. You would have found out the truth eventually, but I didn't expect to spend a second week here."

"The truth about what?" I asked.

He looked at the ceiling. "I'm not really an Oxford student. I'm... a journalist."

He looked directly at me once he had said those words. He was a journalist?

"I don't understand," I said.

He glanced at Jamelia then cast his eyes down at his bowl again. "Winning a place on this masterclass was part of an assignment set by my editor-in-chief. He thought it would make a great story, getting inside the mind of Edith Ramsey, you know, dishing all the dirt. But I never expected it to turn into... all this. My boss insists that I keep my cover and get the dirt on everyone."

"Is your real name Aaron, or is that something you made up?" Hazel asked.

Aaron looked at Hazel and nodded. "Yeah, my name's Aaron. The only thing I lied about was my profession."

I was shocked. Then I remembered his late-night phone conversation. The surprise, he mentioned, must have been the fact that we would find out he was a journalist on the final day.

A revelation that never happened because Edith was found dead.

Jamelia leaned over the table, her teary eyes filled with fury. She aimed her finger at Aaron and retorted: "I told you those things about me in confidence. And you blab it to the press! You two-faced, conniving, snake-in-the-grass!" She picked up her cereal bowl and smashed it on the floor. As she stormed out of the room, she scowled at Aaron: "You better watch your back!"

The kitchen became dead silent. I honestly didn't know what to say. Neither did Hazel.

After a few moments, the kitchen door swung up. Shirley popped her head inside. "Um, DCI Wallace has offered to drive me into the village to do some grocery shopping. I'll pick up a few ready-meals for our dinner tonight. Does anyone want anything?"

Shirley stood in the doorway waiting for a response.

"Alrighty then," she finally said. "I'll be back in a while. See you later."

She left the room. I stared at Aaron. I'd really thought he was a genuinely honest person. But how wrong I was. How wrong I was about many things on this writing course. My confidence in my ability to judge people was crashing.

Perhaps it's normal for a detective to have a confidence crisis?

Without saying a word, I got up and left the kitchen.

*

In the living room, I found Rita sitting on her own, looking despondent. Putting aside my dismay over Aaron's revelation, I sat down next to her.

"Rita, are you alright?"

She looked at me. Her eyes were quite red. It was obvious she had been crying a lot.

"What's wrong?" I asked earnestly.

She sighed heavily as I took a seat beside her.

"Nothing. Just thinking about Rob. This must be a nightmare for him."

"Have you heard from him today?"

She shook her head, looking down at her feet.

"Don't know where he is," she said.

I looked towards the doorway and spoke at a deliberately low volume. "I spoke with him last night. He was outside under the sycamore tree."

She looked at me, seemingly unsurprised by my disclosure. "Yeah, he told me earlier he wanted to speak with you. He trusts you. I know the two of you don't get along but..." she looked away momentarily, as if she was about to cry. Taking a few deep breaths to regain her composure, she looked at me. "Can you help him?"

I looked at the board game boxes stacked on the table. "I was surprised that he asked for my help, since, as you say, we don't get along. But, at the same time, I'm not surprised since he thinks I believe he's innocent."

She raised her eyebrows. "Do you really think he's innocent?"

Pursing my lips, I nodded.

She looked down at her feet again and smiled. She was definitely relieved to hear that.

"I know Rob has a dark side," she lamented, "but that doesn't make him a murderer."

"No, indeed," I said.

She tapped her feet nervously on the floor. "I really like him. I think... I'm in love with him."

I felt that she could do a lot better than Robert, given his twisted sense of humour and provocative behaviour. In fact, deep down I worried if I could be encouraging a toxic relationship. Rita was probably better off without Robert in her life, but this was not an appropriate time for such a conversation. Robert was being hunted by the police for the murder of Edith Ramsey.

Rita looked at me again. "So, can you help him?"

I didn't know what to say. I didn't want to give her false hope. Above all, I was not a real detective. What could I possibly do to help? And yet, out of all the residents staying in the house, Robert chose me to ask for help. For all his faults, I had a strong inkling he was innocent of Edith's murder.

Shrugging my shoulders, I gave Rita the only answer I had any confidence in. "Can't hurt to try!"

She smiled tentatively, as her feet became still.

"There's one thing I could do," I said to her. "But I would need your help."

"What's that?"

"I'd like to look inside Shirley's room. I'm not sure what I'll find but I think she's hiding something. Do you have the keys to her door?"

"Yes," she nodded. "Well, I've got the skeleton key. But why do you think Shirley is hiding something?"

"Let's just say, I'm acting on a hunch."

"Okay," she said. "I'll get you the key."

"Great," I said, then looked at the time. "Shirley's gone into town with DCI Wallace to do some shopping. That gives us maybe ten to fifteen minutes to get in and get out without being detected. Are you willing to be a lookout?"

She nodded her head. "Sure, I guess. If it'll help Rob, then I'm in."

*

Ten minutes later, Rita and I were outside Shirley's bedroom door. Rita quietly slipped the key into the keyhole and opened the door very slowly. As I tiptoed inside the bedroom, she handed me the key and whispered: "Bring it back to me when you're finished." I nodded in agreement and closed the door, locking it behind me.

The first thing I noticed inside the bedroom was the stuffiness. It was if Shirley hadn't opened the window the entire time she stayed here! The room was quite messy, with several garments such as shirts, bras and stockings, strewn carelessly on the bed and on the floor.

Wary of the limited time I had to look around, I went

straight for the drawers in the bedside locker. The upper drawer contained mainly underwear. The lower drawer was cluttered with miscellaneous things like jewellery, make-up, and stationery, such as pens, pencils, erasers, stapler etc – and a small diary. My curiosity roused, I flicked through the diary pages, which were filled with inane notes about the masterclass, until I came across something really interesting. Several of the pages towards the back, contained the line from Robert's assignment card ("Kill the teacher and frame her stalker") written many times. Initially, I was puzzled. Then it dawned on me: Shirley had been practising Robert's handwriting. *She* must have written *this* version of the card.

I returned the diary to the drawer, then turned my attention to the wardrobe. A wave of mustiness hit me as soon as I opened the door. Inside was filled with typical Shirley-style clothes: bland-coloured blouses, pearl-button cardigans, and an ankle-length dress, all of which epitomised conservative fashion. Behind all the clothes was a turquoise handbag. Unstrapping it from the hanging rail, I quickly rooted through it. There was a lipstick, a pocket mirror, a shopping receipt and... *wait, what was this?* An empty bottle. I read the label: it was Zopiclone pills for Edith Ramsey.

Hoorah! The detective makes a compelling discovery!

Edith's empty bottle of sleeping pills. In the possession of her trusted assistant. This was compelling evidence that Shirley may have drugged Edith – and Gregory – and put the rest of the pills in a plastic bag for the police to find in Robert's room. I was excited. I closed the wardrobe and began walking towards the door with the empty bottle in hand, when something caught my eye. On Shirley's writing desk was a limited edition of Edith's bestseller *Shedunnit*, next to a stack of papers. Intrigued by the rarity of this edition, I picked it up and sat down on her bed, placing the bottle beside me.

Inside the front cover was an inscription by Edith to Shirley:

> *To Shirley,*
> *As only you and I know,*
> *this work was not possible*
> *without you. Your efforts*
> *will live on through the*
> *ages,*
> *Gratefully yours,*
> *ER*

Admittedly, it was a confounding message. What exactly did Edith mean? Did Shirley edit her work? Or contribute to the story in some way? Yet Shirley was not credited in the book for making any contribution.

As I pondered this perplexity, Rita whispered through the door: "She's back! Shirley's back!"

Time to skedaddle!

As I hastily placed the book back on the table, I knocked the stack of papers onto the floor, which scattered everywhere.

No, this can't be happening!

Panic-stricken, I began picking them up and placing them back on the table in a pile. As soon as I had finished, I heard Rita's voice.

"Hi, Shirley, how was your trip to the village?"

"Fine, fine," said the voice of Shirley. "Easy in and out."

It's too late. She's at the door. Better hide!

Yes, indeed, and there was only one place I could hide. I popped inside the wardrobe, burrowing past Shirley's clothes, and stationed myself in the corner.

"Can I get you anything from the kitchen?" Rita asked loudly.

"I'll be down in a while. I'm just going to change my clothes."

I heard the key being inserted into the keyhole; the door handle turning; Shirley entering the room. Then Rita's heightened voice: "Okay then, I'll put the kettle on." The door closed. I stayed absolutely still and quiet, to the point where I could hear my heart beating rapidly in my chest.

Shirley's feet shuffled around the bedroom. I opened the wardrobe door ever so slightly to peer out. Shirley stood at her desk, stretched her arms, then yawned. She took off her cardigan then approached the wardrobe. I gently closed the door and recoiled into the dark. I heard her footsteps walk right up to the door.

Blimey! This is going to be awkward if she catches you in here!

Then there was a knock on the door. Rita had come to the rescue! Shirley turned from the wardrobe, walked to the door and opened it.

"Hello Shirley?" said DCI Wallace.

There goes my escape plan!

"Oh, detective. Is everything alright?"

"Everything's fine," he said merrily. "You mind if I come in?"

Shirley paused for a few moments. "Em, yes, sure... if you'll excuse the mess."

The detective's heavy footsteps entered the room. "Not half as messy as my room," he joked.

"What can I do for you, detective?"

"Ah well, let's see. I really just came here to check on you. I know all this mayhem must be hard to deal with. You mind?"

"Eh, um, yes, sure go ahead."

There was very loud and sudden creak on the bed, followed by a prolonged sigh by DCI Wallace: "Ahhhhhhh." Evidently, he had just sat on the bed. "Come here, Shirley. Have a seat. Don't be afraid, I won't bite."

There was another loud creak on the bed. Evidently Shirley had sat down on the bed beside the detective. There were a few moments of silence. The most awkward silence I've ever experienced in my life.

Could this situation get any worse?

"Did anyone ever tell you that you have beautiful eyes?" said the detective.

More awkward silence followed. Although I couldn't see, it was obvious Shirley's face had turned scarlet.

"Ooh detective. I... I... I don't know what to say. Nobody ever really notices me."

"I find that hard to believe!" said the detective with exaggerated overtones. "You're such a lovely woman. Such a pretty face... behind those big glasses."

Shirley giggled.

"Mind if I take them off?" asked the detective. Silence. "Oh, there you are. Look at those pretty, little eyes. They're like two precious pearls plucked from the ocean."

Shirley giggled. "Oh, detective, that's so nice of you to say."

"And you've got a lovely round bottom!" he added. Shirley sounded like she hiccupped when the detective had said these words, such was her embarrassment.

Her embarrassment? Think of your own!

This was the singular most cringeworthy event of my entire young life.

How will this end, I thought? I shuddered thinking about it.

Please don't let it end like that!

I was loath to see the unfolding romantic scene taking place on the bed, but, nevertheless, I found myself opening the wardrobe door again to peer out. I could see them, sitting side by side on the edge of the bed. Then, the detective noticed the bottle I had left on the bed.

"What's that?" he asked, nodding towards the bottle.

Shirley eyed the bottle then picked it up, glancing at the label. Immediately, her face grimaced.

"Oh, that's just my medication. I take it for... migraines." She quickly opened the upper bedside drawer and flung the bottle inside.

"Migraines?" said the detective. "You poor woman! My mother used to get migraines, God rest her soul."

The detective placed his hand on Shirley's back and patted it. He then caressed her back, working his hand downward. Shirley shifted on the bed, looking extremely uncomfortable.

"Eh, detective, why don't we go to the dining room?"

The detective leaned back. "The dining room? Why the dining room?"

Shirley cleared her throat. "Well, it's just that there's a bottle of gin there. I thought maybe we could have a drink together."

"A drink together?" Wallace said, then chortled loudly. "You naughty woman! Are you trying to get me drunk?"

Shirley chortled awkwardly along with him.

"Alright then," he said. "Let's have a drink together. No point in letting good gin go to waste. Lead the way, my dear." He patted Shirley firmly on the lap then stood up from the bed.

I closed the wardrobe door and waited until I heard them leave. Having waited a few minutes for the coast to be clear, I emerged from the wardrobe and tiptoed to Shirley's bedside drawer. I recovered the empty bottle and left the room.

When I entered my room, I found Rita sitting at my desk. She jumped to her feet. "Well, what happened?"

"Just had a very strange experience."

"Did you find anything?" she asked.

"Yes, I did. This." I handed the bottle to Rita. "It's a bottle for Zopiclone, Edith's sleeping pills. Found it in Shirley's wardrobe. This could prove Rob's innocence."

Her face lit up with amazement. "I can't believe it. This is great! I can't wait to tell Rob!"

"I also came across a diary in which Shirley had been practising Robert's handwriting. I believe it was Shirley who wrote that threatening note to Jamelia. Clearly, she's trying to cast suspicion on Robert."

"I don't believe it. She's a right trollop."

I was in complete agreement. "How will you communicate this with Robert?"

Rita pursed her lips and looked at me sternly. "Can you keep a secret?"

"Of course," I said.

She glanced momentarily at the door, then spoke in a whisper: "He'll be staying in the coach house tonight. I've made arrangements. You won't tell anyone, will you?"

"The coach house?" I said. "Hasn't that been taped off?"

"Yes, but no one's watching the place and I've got the key. Besides, they'll never think to look for Rob at a crime scene."

It was a good choice for a hiding place, I had to admit. Albeit a very risky one.

"You won't tell anyone, will you?" she asked.

"No, of course not. Mum's the word."

She smiled. "Thanks, Belinda. I better go. I've got a secret meal to prepare."

"Good luck," I said.

She smiled excitedly as she then left my room. Having endured enough excitement for one day, I decided to pay a visit to Hazel to update her on my adventure in Shirley's bedroom.

*

It was approaching six o' clock in the evening when I yawned on Hazel's bed, having spent the last few hours doodling in my notebook. Hazel sat at her desk, updating her work with details of my covert investigation into Shirley's bedroom.

"Who would have known Shirley would be a suspect," Hazel said, as she typed fervently.

"Clearly, not the local police," I said cynically, listening to the furious pace at which she typed. "Sounds like you're making excellent progress, Hazel."

She nodded, completely absorbed in her task. "This new information about Shirley makes a great twist in the plot."

I checked her bedside clock. "I think I'll go and check on Jamelia. Aaron's revelation must have hit her hard."

Hazel pulled her head away from her laptop to shoot me a cursory glance. "That really was a bombshell. Nothing's what

230

it seems on this writing course," she said, then returned to her writing position. She seemed genuinely happy, immersing herself in her authorial task. Perhaps writing provided a refuge for her from the cruel judgemental world, as evinced in that tabloid exposé earlier this morning.

She remained steadfastly glued to her computer, as I got up to leave her room.

"Talk to you later then," I said, as I opened her door.

"Later, Bel." I walked to Jamelia's bedroom and knocked on it. Within moments, she opened the door, looking jaded and extremely sullen.

"How are you?" I asked kindly.

She glared at me in total silence, like a cat ready to claw my eyes out. After a few moments, she rasped: "Get lost!" then slammed the door on my face.

Woah, that was hostile!

I stood at her door, stunned. She was clearly too incensed over Aaron's betrayal to talk. I hoped she wasn't going to do anything drastic.

Like try to kill Aaron?

Deflated and tired, I returned to my room to grab a power nap. I was beat from my detective work today. But my investigation wasn't quite finished. I set my alarm to wake up later in the evening, since I planned to pay Robert an unexpected visit in the coach house. I was eager to know what he thought about the evidence I had uncovered to clear his name.

*

The muddy grass squelched under my feet as I trudged across the back garden towards the coach house, which was cordoned off with police tape. Looking warily around me, I lifted the police tape up and entered an official crime scene, making my way around the back of the house. Luckily the back door was unlocked. I entered and was immediately greeted by the smell of cooked food. Rita must have been here already.

The house was eerily quiet as I entered the hallway. Standing outside the living room door, I paused. The harrowing memory of Gregory's body lingered vividly in my mind. I shook my head to rid myself of that horrible image and turned the doorknob.

As soon as I entered the room I met a familiar face, standing beside Gregory's armchair: *the one and only Robert!* I smiled at him, anticipating that he'd be relieved to see me. But he didn't smile back. Instead, his face became perturbed. Something was amiss.

Wait, what's that on his hands? It looks like... blood!!!

Immediately my heart rate picked up. My eyes trailed from Robert's hands down towards the floor, where a pair of feet lay behind the armchair. My heart began thumping in my chest as all the detective novels in the world could not prepare me for what I saw: Rita was sprawled on the floor; her shirt soaked in her own blood. A bloody kitchen knife lay close to her on the floor. My gaze trailed back to Robert's eyes. He raised his bloodied hands in silence, as if trying to persuade me not to run.

But run I did!

I bolted out of the living room, through the kitchen and out the back door. As I sprinted towards the country house, I burst into tears. Poor Rita! Poor, sweet, innocent Rita. I cried out as I got to the hallway of the main house.

"Help! Someone help me, please," I cried. "Please help me!"

Within moments, everyone gathered around me in shock.

"Bel, what is it?" Hazel asked.

I sobbed profusely on my knees. "It's Rita... she... she... she's been..."

"Murdered?" repeated Aaron.

I nodded my head in mute agony.

"What's all the fuss here then?" A dishevelled, sleepy-eyed DCI Wallace staggered out of the dining room and joined the gathering in the hallway. He crouched beside me. "What's the matter, dear?"

His breath stank of gin. Lowering my head, I forced myself to stop crying. Once I had regained some level of composure, I looked straight into the detective's eyes and said: "It's Rita. She's in the coach house. There's nothing you can do."

The detective rose to his feet and announced to everyone: "Right, everyone back in your rooms. Lock your doors. No one leaves until I return!"

Everyone proceeded back upstairs silently. Hazel and Aaron helped me off the floor and assisted me up the stairs. The detective left in a hurry toward the coach house.

12

No Escape from this Madness

I didn't sleep a wink. I had heard the police come and go throughout the night, while I remained in my room, curled up in bed. My mind was plagued by what I'd witnessed the previous day: Rita's body lying on the floor in the coach house. Robert standing over her, his hands covered in her blood. Robert's eyes were vividly burned into my mind. I will never forget them.

The eyes of a cold-blooded killer.

Deep down, I blamed myself. It was my own stupidity that led me to believe that Robert might be innocent. A stupidity owing, in no small part, to the illusion that I would be a great detective one day. How did I allow myself to be duped by that awful, dastardly person? A person who was openly callous, arrogant, unempathetic and who routinely boasted about the genius of murderers. How could I think that was all just a façade?

The boy was sick in the mind, everyone saw it.

Everyone saw it, yet I chose to believe it was an act. How tragically naive I was! And now Rita was dead. I could have done something to save her. I should have warned her to stay away from him. I should have prevented her from going to the coach house. But I didn't. And now she was gone. Body number four on this never-ending nightmare masterclass.

There was a knock on the door, which I didn't answer at first, since I didn't want any contact with the outside world. I felt safe inside my bedroom. The second knock, however, was accompanied by Hazel's voice.

"Bel? Bel? Are you okay in there? Bel? Can I come in?"

Although I remained silent, the door nevertheless opened. Hazel peered inside and became quite concerned, seeing me curled up in my clothes. She closed the door quietly behind her and stood by my bedside, frowning.

"Aren't you getting up today?"

Turning over on my back, I stared straight at the ceiling and shrugged. "Not really in the mood to get up today. Too much darkness out there."

Hazel glanced out the window. "It's quite sunny today. The skies have cleared."

"I meant existential darkness."

"Oh," Hazel uttered, as she wandered over to my desk. "Have you seen the news today?"

I really didn't want to hear about the news. "No," I said bluntly.

"Robert's now a possible serial killer," she explained. "According to Scotland Yard. He's wanted in connection with the deaths of at least three people. Rita being his latest victim. It's so awful. They interviewed Rita's mum, who was crying on TV. As were her two sisters, and they also had..."

"I don't want to know!" I bellowed.

She fell completely silent and turned toward my desk. My eyes remained glued to the ceiling. Hazel began flicking through the pages of a notebook. With great reluctance, I sat up in bed.

"I'm sorry for snapping at you, Hazel. I'm just really tired and fed up with all of this. I just... can't get the image of Rita lying dead on the floor out of my mind. She was such a lovely soul. Such a gracious, cheerful, beautiful person. How could anyone..." I burst into tears. Hazel shuffled over to my bedside and threw her arms around me.

"We all miss her, Bel, we really do. We're all in this together. You've been so brave. Out of all of us, you've been the bravest."

I knew she was trying to be supportive, but her generous sentiment made me feel worse. "The bravest?" I exclaimed. "Rita's dead because of me."

Her eyes opened wide in bewilderment. "Why do you say that?"

"Nothing," I said, shaking my head. "Just... leave me alone." I turned over and sank my head firmly in my pillow. Hazel sniffled, then cleared her throat.

"You were the one who stood up to Robert when I couldn't," she said, with unwavering confidence in her voice. "You always knew he was a scumbag. You never doubted it. If more people thought like you and had your courage, maybe all this wouldn't have happened."

I turned over and looked directly at her. "Rita *is* dead, despite my misgivings about Robert. Furthermore, I was actually beginning to believe he was innocent. That he'd been set up. What a complete idiot I've been."

Hazel sat down on the side of the bed. "No, Bel, you're not an idiot. You were drawing conclusions from the evidence at hand. That's all. Other detectives would've drawn the same conclusions. Don't you think?"

"Other detectives?" I said. "Well, that's the point, isn't it? I'm not a detective. I'll never be a detective."

Hazel placed her hand on my hand. "If it makes you feel any better, you *are* a detective in my book." She paused for a few moments, before she clarified herself. "I mean, the book that I'm writing. Not the figure of speech."

Closing my eyes, I slowly drew my hand away from Hazel's and turned on my side. My belly rumbled. I was hungry but didn't want to eat. I didn't want to do anything except lie in my bed.

Can you imagine Sherlock Holmes lying in bed all day and not getting up to eat, or smoke his pipe?

"Bel? Bel? Please get up. Let's go for a walk," Hazel pleaded.

"A walk?" I said incredulously. "Where would we walk? This entire house is one big crime scene. And it's surrounded by the media, camped outside in droves. There's no escape from this madness."

Hazel remained silent as she considered my desperate attitude. "Alright then," she eventually conceded. "I'll go to my room. See you later."

My eyes remained closed as she left the room.

*

The rumbling in my stomach woke me up an hour later. I couldn't put off eating any longer. Despondently, I rolled out of bed, slipped on my shoes, and lumbered out of my bedroom. As soon as I arrived at the bottom of the stairs, the doorbell rang. Then rang again. Who could it be? I hoped it wasn't the police to ask more questions. I had had enough of questions! I had explained everything to them in fine detail yesterday and didn't want to think about it anymore. The doorbell rang a third time. Before it could ring a fourth time, I swiftly opened the door and was met by a woman in her late forties clutching a dark brown leather briefcase. Her piercing cold blue eyes and narrow lips gave the immediate impression of someone who had very little patience with things in general. She wore a stunning beige trench coat that hung just above her suede high-heel boots. Behind her, a spectacular-looking silver sports Mercedes was parked in the courtyard.

"Hello there," she said abruptly. "I'm looking for Shirley Atkins."

"Shirley?" I repeated. "And who might you be?"

Pursing her lips, she appeared to be somewhat annoyed by my question. "My name is Annabelle King. I'm Edith Ramsey's literary agent." She paused briefly before adding: "From London."

"Oh," I said, "Please, do come in."

"Thank you," she said, as she marched presumptuously into the hallway. "It's truly mayhem back there. Took me ages to get past all those journalists. That young policeman they've put on the gate is completely out of his depth. He spent almost half an hour trying to confirm my identity!"

Closing the door, I nodded to pretend I agreed with her brief rant. The truth was I didn't want to know about all that mayhem. We stood in silence for a few brief moments, looking at each other. Finally, she raised her arms and said in a demanding voice: "So, where is Shirley?"

"Oh," I said, scratching my head. "I'm not sure."

She exhaled impatiently through her nostrils. I almost expected fire to come out. "Well, would you mind finding out where she is?"

She came across as quite bossy, which annoyed me. Nevertheless, I was willing to assist. "Um, let me check her room," I said broodily, then sauntered up the stairs. After knocking repeatedly on Shirley's bedroom door and getting no response, I sauntered back down the stairs.

"Not in her bedroom then?" she said snappily.

"I'm afraid not," was my lame response. "I'll try downstairs."

Less than a minute later, having checked all the rooms downstairs, I returned to the hallway where Annabelle stood. "I can't find her anywhere," I said with a shrug of my shoulders.

She tsked, and seemed increasingly bothered that she was still standing in the hallway.

"Is there anyone in this house who may know where she is?"

"I have no idea."

"You have no idea?" she retorted. "Can you find me someone who runs this place? This is becoming a farce!"

Her scolding attitude was beginning to infuriate me.

"Excuse me, I really don't appreciate your tone. I barely know your name or the reason why you're here, and you're speaking to me in a very demeaning manner. I don't know where Shirley is and, frankly, I couldn't care less. Now, if you don't mind, I'm going to get something to eat."

I marched straight past her towards the kitchen, leaving her standing alone in the hallway with her fancy briefcase.

My stomach continued to growl with hunger, as I rooted through the fridge for food. Thankfully, I discovered a plate of leftover cottage pie and popped it in the microwave. As I watched the timer counting down, Annabelle entered the kitchen.

What now? Does she want me to fix her a sandwich?

She cleared her throat. "Perhaps, I spoke with a little too much haste," she said apologetically. "You see, everything that's happened is very, um, unprecedented. Edith's death, while shocking and untimely, has left the agency in quite a predicament. Legally speaking. Em... may I sit down?"

Shrugging my shoulders, I replied: "If you want."

She took a seat at the top of the kitchen table and placed her briefcase beside her chair. With a flick of her wrist, a gold wristwatch appeared from under the sleeve of her coat.

"Good heavens, look at the time! Listen, I don't mean to be a bother, but have you seen Shirley at all today? I really need to speak with her."

"I haven't seen her," I stated blankly. "What do you need to speak about?"

"Oh, I just need to clear up some issues with Edith's contract," she said plainly.

"What kind of issues?"

"I can't really discuss it with you. It's confidential."

Unimpressed by her reticence, I turned away from her and stared at the cottage pie rotating in the microwave. After a few seconds, I could smell nicotine in the air. I swung around on my feet. She had casually lit up a cigarette.

"Who are you anyway, dear?" she said, as she took a drag.

"Belinda Boothby is my name. And I would appreciate you not smoking in this room."

"Belinda Boothby. That's an interesting name," she said, completely ignoring my request to stop smoking. "I like the alliteration. It gives you a certain... literary appeal."

What an arrogant wench!

"So, you must be devastated about Edith?" I asked.

She nodded indifferently as she took another drag. "Yes, it's very sad. Very sad indeed. It leaves the agency with large shoes to fill." She drew her head back as she blew smoke towards the ceiling. "So, um, this Robert they're after. You know him well? What kind of fella is he?"

I narrowed my eyes at her impertinent line of questioning. "He's the kind of fella who apparently kills people. He's got quite the high body count so far."

Smiling at my sarcasm, she picked up a jar of honey on the table and took the lid off, into which she tipped the excess ash from her cigarette. She was now getting to be intolerable. "Yes, he sounds quite... prolific," was her equally sarcastic reply.

"If you don't mind me saying, you don't seem to be sad about Edith's passing at all."

Annabelle frowned. "I am sad. Like I just told you. But, honestly, we weren't close. When it came to her legal affairs, I dealt mainly with Shirley."

"Shirley?" I said. "Why did you deal with her? She's merely Edith's assistant."

At that very moment, Shirley's head popped in the door.

"Oh, Annabelle!" she exclaimed, as she approached the kitchen table. "I'm so sorry I'm late. I was down at the station with DCI Wallace."

"Not to worry, Shirley," Annabelle replied, putting her cigarette out in the honey jar lid. "Is there a room we can go to, to discuss things in private?"

"Well, of course. If you'll follow me."

Annabelle picked up her suitcase and brolly and smiled condescendingly at me. "It was nice meeting you."

"Likewise, I'm sure." As soon as they left the room, the microwave beeped repeatedly. The cottage pie was ready.

*

After I'd eaten, I decided to pay Hazel a visit, since I wanted to make up for my stroppy attitude to her earlier. Coming up the stairs I could hear the voices of Shirley and Annabelle from inside Shirley's bedroom.

Should I eavesdrop for a few moments?

Choosing to mind my own business, I continued to Hazel's door and knocked.

"Come in!"

I expected her to be busy writing at her desk when I opened the door but instead found her lying on her bed, with a pen in her mouth. She looked decidedly glum, as I'm sure I had looked when she had been in my room. She wasn't particularly enthusiastic to see me.

"Do you mind if I come in?"

She shrugged her shoulders, which I took as a yes. I sat down on the edge of her bed.

"Hazel, I'm sorry for my mood earlier. I feel devastated over Rita. As I'm sure you are. And everyone else. This masterclass is the worst thing that's ever happened to me. Probably to any of us. I wish I'd never entered that bloody writing competition. So much for wanting to be a mystery writer. Or, indeed, a detective. If I never see another body, I will die a happy death."

Hazel took the pen from her lips and held it like a cigarette in her fingers. "You can't blame yourself, Bel. Even great detectives have bad days."

There was no point in reminding her that we were writers, not detectives. And amateur writers at that. Heaven knows I, too, was guilty of confusing crime writers with crime detectives, as if both professions were existentially indistinct. But the horrid events of last night reinforced the distinction. Murder was not an armchair hobby of any kind, nor an excuse to indulge in amateur sleuthing, as it is often portrayed in mystery novels. It was painfully abhorrent and vile, in which a real-life human being has been treacherously robbed of life and stolen away from his or her loved ones. I decided to change the subject.

"Edith's agent is here."

"Edith's agent?" Hazel said.

"Yes, her literary agent. Annabelle. She's with Shirley in Shirley's bedroom, discussing something about Edith's contract."

Hazel sat up on the bed, frowning. "Where did she come from?"

"London. She travelled here in style. There's a sports Mercedes parked out front. She's quite a character."

"Huh," Hazel uttered. "So, the roads are back open?"

The roads must be open again if she drove here from the capital.

"I suppose they must be."

"And yet we remain confined to this house. Like prisoners. Getting knocked off one by one." Her tone was quite cynical. Yet quite justified.

I sighed deeply, acknowledging her frustration. "As the DCI said last night, they want us to remain here until they apprehend Robert."

Hazel flung herself back on the bed. "I need to leave here as soon as possible."

"I understand. We all do. I'm sure they'll catch him soon. He can't have got far on foot. And given that he has limited experience with..."

"No, that's not what I meant," she interrupted. "I need

Ventolin for my inhaler. If I have an asthma attack, I'll be in serious trouble."

That was worrying. "Can you get it delivered here?"

"I'm not sure. That could take some time, if all the police are out looking for Robert. But there's a pharmacy in the village. I could ring my GP and have her send a prescription to them and pick it up today. If only we could leave the house."

I stood up from the bed and gazed out the window. "We could slip out the side-gate by the coach house, as long as the coast is clear."

"I guess we could," Hazel said. "You think we'll be seen?"

I turned to her and smiled. "Only one way to find out."

*

It seemed that myself and Hazel were back in detective-team mode, having successfully reached the village pharmacy later that day, without being seen by the media or the police. At least, I hoped we hadn't been seen. Hazel spoke to the pharmacist at the counter about her medication, while I lingered around the vitamin aisle, keeping an eye out the window in case anyone spotted us. Twenty minutes later, as I examined the manifold types of lotions in the skincare section, Hazel tugged on my elbow.

"Let's go," she said, holding a small paper package.

"All good?" I asked.

"All good."

As soon as we left the shop, we spotted a group of journalists approach us from across the street. They crowded around us like a pack of vultures as we left the pharmacy.

"Excuse me, are you residents of the Ainsley Manor

House? Excuse me? Excuse me? Are you a friend of Robert Eccleston, the man wanted in connection with the murder of Edith Ramsey and two other people?"

A small blonde woman aggressively shoved a microphone in my face, as we kept our heads down, trying to navigate around them. They stuck to us, however, like a cheap suit. Within moments we were mobbed. We tried to make our way down the street.

"Were you involved with Mr Eccleston while you were inside the house?"

"Did he sleep with the teacher, Miss Ramsey?"

"What was his relationship like with his mother?

"Some think that he murdered the maid during a wild sex game. Can you confirm if this is true?"

Steadfastly I held my tongue. Up ahead, I noticed a small laneway that led towards the woods. It would be perfect for a getaway. Under my breath, I said to Hazel: "On three, turn right and run!" Hazel glanced towards the laneway and nodded.

"One... two... *three!*"

We abruptly turned right and sprinted down the laneway, leaving the journalists in our dust.

"To the woods!" I shouted as we reached the end of the lane.

"Aye, aye, detective!"

As soon as our feet touched the dark foliage of the woodland, we slowed down to a halt. Behind us, the journalists were out of sight. Hazel bent over, struggling to catch her breath. She sounded wheezy.

"Hazel, are you okay?"

She looked up at me as her cheeks puffed in and out, nodding. I waited a few minutes to make sure she was alright.

"Do you need your inhaler?"

"No. I'm fine," she said reassuringly. "Got my breath back. Where to now?"

My eyes scanned the dark, dense landscape of trees. With the evening sky darkening above, the sensible thing to do was to walk among the trees near the road. That way we couldn't get lost.

We had walked in silence for about fifteen minutes, when Hazel stopped.

"What's wrong?" I asked.

Her head repeatedly turned side to side, like an owl scrutinising its surroundings.

"Feels like we're being *followed*."

I gazed around me but couldn't see anyone.

"You're being paranoid," I said flatly.

She pursed her lips. "Perhaps I am."

We continued to walk without conversing for another few minutes, until Hazel stopped in her tracks again. This time her head was fixed in one direction. Her face suddenly turned pale and her eyes became fearful. I turned in the direction of her gaze and my heart stopped. We *were* being followed: no more than twenty metres behind us, a dark shape fast approached us. A dark shape that exuded a bone-chilling familiarity: It was... *Robert*. He hastened his ominous stride towards us. Hazel and I ran for our lives.

"What the hell is he doing here?" Hazel screamed.

"No idea! Don't want to find out!"

We dashed through the trees and foliage until Hazel tired out. She stopped and wheezed loudly. We were at least a half mile from the lane that led back to the house.

"I won't make it," she said breathlessly, "you go on."

"Don't be ridiculous. I'm not leaving you behind."

"Where do you think he is?" she said, fraught with worry.

Looking around, I couldn't see any sign of Robert. Perhaps we lost him. But I couldn't be sure. I felt very unsettled. Hazel was still crouched over, trying to catch her breath. Standing next to her, I placed my hand on her back.

"Take your time, Hazel. We haven't far to go. You'll be drinking a nice, hot cuppa in no time."

She took out her inhaler and took a few puffs. Her wheezing died down. She looked at me and smiled, relieved she had got her breath back. Then, suddenly, her smile fell. Her face filled up with terror. Robert appeared from behind a tree, having crept up on us like a silent predator. He slowly walked towards me, holding out his hands.

"Listen, I only want to speak with you," he said in a desperate tone. "Please, don't run."

Think fast. As long as you're with Hazel you can't outrun him.

No, indeed, but I can draw him away from her. Without warning her, I sprinted away from Hazel, into the darker recesses of the woods. As I hoped, Robert immediately chased after me. Hearing him hot on my heels, I shouted back to Hazel:

"Get back to the house! I'll meet you there later!"

My sprinting feet smashed through thick leaves, as I headed deeper into the dark woodland. I had no idea where I was going but I needed to prioritise Hazel's safety. Having ran at full speed for about ten minutes, I summoned the courage to look behind me. There was no sign of Robert. Relieved and weary, I stopped in my tracks, panting heavily. Surrounded by the ominous presence of dark and brooding trees, it was evident I was alone. But alone exactly where? Darkness was quickly enveloping the sky above me. The thought of having to survive a night in the woods for the second time filled me with dismay.

Déjà vu. Only this time you'll have Robert Eccleston hunting you instead of Jack Burley.

I wandered through the woodland for about an hour, coming to terms with the fact that I was hopelessly lost. That is, until I heard the faint echo of a car, beeping its horn in the distance.

The blissful sound of traffic!

I ran in the direction of the horn and became ecstatic to find the beginning of Turnpike Road. Wading through the briars and brambles that led to the rear of the house, I slipped through the side-gate and into the back garden.

What a relief! Home safe and sound. Time for a nice, hot cuppa!

I trotted halfway up the stairs and glanced out the window that overlooked the courtyard. Annabelle's sports Mercedes was gone. I continued up the stairs and knocked on Hazel's door to ask her to join me for tea. Worryingly, there was no response. I entered her room but there was no sign of her. That only meant one thing: *she was still in the woods*. I would have to go back out there and search for her. This was going to be a nightmare! Should I get Jamelia to help me find her? That would be the best course of action. I was about to leave Hazel's bedroom when my phone vibrated in my pocket. I took it out and looked at the screen: it was an incoming call from Hazel.

Thank Heavens for that!

"Hello, Hazel?"

There was silence on the other end.

"Hazel?" I repeated. "Hazel, are you there? Can you tell me where you are?"

"It's me," said a male voice.

That's not Hazel!

"Who... is this?" I asked, anticipating my worst fears.

"You know who this is," said Robert's masterly voice.

Silence resonated from my end for a few moments, accompanied by a cold chill down my spine. Immediately, I panicked about Hazel's well-being. *What had this sick, twisted psycho done to her?*

"Where's Hazel?" I asked with growing trepidation.

"She's okay for now. Here, I'll put her on."

Rustling on the other end.

"Hello Bel," said Hazel in a shaky voice. "He's got my phone. There's nothing I can do. He won't let me..."

Hazel was abruptly cut off. Robert's voice returned. "As you can hear, she's fine. For now. Do exactly as I say and nothing will happen to her."

"You listen to me," I said in an extremely determined tone. "If anything happens to her, I swear I'll..."

"Yeah, yeah, yeah, I get the idea," interrupted Robert's arrogant voice. "If you want to see your friend again, you'll follow my instructions."

"What are your instructions?"

"You know the old windmill you can see from the house?"

I turned towards the window. Vaguely, I could make out the rotating blades in the distance, beneath the dusky sky. "Yeah, I know it."

"Meet me there. I'll explain everything to you."

"Explain what exactly?"

Silence followed for a few moments.

"Be there in the next half hour," he said in a demanding manner. "Do not think of calling the police. If you do... *you'll never see your friend again.*"

The line suddenly went dead.

"Hello? Hello?" I looked at my phone. The call had ended. This was bad. Very bad.

This is bloody awful. He's got poor Hazel! What's he planning to do with her?

Many possible scenarios flooded my mind, all of which spelled danger for Hazel. It was up to me to save her. I couldn't risk telling anyone else. Calling the police could put Hazel's life in jeopardy. There was no doubt in my mind that Robert was capable of anything... of committing the most heinous deeds. But the question was: what did he want with me? Was I going to be the latest victim on his kill list? What devious scheme did he have planned? I would be taking a big risk – probably the biggest risk of my life – if I met with him. But what choice did I have? Hazel's life was on the line. Right now, I was her best hope.

*

By my estimate, the old windmill was about a half mile from Ainsley Manor House. Leaving through the side-gate, it would be a direct walk through several fields. Pretty straight-forward. Except that it was getting dark, which would make the journey that much more difficult and time-consuming. Nevertheless, I began my trek in determined spirits, putting the welfare of Hazel before myself. Aware that half an hour was barely enough time, I walked at a brisk pace, keeping a close eye on my watch.

Within twenty minutes, I was within a stone's throw of the windmill. The wooden structure looked very run down from the outside, while the rusted metal blades creaked restlessly in the light breeze. The surrounding area was desolate and eerily silent. To the left of the windmill stretched an endless blanket of rolling fields, swallowed up by the encroaching night sky. To the right, a dark abyss of brooding woodland. Robert and Hazel were nowhere to be seen. As I crept towards the windmill, painfully conscious of the noise each footstep I took made, my phone vibrated in my pocket, bringing me to a complete standstill. Hazel's name appeared on the screen again.

"Hello," I said nervously.

"Around the back, there's a door," said Robert's echoey voice. "I'll see you inside."

Slowly and tentatively, I stole around to the back of the windmill and saw the door. As I approached it, the door slowly opened. My heart thumped loudly in my chest.

"Hello? Can anyone hear me?"

There was no response. I drew back the door and shone my phone's torch inside, which illuminated a very old, dilapidated waterwheel. Behind the waterwheel, there was movement. I shone my lamp in the direction of the movement, illuminating the petrified face of Hazel, held hostage by a surly looking Robert. Immediately, my personal fear was replaced by an overwhelming concern for Hazel's well-being.

"Hazel!" I said assertively, which resonated an echo inside the closed space. "Are you alright?"

She nodded, while struggling against Robert's arm, which was wrapped firmly around her neck. I stared intently at Robert, frowning defiantly at his intimidating behaviour. "I'm here now. You can let her go."

"Do not tell me what to do, Boothby!"

I moved closer to the waterwheel to show him I wasn't afraid. "What exactly do you want?"

"That's close enough," he said. "If you come any closer, I'll break her neck."

Hazel squirmed in his grip, clearly upset by her captor's words. I realised in that moment, however, that Robert was unarmed. All he had was a tight grip around Hazel's neck. Boldly, and perhaps a little recklessly, I took another step towards him.

"Rob, it's me you want. Let her go."

He stared at me for a few moments, then looked at his arm, tightly fastened around Hazel's neck. Hazel was starting to cough because of the pressure around her neck, which I feared would trigger a full-blown asthma attack.

"Rob, look at me," I said in a sympathetic tone. "Let her go. I'm here now. I'm not going anywhere. I'll listen to whatever you have to say. Just let her go."

Robert's eyes returned to staring at me. He slowly withdrew his arm from Hazel's neck. Hazel coughed profusely for a few seconds, before rushing over to my side. She was now safe. Then, in a completely unexpected twist, Robert began to cry. It was a truly shocking thing to witness. Robert Eccleston crying like a little boy. And his tears seemed wholly genuine.

There's one for the books!

Never in a lifetime, could I have imagined *this* guy displaying real emotion. Yet here I was, watching the arrogant prince of provocation, bawling helplessly inside an abandoned windmill. Hazel and I looked at each other, amazed. I motioned for her to escape. She quietly slipped outside, while I continued to observe Robert sob. I was beginning to feel sorry for him... until I remembered Rita. The image of her brutally slain body quickly quashed my sympathy.

He's a sicko, a cold-blooded killer.

Yet I wasn't going to run. I wasn't going to hide. I was staying put. *Belinda Boothby doesn't run from cowardly murderers.*

"You killed Rita. What kind of monster are you?"

His bout of crying came to an end as he refocused his stare on me. He raised his hands and spoke in a desperate tone: "I didn't kill her. It wasn't me, I swear. I could never have done that. I loved her. Really, I did."

"I saw you there, your hands were covered in her blood. You expect me to believe you?"

He shook his head. "No, I don't expect you to believe me but I'm telling you I didn't do it. It wasn't me. Someone else was there."

I paused for a few moments to think. Was this another ruse he was spinning? It was time to re-don my detective thinking cap and continue with cautious scepticism. "Who else was there?"

"Shirley," he said.

"Shirley?"

He sighed. "That night, Rita brought me some leftover dinner, which we ate together. There was a knock on the back door. I ran upstairs and hid in the bathroom while Rita went to answer it. After a while, there was an argument. I listened from the top of the stairs. Shirley was extremely angry. She accused Rita of going into her bedroom and taking something. A bottle of pills or something. I couldn't hear their argument clearly. Then there was a scream. I didn't know what to do, so I waited a few minutes, then went downstairs. When I went into the living room, I saw Rita... just lying there. I tried to resuscitate her but... it was no good." His eyes filled up with tears again and his lips quivered. "Then you came into the room. Now, everybody's out to get me." He began sobbing again.

Did I believe him? His story was entirely plausible, coupled with the fact that he was genuinely in bits and didn't seem to want to cause me any harm. Despite my resolution never to be duped by Robert again, I found my suspicions redirected again towards Shirley. What should I say to him?

"Robert Eccleston, we know you're in there," boomed a voice from outside, accompanied by a blindingly bright beam of light that shone through the partially open door. "This is the police. Release the hostage and come out with your hands raised above your head."

Robert's anguished face turned to shock.

"You brought the police?"

I shook my head, completely caught off-guard by the sudden arrival of the police. How did they find us here?

"No, I didn't. I have no idea how they know about this."

"That's bullshit!" he retorted. "I told you not to tell anyone."

"Rob, I didn't tell anyone I was coming here," I said earnestly. "I promise."

Robert sunk his face into his hands. "What the hell am I going to do! I didn't kill her! I'm going to go to jail for something I didn't do."

"Robert, listen to me," I pleaded. "You need to give your-self up. I'll do whatever I can. But you need to surrender now."

His hands slowly fell from his face. He looked at me through anguished eyes. He knew he couldn't escape. The game was up. After several moments, he conceded. "Alright then, I guess I have no choice. You go first."

I turned towards the door. I cleared my throat and said in a raised voice: "I'm Belinda Boothby. I'm coming out with Robert Eccleston. He's unarmed."

There was silence outside which made me feel more nervous. Slowly, I pushed the windmill door open and stepped out into the blinding light. Standing behind the flashlights were several silhouettes of police officers, pointing guns towards me. Instinctively, I raised my arms in the air. One of the officers waved for me to walk forward.

"Come on, move towards me," he instructed. "Come on, this way!"

I stalled outside the door to wait for Robert, who emerged from the windmill, and stood beside me.

"Down on the ground! Down on the ground now!" shouted the police. I turned towards Robert and saw the terror in his eyes.

"Don't worry, it'll be alright," I said to him. "Better to do what they say."

He nodded in agreement. "Here, before I go. You better take this." He reached inside his pocket and pulled out something that glinted in the light.

"Drop it!" shouted one of the officers, which was followed by a *gunshot*! Robert fell to the ground. The police charged towards him, piling on top of him.

Robert writhed on the ground, crying out in agony: "Awwww, Mummy, I've been shot!"

The police unsympathetically turned him over on his stomach, putting him in handcuffs. On the ground beside Robert was Hazel's phone, which had fallen from his hand.

13

Time for Your Final Lesson

As far as everyone was concerned, the story had ended. Robert was in hospital with a serious gunshot wound to his right shoulder. The killer was finally caught and would face the "trial of the century" – the tabloid media's words, not mine – as soon as he was released from hospital. The only person who didn't think the story was at all over was me. And possibly Hazel, although she wasn't present inside the windmill to hear Robert's retelling of the day Rita was murdered. Shockingly, the police didn't seem to be interested when I related what Robert had told me. They dismissed it as fanciful storytelling by a sociopath desperate to get away with murder. Storytelling that I was gullible to believe in, they said. I didn't blame them for their incredulity. After all, there was a good deal of circumstantial evidence that pointed towards Robert being the murderer. But what did annoy me was that none of the detectives were willing to investigate my claims.

It was now almost five o' clock in the evening. The remaining class members of what was undoubtedly one of the most unforgettable writing courses in history, were gathered in the living room, awaiting DCI Wallace to make yet another announcement. Jamelia and Hazel sat at the table, engrossed in a tense game of "Guess Who?". I stood by the mantelpiece, gazing up at the painting of Lord Ainsley, locked in his austere stare. What did his eyes say to me? I could only imagine.

A story may not always have a happy ending, but it should always have a truthful one. Never give up until you uncover the truth!

Aaron entered the living room and was greeted by a cold silence from all three of us. He took a seat in the corner of the room and placed his hands beneath his chin, avoiding eye-contact with everyone else. Jamelia glared at him for a few moments before continuing to play the board game.

"Are you bald?" Jamelia asked in a sullen voice.

Hazel shook her head. Jamelia flipped down a few faces.

"Do you wear glasses?" Hazel asked.

"Yep," said Jamelia.

Hazel flipped down a multitude of faces. Aaron began tapping his foot, looking considerably isolated in the corner of the room. Jamelia surveyed the faces that were still standing on her side of the board, then took notice of Aaron's foot-tapping.

"Do you mind?" Jamelia said.

Aaron raised his head to look at Jamelia, then ceased tapping his foot.

Jamelia returned to the game.

"Do you have grey hair?"

"Yes, I do... although I'm thinking of dying it soon."

Despite Hazel's quip, Jamelia remained steadfastly straight-faced, as she flipped down many faces.

Aaron cleared his throat and began tapping his fingers on the arm of the chair. He clearly was uncomfortable sitting with us in this room.

"Can you shut up!" Jamelia snapped at him.

Aaron's hand became still while his face flinched, stung by Jamelia's snappiness.

"Bloody hell!" Jamelia retorted, staring intently at the game faces. "Breaking my concentration."

The room descended into a cold silence.

"Look, I'm sorry for what I did," said Aaron, with a slight quiver in his voice. "I didn't mean to upset anyone. I was just... doing my job."

"Your job!" Jamelia fired at him. "Spreading gossip to the tabloids... you're a two-faced rat!" Jamelia was quite vicious in her tone. "You bloody lied to us all... you got on this writing course under false pretences!"

"The only thing I lied about was my profession," Aaron said defensively, like a man standing trial. "I won a place on this masterclass fair and square. I still want to be a writer one day."

Jamelia's nostrils flared. "You're the snake of the group!"

Aaron clenched the arms of his chair with his hands. "Hey, I'm by far not the worst person on this course. I mean... it's not like I've killed anyone."

Jamelia gave Aaron a hard stare. "Well, neither have I. But that could change any moment."

On that ominous note, DCI Wallace entered the room.

"Evenin', everyone. It's been quite a day, I must say. As you may have heard, we've charged Mr Eccleston with the murders of Edith Ramsey, Gregory Bramble and Rita Jenkins. He'll be remanded in custody to await trial once he's released from hospital. I'm very happy to say that this dreadful saga has now ended. It's now safe for you to leave and return to your families."

"And the media?" Jamelia asked, casting her suspicious gaze at Aaron.

"Some are still camped outside the gates below," he explained. "But most have moved to the hospital where Mr Eccleston is being treated, which has unfortunately caused significant disruption to emergency services."

Jamelia tsked, saying under her breath: "Geez, trust that guy to put more lives in danger."

"Regarding your departures from this house," continued the detective, "we have arranged for a minibus to collect you from here tomorrow and take you to King's Cross station in London, where you can make arrangements to travel home. Anyone have any questions?"

There was silence for a few moments. I thought about repeating my misgivings about Robert's presumed guilt, but I knew it would be futile. No one wanted to hear anyone defending Robert. Not least, the police.

"Do you have a moustache?" said Hazel.

The detective frowned, while his cheek twitched. "Yes, of course, I have a moustache. What kind of question is that?"

Hazel raised her head from the board game. "Sorry, I was talking to Jamelia. We're in the middle of a game."

"No, I don't have a moustache," answered Jamelia. Hazel, flipped down several faces on the board.

The detective stroked his moustache with a look of fleeting indignation. "Well, since there are no questions, I'll get back to the station." He turned to leave the room, then hesitated. "Oh, I almost forgot. Shirley has invited everyone for tea in the drawing room at seven tonight, to say farewell. She wants to make a special toast before your departure tomorrow. She's a very thoughtful person, I must say." He smiled to himself, as he contemplated Shirley affectionately in his thoughts. Finally, he snapped out of it. "Well, I wish you all the best. Have a safe journey tomorrow and I hope you won't let the last few days put you off returning to Beaglesford. It usually is such a nice, tranquil little village." He smiled, then plodded out of the room.

Once the door had closed, Jamelia lamented. "That's all we need at this time – another get-together. The sooner we get out of this house the better!"

*

At five past seven that evening there was a knock on my bedroom door. I opened it to find Shirley standing there, looking quite anxious.

"Hi Belinda, I'm serving tea for the class in the drawing room now. Won't you join us?"

"Um, no, I ah, have a headache. Really feel under the weather." I smiled as politely as I could, hoping that she wouldn't press me into joining the rest for tea.

She pulled a sour face, clearly dismayed by my answer. "Oh, I see. Well, best you get some rest then. I'll, um, see you later."

She abruptly walked away from my bedroom door, leaving me feeling very relieved. I didn't really have a headache; I had another reason to skip the farewell tea party: I wanted to get back inside Shirley's bedroom.

Tonight was the final night. The last opportunity that I'd have to crack this case. Shirley was hiding something. And I needed to find out what.

I crept towards Shirley's bedroom and opened the door with the skeleton key. Quietly locking the door behind me, I quickly got to work snooping around.

I checked the drawers and the wardrobe but couldn't locate the empty bottle of sleeping pills. However, I did come across a slim leather portfolio briefcase at the bottom of the wardrobe that wasn't there the last time. I placed it on the desk and took out the papers inside. As I'd hoped, I found legal contracts and financial agreements from Edith's literary agent. I sat at the desk and began perusing the paperwork.

On page two of the contract, the author name was Shirley Atkins. A clause below stated that the novels would be released in Edith's name, as her original works. I was utterly astounded. Did that mean Shirley was the true author of the prize-winning mystery novels and Edith merely the famous face that took all the credit? Why would they make such an agreement? Why wouldn't Shirley want to be credited for her own work?

Well, she wasn't the most outgoing, gregarious personality out there!

Could that explain it? Shirley, being the wallflower that she is, allowed Edith to take credit for her work so she could remain out of the limelight? Perhaps she was content to remain in Edith's shadow, while being the backbone to her literary success. Perhaps over the years the relationship became toxic and Shirley couldn't stand being Edith's doormat any longer. Deep down, she must have loathed Edith's persistent demeaning attitude towards her. Loathed it to the point... *of wanting to kill her?*

The financial contract contained even more interesting facts. Shirley and Edith shared a joint bank account into which all the profits from book sales, royalties, prize money and advance payments were paid. However, the percentage share seemed one-sided: Edith owned sixty-five per cent of the account while Shirley owned thirty-five per cent. But there was a caveat: in the event of the death of either party, the other party would automatically become to sole owner of the account.

There is what you'd call motive, my dear amateur sleuth!

With Edith now dead, Shirley was the exclusive owner of this bank account. I took pictures of the contract with my phone then filed all the paperwork back in the leather portfolio and returned it to the wardrobe. I stood at the window and looked outside, mulling over the litany of shocking facts that had just come to light. Was Edith Ramsey really a fraud, and Shirley the true, underappreciated genius behind her works? I almost expected an answer from the silence. I desperately wanted to hear the ethereal voice of Edith speak from beyond the grave and tell me the truth. But with no answer, her murder remained a mystery.

Outside, an owl hooted. I hadn't heard that sound since the night... I saw Edith standing in the garden, while she was asleep. She kept repeating the same phrase... what was it again?

She writes everything.

That was it! She writes everything. It was mind-boggling at the time, but now... *it made sense.* In her sleeping state, she was referring to Shirley. Shirley writes everything. At that moment, other memories of the week came to my mind.

During Edith's drunken rant, in which she fired a gin bottle at Shirley, she had said the words, if I recalled correctly: "Learn from my trusted assistant here. She'll teach you all about being a writer..."

Then there was Edith's shocking blunder about the character Mr Granger being the murderer in her bestseller *Shedunnit*, which Shirley corrected in front of the class. At the time, I put it down to Edith being under a lot of stress, but, in hindsight, it must have been because she didn't actually write the story.

And, of course, the note Edith had written to Shirley in the limited edition of her bestseller, in which she said that her efforts would live on through the ages.

Outside the window, the dusk was beginning to set across the sky. It reminded me of the sky beneath which I saw Edith reading on her own in the herb garden, the day before her body was discovered. As I peered at the cypress trees, something dawned on me. Edith was wearing sunglasses that day. Yet the sun had gone in at the time I saw her. I remember I waved at her and she didn't wave back. It was as if she ignored me. But perhaps she didn't ignore me. Perhaps... she wasn't awake at all.

How do you figure?

Beside where she sat, there was an empty glass. Perhaps a high quantity of Zopiclone had been in that glass and Edith was in fact unconscious at the time I waved at her.

And something else too: that bench where she sat was where I found that button later. A button, seemingly, from Edith's nightie. The same nightie she was found dead in, which was on back to front. But how did that button end up there?

I looked at the drainpipe outside Shirley's window and recalled the night Shirley scrambled up it, onto the roof.

If she could climb up it, she could easily climb down it.

That would mean she didn't need the keys to downstairs, which were in Rita's possession, a point she made sure we would take note of when she reminded Rita to lock up everywhere the night Edith was murdered. So then – and my mind was racing at this point – Edith was unconscious in the herb garden when Rita locked up downstairs at night. No one must have known or realised Edith was still outside, since the bench where she sat was not visible from the house. No one, except for Shirley. Then, sometime during the night, Shirley climbed out her bedroom window, down the drainpipe, into the back garden, and over to where Edith sat heavily sedated. There, she undressed Edith, slipped on her nightie (losing a button in the process) dragged her into the labyrinth, where she plunged a knife into her back. She then came back up the drainpipe, into her bedroom, having committed what she thought was the perfect murder.

That's quite a theory!

Yes, it was. And it did solve a lot of questions surrounding Edith's death. My heart raced inside my chest with excitement: had I solved the mystery? I was on the verge of being ecstatic.

Wait a second. You forgot something.

What's that?

You saw Edith upstairs that night, remember? She was sleepwalking and knocked over the glass peacock.

Oh yes! I did see her. The glass peacock was smashed on the floor.

Blast! There goes my theory!

All of a sudden, I was hugely disappointed.

Whoever said mysteries were easy to solve?

I fumed at my inner voice. I needed to think more. Don't give up, Belinda. Wait! Hold up a second! What if – and this was a big what if – what if... that wasn't Edith I saw sleepwalking that night. What if it was in fact... *Shirley.* I didn't see her face that night. All I saw was the back of someone walking into Edith's room, wearing Edith's nightie and nightcap. Edith and Shirley were almost of equal shape and size. What if Shirley deliberately knocked over that peacock to bring attention to her sleepwalking that night, so it would appear Edith was indoors after Rita had locked up.

Quite convoluted, to say the least... yet it does offer an explanation to the locked-room mystery of Edith's murder.

Shirley was a mastermind. A genuine mastermind. She was the spinster version of Moriarty. And I...

The young, ambitious, albeit unemployed, female version of Holmes?

I needed to take this to the others. But they were with Shirley in the drawing room. What was going to be my plan? Should I play it like Poirot and divulge my theory in front of everyone and wait for Shirley's reaction?

Can't hurt to try, right?

Save for the fact that Shirley may be a fiendishly clever, calculating, cold-blooded killer. But I had no other choice. My working theory was almost entirely circumstantial, which the police would no doubt ignore. I needed to somehow get Shirley to confess her crime in front of the others. That was the only way this mystery would finally get solved.

*

Aaron and Jamelia sat at opposite ends of the drawing room, while Hazel and Shirley sat together around a table with a teapot and a misshapen chocolate cake. Hazel looked up at me as soon as I entered and beamed a smile.

"Hey Bel, fancy a slice of chocolate cake? Shirley baked it herself. It's really scrummy."

Nodding silently, I agreed. Hazel proceeded to cut a slice

of cake with a large kitchen knife. Shirley narrowed her eyes at me through her bright red specs.

"How are you feeling now, love?" she asked.

"Oh, much better."

She pulled a chair up to the table. "Have a seat."

As I sat on the chair, Hazel handed me a slice of cake on a plate.

"Fancy a cuppa to go with that?" Hazel asked.

"Please," I said.

She picked up the silver teapot and poured me a rich-looking cup of tea.

"So, Shirley," Jamelia said, "what is it you wanted to tell us?"

Shirley pushed her glasses up her nose. "Well, I thought it might be interesting if I read out each of your assignment cards."

"Assignment cards?" Jamelia exclaimed.

"Well, yes," Shirley said, as she reached inside her cardigan and pulled out the five cards. "The assignment cards you each completed, before..." she coughed nervously, "well... you know..."

"Before Edith was murdered," I stated emphatically.

She looked at me.

"Yes, indeed." She laid the cards on the table, face down and looked at each person present. "Well, what do you think? Do you want to know what you each wrote?"

"What's the point?" Jamelia said. "The masterclass is over and there's no prize anymore."

Shirley nodded. "Yes, you're quite right. But I thought that, since this is the last time we'll be together, it would be a nice homage to Edith's memory and to each other's writing talent."

Jamelia, Aaron and Hazel looked puzzled.

"Isn't it a bit weird doing this now, with everything's that happened?" Aaron asked.

Shirley furrowed her brow: "Well, yes, I see your point... I guess we don't have to..."

Before she could finish her sentence, I intervened. "Yes, you're quite right, Shirley. I think it's a very fitting idea. We're all here now, gathered in the drawing room on the very last night. It can't hurt to reveal what everyone wrote."

She smiled tentatively at me, then picked up the cards. She shuffled them in her hands. "Let's see, who do we have first... Hazel Griffin."

Hazel's eyes widened, as she gulped deeply.

Shirley continued: "Write in one sentence how you would commit the perfect murder? To which Hazel wrote: 'After blackmailing someone for lots of money, I would kill them and hire the best team of lawyers to get acquitted.'"

There was a moment of silent reflection. Beneath the silence however, I could sense everyone was underwhelmed by Hazel's answer. Hazel pursed her lips and nodded humbly, acknowledging the collective lack of enthusiasm for her answer.

"Probably not the best answer. But, then again, the assignment was sprung upon us without warning," Hazel said. I smiled at her to show I understood where she was coming from.

Shirley moved on to the next card. "Okay, up next is... Aaron James. Aaron wrote: 'I would hire a contract killer, under an assumed identity, to kill me, who, upon having tracked me down, I would kill in what would appear to be self-defence.'" Shirley looked up from the card and smiled. "Quite clever, Aaron, quite clever indeed."

"Yeah, clever for a fraudster," Jamelia said under her breath.

Aaron shot an indignant stare at her.

"Next up," Shirley announced with growing confidence, "Jamelia Lewison. Jamelia writes: 'After years of taking acting classes, I would kill my ex-boyfriend and feign temporary insanity.'" Shirley looked at Jamelia. "Hopefully life won't come to imitate art in your case, Jamelia." Shirley tittered.

Jamelia and I looked at each other and winced at Shirley's attempt at humour.

"Right moving on to contestant number four," Shirley continued, beginning to sound like a gameshow host: "Belinda Boothby. Belinda writes: 'To attempt to commit the perfect murder is to commit the perfect fallacy, since the perfect crime relies, not on the perfection of the criminal's method, but on the imperfections of the criminal investigation, which lacks the one thing that makes mystery fiction worth reading: the great detective.' My word," Shirley exclaimed, "that's quite an answer. Very academic, may I say." She looked at me and smiled, while her glasses slid slightly down her nose.

"Well," I said. "I wasn't sure what Edith was looking for, so I just wrote an answer that was true to myself."

Shirley blinked repeatedly, as she pushed her glasses back up her nose. "Ah, spoken like a true artist."

I smiled vacuously at Shirley's comment, as she held the final card in her hand. There were a few moments of silence. "The last card is from, erm, well... Robert." She looked at us. "Would you like me to read it out?"

The four of us remained silent. Shirley refocused on the card and proceeded to read: " 'Since practice makes perfect, to commit the perfect murder I would have to kill many times over.'"

The room continued to be silent. Shirley quietly placed Robert's card on the table and sighed. "Well that's it then," she said in a deflated manner, placing her hands on her lap. "The adventure is over. Tomorrow we all go home. And life goes on." She yawned.

Okay this is it. Now's the time to unveil this scheming vixen.

"Excuse me, Shirley?" I said.

She turned towards me. "Eh yes, what is it?"

"Didn't Robert have two cards?"

"Excuse me?"

"Robert," I repeated. "Didn't he have two cards? The one you just read... and *another* version?"

She narrowed her eyes. "Another version?"

"Yes," I replied. "It went something like: 'Kill the teacher and frame her stalker. Signed Rob the lady killer.' Do you remember that?"

She jerked her head back and cast a befuddled look around the room. "Erm, I don't think I know what you mean?"

I sat forward in my chair. "A few days ago, you bumped into me on the upstairs landing, if you remember? You made it look like an accident. After you had left, there was a card on the floor. You wanted me to find it."

Shirley frowned, giving me a stern look. In that moment, her gaze reminded me of the gaze of the fox that was mounted on the wall.

She cleared her throat. "What are you trying to say, Belinda?"

The other three sat forward in their chairs. This was the moment of truth. I was extremely nervous to say the least.

Now's your time to shine, Miss amateur detective! Don't let nerves stop you!

"You wanted to cast suspicion on Rob," I said.

Shirley's face grimaced slightly. "Cast suspicion for what?"

"For the murder of Edith."

"Why would I want to do that?"

"Probably for the same reason you wanted to frame Jack Burley... *you* wanted to get away with murder."

There was a simultaneous gasp from Aaron, Jamelia and Hazel. My heart thumped loudly in my chest. I feared my nerves would get the better of me.

Relax! First-time denouements are always nerve-wracking. Just try to stick to the facts!

I looked at Shirley's feet, which were crossed under the chair. Then I noticed that she was wearing clogs. *Clogs!* Suddenly I remembered what Gregory had told me under the sycamore tree.

I paused for a few moments to think about my opening argument. "The night Gregory returned from the hospital after being assaulted in the woods, he told me that his assailant wore navy clogs. Navy clogs for a woman's feet. A very strange fact, since we all were convinced that Jack Burley was the person who assaulted him. Fast-forward to the night Jack broke into this house: although we were all terrorised, he mainly went after one person. You, Shirley. It was you he chased onto the roof, and as he did so, he mentioned something about you having tricked him. During the struggle, if you remember, one of your shoes fell from the roof onto the ground. Soon afterwards, Jack himself fell from the roof, smashing his head open. Before he died, he whispered something into Gregory's ear. To this day, I have no idea what exactly he whispered but I can make a pretty good guess. When I asked Gregory if Jack was dead, he didn't answer me. He just stared at the ground. At the time, I presumed he was too shocked by Jack's death to answer me, but now I think that's not the case. The truth is, Gregory wasn't staring at Jack on the ground. He was staring at your fallen shoe... A *navy clog*."

Shirley uncrossed her feet under the chair.

"Despite all the madness and mayhem Jack brought to this village," I continued, "the mystery of Edith's murder did not go away when he died. Turns out, he had an alibi the night Edith was killed, which ruled him out as the murderer. Added to that, the coroner's toxicology report stated that Edith and Gregory both had Zopiclone in their blood at the time of their deaths, thus establishing a link between the two deaths. Or two murders, I should say. At which point, we had ourselves a serial killer.

"I submit that Jack's final words into Gregory's ear were that Shirley killed Edith, since Jack worked out that he'd been lured to the village by Shirley, only so he could be blamed for Edith's murder. Upon seeing the fallen shoe, Gregory realised that the navy clogs worn by the woman on the night he was assaulted belonged to Shirley. When Shirley realised that Gregory could cast suspicion on her for the murder of Edith, she drugged him with Zopiclone, then staged his suicide. The staging however was flawed, since the suicide note she wrote referred to Harry rather than Henry as the name of Gregory's dog."

I took a sip of my tea. The tea had all but lost its warmth, which made me wince slightly. Upon noticing my disgust, Hazel immediately picked up the silver teapot.

"Refill, Bel?"

"Sure," I nodded.

She poured hot tea into my cup, topping up the temperature nicely.

"Where was I?" I said to myself, after taking a sip. Hazel, Jamelia and Aaron stared at me wide-eyed, fascinated by my narrative. Was I convincing them? I turned in my chair toward them. "Oh yes, the mystery of the Zopiclone pills, which partially explains Robert's absence tonight. You see, it was I who had found an empty bottle of Edith's sleeping pills in Shirley's bedroom, which I gave to Rita who then planned to give it to Robert in the coach house, to prove his innocence. However, Shirley confronted Rita in the coach house about it, while Robert hid upstairs. When Shirley killed Rita and fled the scene with the empty bottle, Robert was left behind to take the blame."

I picked up my cup and drank the warm tea. I was about to present the most shocking part of my case, for which I turned in my chair to face Shirley directly.

"We all know Edith was a sleepwalker. I had in fact seen Edith sleepwalking the night she died. Or at least, I thought I had. Looking back, I am now convinced it was *you*, Shirley, I saw that night. You deliberately knocked over the glass peacock in the hallway to draw someone out of their bedroom, so they would see you enter Edith's room. Edith, in fact, wasn't in the house the night she was killed. She was sitting below in the herb garden, passed out from an overdose of sleeping pills that you put in her drink earlier that day.

"When you entered Edith's room, you got undressed and slipped back into your own clothes. You then waited, like a clever fox, then snuck back into your bedroom with Edith's night clothes. From there, you went out the window and down the drainpipe. You walked to the herb garden and dressed Edith in her night clothes. I submit that you dragged Edith into the labyrinth, where you maliciously and most villainously plunged the knife into her back. You then climbed back inside your bedroom, taking Edith's day clothes with you."

Everyone stared at me in disbelief. They were stunned. But I hadn't finished.

"And now," I announced, turning back to Jamelia, Aaron and Hazel, "we come to the question of motive. We all know Shirley endured some horrible behaviour from Edith during this writing course. They had a far from perfect relationship. But there was more to their toxic relationship than meets the eye."

Shirley folded her arms and glared at me through her large spectacles.

"No one here would disagree that Edith Ramsey was an internationally renowned, award-winning author of many great works of mystery fiction, and had a huge fanbase of crime fiction lovers the world over. Only problem is... she didn't actually write any of her books."

Aaron, Hazel and Jamelia's all raised their eyebrows simultaneously. At the same time, Shirley's nostrils flared, emitting an emphatic exhalation.

"It may be hard for us to hear this, but *Shirley* is the true author of the books that were published under Edith's name. Shirley did the work. Edith took the credit. I've been inside Shirley's room and have seen the contract from the literary agency."

Shirley's face grimaced. "You were in my room? How did you get inside there?"

Taking the skeleton key out of my pocket, I held it up in

my hand. "With this key. Rita had given it to me some time ago. I never got the chance to give it back to her."

Shirley looked enraged.

"What's more," I continued, "you and Edith have a joint bank account that all profits and royalties from book sales go into. Edith owned a majority percentage of this account. But now that Edith is dead, *you're* the sole owner. You're now very wealthy and, with Edith no longer here to boss you around, you're free to do whatever you want. To go wherever you want. To be the person you always wanted to be. Tired and frustrated with living in Edith's shadow, of playing second fiddle to her success, and the perpetual target of her gin-fuelled temper tantrums, you murdered her. You staged this entire masterclass so you could commit... *the perfect murder.* But no murder is ever perfect, is it, Shirley?"

A tense, deadly silence dominated the drawing room when I had finished. I felt I had presented my case in the best possible way.

Poirot would be proud!

Shirley remained completely still and quiet for the next few moments. Jamelia, Aaron and Hazel stared at her intensely to see how she would react. Finally, Shirley cleared her throat. What was she going to say? Would she confess? I hoped so.

"Goodness me," she began. "This is a lot to stomach. Erm, may I have a slice of cake?"

She wants a slice of cake?

Hazel pushed the plate with the chocolate cake towards Shirley.

"Erm, may I also have a knife?"

Hazel handed Shirley the kitchen knife. Shirley took the knife and cut herself a thick slice of chocolate cake.

She devoured it quickly, smearing chocolate icing on her lips and chin. "Mmmm," she hummed, as she swallowed everything in her mouth. "Gosh, that's so delicious. Belinda, would you like another slice of this cake. It is so rich and succulent."

I remained steadfastly silent.

Shirley tsked. "I have to say I am quite offended by you refusing to have a second slice. I spent many hours preparing this." She wiped the kitchen knife clean with a handkerchief. "You remember what it says below in the kitchen? Beware of hurting the cook's feelings because he has access to all the knives? Well, as of now, I have access to the knife!"

Suddenly, she leapt from her chair and lunged at me with the knife. Instinctively, I put my arm up in defence. The blade ripped through the flesh of my forearm, which made me *scream*. I looked at my arm. It was bleeding badly. Jamelia leapt from her chair and pounced on Shirley, grabbing her by her hair. Shirley and Jamelia wrestled with each other, until Shirley flung Jamelia to the floor. Poised with the knife, Shirley was about to drive it into Jamelia while she was down, when Aaron intervened, shouting "Noooooo!" Aaron grabbed Shirley's arm and tried to wrench the knife from her hand. Shirley, who possessed considerable upper-body strength, broke free and pushed Aaron back against the wall, causing the fox's head to fall to the floor.

A terrified Hazel ran behind Jamelia and I as Shirley and Aaron fought. Aaron punched Shirley in the stomach causing her to drop the knife. Aaron tried to run to the other side of the room but tripped over the fallen fox's head and slammed his head off the table as he fell to the floor. He was out cold. Shirley picked the knife off the floor and observed Aaron lying on the ground. She then turned towards us and snarled.

"Let's get out of here!" shouted Jamelia.

We bolted out of the drawing room as fast as our legs could carry us, leaving Aaron behind. As we scurried down the stairs, Jamelia exclaimed: "She's batshit crazy that woman! I knew it all along!"

"Where will we hide?" said a perturbed Hazel, as we reached the bottom of the stairs.

"To the library!" I declared.

We scrambled into the library and shut the door firmly behind us. Hazel and Jamelia pushed the old writing desk up against the door and leaned against it. I applied pressure to my forearm, to stop the bleeding. It wasn't a critical wound but it hurt like crazy. Within moments, the door was being pushed open from the other side, despite Hazel and Jamelia pushing back against the desk. Shirley squeezed her arm inside the door and started swishing the knife ferociously in the air, almost catching Jamelia in the neck. Shaken by her maniacal knife-wielding arm, Hazel and Jamelia backed away from the desk. Shirley forced the door open wider, slowly squeezing her entire figure into the library.

"What do we do now?" Hazel said.

"Move to the back!" answered Jamelia.

We ran to the back of the library and hid behind the final bookcase. We huddled together behind the local history section, as Shirley's footsteps approached.

"Come out, come out, wherever you are, little book-worms!" she said ominously. "It's time for your final lesson: *how to die!*"

Shirley appeared at the beginning of the bookcase aisle where we hid. Hazel gulped loudly: "We're history!"

"Not quite," I said. An idea struck me. I whispered my idea into their ears. They immediately fled the aisle from the other end, towards the top of the library. I stayed put, drawing Shirley towards me. Glancing at the books on the shelf beside me, I picked out the thickest hardcover and looked at its title: *The decline of fox-hunting in Beaglesford: Examining the impact of the Inclosure Act of 1801.*

This will do, I thought.

Shirley paced towards me, raising the knife in the air. "You're quite the detective, Belinda Boothby. Quite the detective indeed. Pity you won't live long enough to tell your tale!" Just as she lunged at me, I raised the book in the air. The knife plunged into the hardback cover, at least two inches deep. I flung the book to the floor, successfully disarming Shirley. Enraged, she grabbed me by my hair and dragged me to the floor. Placing her knee on my chest, she dislodged the knife from the book and held it right under my chin. Her eyes were filled with bloodlust.

Is this really how my life ends? Murdered by a madwoman in a library?

As I turned my head away in fear, I saw something underneath the bookcase: Robert's Montblanc pen. I reached in and grabbed it. Popping the lid off, I spun it once in my hands, then plunged it into Shirley's eye, causing her to fall back. As she clutched her wounded eye, I picked myself up and ran out of the bookcase aisle.

"Now!" I shouted at Jamelia and Hazel.

They pushed against the first bookcase causing it to fall against the next bookcase, which caused that bookcase to fall against the next one, creating a domino effect. The bookcases toppled over one by one, cascading towards the final bookcase. Just as Shirley had picked up the knife, the bookcases came crashing down on her, burying her under a heap of old books. This was followed by dead silence. Jamelia and Hazel rushed to my side and beheld the sight of the book pile, beneath which Shirley lay buried.

"Is she dead?" asked Jamelia.

We listened for a few moments, until we heard a very faint groan from beneath the book pile.

"I guess she's still alive," said Hazel. "But she's definitely not going anywhere."

"Bel, you need to get to a hospital," said Hazel.

I looked at my arm. My entire shirt was covered in blood.

"Yeah, that's probably a good idea," I replied. "Wait, what about Aaron?"

Jamelia and Hazel looked at each other, raising their eyebrows. "I'll check on him," said Jamelia, who seemed genuinely concerned about Aaron's welfare. She rushed out of the library.

Hazel and I remained staring at the pile of books.

"This will make some story, eh, partner?" I said to her.

Hazel looked at me. "The murderer of a famous author buried beneath a pile of books. Even that's too much for a mystery novel."

I placed my good arm around Hazel and together we walked out of the library.

14

Friends Forever

Spending a night in hospital wasn't my idea of a getaway. But it was a welcome change to Ainsley Manor House. They put eight stitches in my arm and, because I lost so much blood, they kept me overnight for observation.

For most of the morning, Hazel sat in the corner of the room with a stack of newspapers, reading out the main headlines, which focused on the same breaking story: the arrest of Shirley Atkins for the murders of Edith, Gregory and Rita. The press also revealed that Shirley was the actual author of Edith's novels, having received a leaked copy of the confidential contract I discovered in Shirley's room. Although the papers credited the police with making the arrest, some of them did mention a young woman from Brighton as having helped with their investigation, which made me feel a little appreciated, after all the trouble I had been through. As for Shirley, she'd been transferred to a London hospital for emergency surgery, whilst under police arrest.

Hazel folded up the newspaper in her hands and looked at me like a worried owl. Clearly, it was hard for her to see me lying in a hospital bed.

"Don't look so sad, Hazel," I said, straining a smile. "I'm not the only one that ended up here."

Aaron had been kept overnight as well after being admitted with a concussion. As far as I was aware, Jamelia was at his bedside.

"You think Jamelia has forgiven Aaron?" Hazel asked.

I looked up at the ceiling and recalled Aaron stepping in front of Shirley's knife, as she was about to stab Jamelia. "I'm sure she has. She's been with him all night, right?"

"I think so," said Hazel. "And then there's Robert."

Of course, there was. Robert was still a patient somewhere in this hospital as well. What an ending to the masterclass: three out of five class members admitted to hospital.

That has to be a record.

"What's the first thing you're going to do, Bel, when you go home?"

I stretched my good arm behind my head to perk up my pillows. "That's a good question. Maybe... arrange my bookshelf?"

Hazel chuckled. "You might need a hand while your arm heals. That might take weeks to get back to normal."

I looked at my bandaged arm and agreed with her assessment. Then I realised something else: Hazel wanted to meet again. Neither of us was used to making friends.

"I may need a hand, who knows?" I said. "I have Mum to help me out."

"Oh, that's good," she said in a deflated manner. Immediately, her face became glum.

"And, of course, you Hazel. If you're willing to make the trip to Brighton."

Hazel's face lit up with glee. "Brighton's easy to get to."

"You can visit me anytime. And I can visit you."

"I'd love that, Bel." She hopped out of the chair and skipped over to my bedside and held out her small hand. "Friends forever?"

I shook her hand and smiled: "Friends forever."

"You'll probably be busy through, over the next while."

She looked puzzled. "Why's that?"

"Aren't you going to finish your book? You know, about everything that happened in the masterclass. No one else has kept a record like yours."

She grinned. "I'll try my best. It's going to take a lot of work to get it finished. Especially how you expertly pieced together all the evidence in the drawing room to reveal Shirley as the mastermind villain."

"I'm sure we can collaborate on that part."

She beamed a broad smile. "I think I'll pay Aaron a visit. Just to see how he's doing."

"Sounds like a good idea. Send him my wishes."

"Will do," she said. "Catch you later." She began to walk towards the door, then stopped and turned back. "Hey Bel, can I ask you one thing?"

"Sure."

"Who do you think would have won the assignment? You know, if things had turned out differently."

I frowned, confused. "What do you mean?"

She placed her hands on her hips. "You know, the perfect murder assignment. When Shirley read out everyone's card last night, who do you think had the best answer?"

It was a perplexing question. One which I hadn't given any thought to, given all the mayhem that followed Shirley's reading. I gazed at the ceiling and shook my head. "I honestly could not say."

Hazel stayed silent for a few moments, staring at me. She then put her hands in her pockets and said: "Maybe it's a question for another day." She sauntered out of the room.

My eyes remained fixed on the ceiling as I thought about Hazel's question. Who indeed had the best answer? After a few moments of honest reflection, I chose a winner which seemed to go against my better judgement.

Go on then! Reveal the mystery winner!

I closed my eyes and said to myself: "Robert."

"Did I just hear my name?"

My eyes opened wide and darted toward the doorway. Robert was standing there, with his arm in a sling.

"Mind if I come in?"

Taken aback by his sudden presence, I smiled hesitantly. "Sure, be my guest." He walked to my bedside and smiled. "How's the arm?"

"Oh, it's not so bad. Few stitches. How's yours?"

He wiggled his arm ever so slightly inside his sling. "Hurts like hell. Luckily, the bullet went in and out. Oh well, at least I can brag to my mates about being shot. Should boost my street cred."

A grin lingered on his face for a few moments then quickly faded. He became serious. It was obvious he couldn't joke his way out of the trauma he had been through. He closed his eyes, as if preparing for an emotional speech.

"Look, Belinda, I owe you my life. If it wasn't for you, I'd have gone to jail for something I didn't do."

He opened his eyes, after having said those quivering words. I could see they had become faintly teary. I was beginning to feel sorry for him. "Hey, I was just sticking to the facts," I said, trying to sound upbeat.

His face remained serious. He placed his hand on my good shoulder and looked at me with genuine gratitude.

"You've made me realise that the world needs good detectives more than it needs villains. Thank you for believing in me."

He patted my shoulder gently then left the room. I was speechless. A giant lump formed in my throat. Had I really converted his way of thinking? Was he being genuine?

He seemed genuine. Maybe he's not the sociopath he tried hard to make himself out to be.

Maybe so. I felt uplifted. For a moment, at least. If a guy like Robert can change, then there's hope for everyone. I only wished Rita had lived to see such a change. A heavy sense of sorrow immediately entered my heart as soon as I thought of Rita, whose young, vibrant life was cruelly stolen from the world. Then I thought about Gregory, the kindly groundskeeper, who left behind his beloved bloodhound Henry. And then, of course, Edith, whose vivacious and eccentric persona lingered vividly in my mind. Their tragic deaths would remain with me forever.

I closed my eyes as I fought back the tears. In that moment of personal darkness, I realised that one thing mystery novels can never teach you is how to deal with the turmoil that accompanies the loss of innocent life.

But you did catch the villain!

Yes, but that gave me little comfort. Despite my obsession with detectives, unravelling Shirley's devious plan was a thin concession for experiencing first-hand the loss of human life. I realised that a murder mystery shouldn't be about the hero that solves it but about bringing justice to the families and loved ones of the victim. And perhaps that's what makes a truly great detective: it requires not only a talent for deduction but the willingness to place that talent in the service of victims and the people left behind.

*

Feeling exhausted, I stretched my arm behind my head to adjust my pillows again, then settled down to sleep. As soon as I closed my eyes, another familiar voice entered the room:

"Hello, Belinda."

I opened my eyes and looked towards the doorway. Mum! She entered the room with a shopping bag and smiled. She laid the bag on the floor and gave me a tentative hug, careful of my injured arm.

"It's great to see you, Mum!"

"How's your arm?" She looked deeply distressed at the sight of the bandages.

"It's fine. It's a minor wound."

"Oh God, Belinda. I was so worried about you. You have no idea." She started to cry.

Sitting up, I stretched out my good arm to touch her. "Hey, it's okay, Mum. It's okay. Everything's fine. I'm safe. Come on, pull up a chair."

Taking out a tissue from her pocket, she wiped her eyes then blew her nose. She pulled the chair that Hazel had been sitting in over to my bedside. As soon as she sat down, she yawned several times. She was exhausted.

"How was your journey?" I asked.

"It was fine. I'm very tired after it but I'll live. I'm just so glad to see you. You have no idea what it's been like reading about you in the news and not being able to see you."

"I can only imagine."

She leaned towards me. "Tell me everything, Belinda,

from the beginning. I want to know everything that went on inside that house."

I smiled at her. She really was eager to hear my story. Despite my exhaustion, I went back to the very first day of the masterclass and recounted the events the best I could. I talked for over an hour. She remained on the edge of her chair throughout, hanging on my every word. When I finished, Mum was enthralled. She couldn't believe that I had outsmarted the villain. She stood up from her chair and tucked me into my sheets and kissed me tenderly on the forehead.

"You've been through so much, dear. I'm so proud of you. You'll have to introduce me to your new friends later. Maybe we can arrange a get-together?"

"Yeah, sounds like a good idea."

A class reunion? That doesn't sound like a good idea!

"Oh, I got you something from the bookshop downstairs." Mum rummaged in the shopping bag she had brought with her and took out a book. "It's that new mystery novel by Brigit Harris that everyone's talking about. Thought you might like to read it."

"No offence, Mum, but the last thing I want to do is to read a mystery novel."

"You sure?" she said. "It's number one in the charts. Critics are saying Brigit Harris is the next Edith Ramsey."

The next Edith Ramsey?

I rolled my eyes. "I don't believe it!"

"You don't believe what?"

I shook my head and smiled. "Nothing, Mum. It's nothing. Why don't you start the first chapter and I'll listen."

"Alright dear," said Mum, sitting down on the chair. She

began reading the opening line. "It was a cold and stormy night at the manor house..."